THE
BEAUTIFUL
BEING

THE
BEAUTIFUL
BEING

JESSICA INCLÁN

ZEBRA BOOKS
KENSINGTON PUBLISHING CORP.
www.kensingtonbooks.com

ZEBRA BOOKS are published by

Kensington Publishing Corp.
119 West 40th Street
New York, NY 10018

All Kensington titles, imprints, and distributed lines are available at special quantity discounts for bulk purchases for sales promotion, premiums, fund-raising, educational, or institutional use.

Special book excerpts or customized printings can also be created to fit specific needs. For details, write or phone the office of the Kensington Special Sales Manager: Kensington Publishing Corp., 119 West 40th Street, New York, NY 10018. Attn. Special Sales Department. Phone: 1-800-221-2647.

Zebra and the Z logo Reg. U.S. Pat. & TM Off.

ISBN-13: 978-1-4201-0116-4
ISBN-10: 1-4201-0116-1

First Printing: October 2009
10 9 8 7 6 5 4 3 2 1

Printed in the United States of America

THE
BEAUTIFUL
BEING

Prologue

There is nothing but nothing. Everything is simply darkness, a black swirling hole in the middle of a void that is enormous, bigger than all the words that could possibly describe it. In this monstrous darkness, there is no light, no swirl of stars, no planets blinking in the reflection of a sun.

But as he looks more closely, as he stares into the nothing, he sees an eddy, a movement, a pooling of the black fabric of the nothing. The pooling intensifies, grows more vigorous, turns into a stream, a current beating against rocks, the shore, beating against the blackness. Becoming denser, it forms an orb, a circle of molten night, swirling against itself, until the colors begin to change, to shift. It pulses, flickers, flares black and red, pulses into being, spinning fast, a whoosh of matter. The orb grows larger, enough so that when it spins, it seems to pull the fabric of darkness with it, turning the darkness into colors—brown, green, blue, red, white—colors that now form and cover the orb.

Behind and around the orb, the darkness fills with light, first the tiny pinpricks of stars and then the glow of a much larger star, a star that must be warm, that must give life, the light hot and orange and bright. The slowing orb seems to absorb the light, taken in the warmth, slow into a regular spin, beginning it seems to orbit the large star.

He wants to go down to this world. He can imagine what it is like, teaming with animals and full with plant life. Enormous, dense forests, wide plains of grasses, mountains with snowcaps. He can almost feel the salt tang of the many oceans, full of fish, of whales and seals and dolphins. Under the water there are more colors: aqua, indigo, vermillion, topaz, sunflower, pink. This world is perfect, pristine, lovely, and his, a place that he wants to take care of and honor and live on. All he wants is to be on this world, to run on it, roll on it, breathe in the sweet air, but just as he's about to push himself there, the orb begins to change again, spinning slightly as it does. It's morphing from an orb into a shape, and figure, a form. It's still brown and green and blue and red and white, but it is now an hourglass, no, a body, no, a woman.

He stares at the shape, watching the colors slowly fade to neutral, to beige, to sun-kissed taupe. The woman now has hair, hair long and blond and flowing. As he stares at her, the woman looks up at him with eyes the color of warm earth. She knows him. She's waiting for him. She wants him. She's the world, his world. She's what he wants, more than anything.

But as he moves toward her, this woman who is his world, the only world he wants, the dream breaks into shards, one dark eye caught in a shining reflection of glass and light. And then he is awake.

Chapter One

Watch this! a Cygirian thought, his joyful idea hitting Ava Arganos as if he were yelling directly into her ear instead of standing hundreds of feet away from her and simply thinking.

Keep your focus, his partner thought back, her intensity a crackle in the air. But she was happy, too. *We aren't moving surfboards like we did back on Ocean Beach. Focus please!*

Ava listened to their back-and-forth thoughts and looked upward at the impossibly heavy object that sailed through the sky. She stood in the middle of the Upsilian desert construction site, her hands on her hips, her head tilted up, the hot wind blowing back her hair. Five hundred feet above her, the large column of metal that the two Cygirians were moving with their minds passed by as if it were nothing more than part of a childhood toy, finding its way to a structure where it came to rest on top of two other steel columns. Once settled, a group of Cygirians seemed to fuse it to the other columns, sparks flying in a spray of heat and flame, the building growing right in front of Ava's eyes.

The sand mound she stood on gave Ava enough of a perspective to see most of the construction going on, the back and forth of Upsilian aircraft and earthmovers, the movement of Cygirian power and Upsilian technology. In just a few short months, a hastily formed temporary encampment was slowly being transformed into permanent housing and business buildings, the small town full of meandering paths that wound between the structures, Cygiria powers managing to keep the planted shrubbery and landscaping alive and flourishing.

This town slowly becoming a city that the Cygirians called Talalo, a word that meant *home*. A word that gave Cygirians a place, a permanent place for the first time in decades.

Ava smiled, happy to see the work. Together, Upsilia and Cygiria were building a place for the lost and abandoned Cygirians to live. To regroup. To form a plan against the Neballats, the race that wanted Cygirians for their powers.

But all Ava was able to do was watch. The air was hot and held her in sandy arms, and if she were smart, she would leave the desert and return to downtown Dhareilly and sit down with the group who was planning their next move. But she was tired of being confined, of talking, of sitting and thinking. She wanted to move. To do something. To help! But she was of no use whatsoever. The two Cygirians moving the steel beam didn't need her, nimbly pushing around three tons of steel with no more than a thought. And they didn't need her to join with them in power, to Converge, because, well, they were doing fine on their own.

This is horrible, she thought, turning to look south, where she saw that another pair of Cygirians were filling a water tank, the necessary water coming from seemingly nowhere.

And really, all around her, Cygirians were working, using their powers to help the Upsilians create the outpost. But all Ava knew was that it would be home. Home for all the Cygirians who were left in the universe, on the planets they'd been left on, those who had been scattered, abandoned, orphaned. Here they would find their culture, remember their roots, work with each other to form a plan that would once and for all keep their enemies the Neballats away.

But she felt like a waste of space, knowing that her power—while one that the Neballats craved—was not helpful in building anything of service. Closing her eyes against the flat hot sun, Ava knew she should go back and help where she could. She should stop whining about what she couldn't do and be thankful that the Upsilian government had granted the Cygirian refugees a place on their planet—something Ava had imagined impossible. Upsilia had never been friendly to them, afraid of their powers. In fact, they'd been so afraid they'd hidden the orphaned Cygirians away, forced them to go into the Source, a place of immeasurable beauty, of infinite possibility. But it wasn't life. And with the Cygirians there, the Upsilians didn't have to think about them.

Every day, Ava played out this constant thought stream. She should, she should, she should . . . Work, help, be someone else. But for this moment, for this amazing second, she wanted to stand on the desert and watch. After five years in the Source, she needed the feel of the hot dry air on her skin that was somehow like the whirl of energy in that place where all souls met. Swirling and wild and exciting. She wanted to forget her deficits, her problems, her "issues," as a woman from Earth had once said.

"We all have our work to do," she'd said after listening to Ava's story. "But you have more than most. You clearly have issues."

The woman had gotten up and left Ava sitting alone on a bench in a spacecraft. At that moment, Ava had wished for a mind that could spew out quick, cutting rejoinders, but all that came to her was confusion and the understanding that the woman was probably right.

She couldn't figure out how to stop wishing for what wasn't. And she was also tired of imagining her double, or twin, as those raised on Earth called them. The sad, tired, repetitive thoughts of her imagined other half were irritating and sad. With more Cygirians arriving daily, she'd expected to feel a pull toward one of them, a call out of the ether to alert her that finally, he was here. Even as she stood outside in the desert, sweat trickling down her spine, she thought she'd hear him alert her, knowing her name from some well of remembrance deep inside him. His voice would be like a bell, a beacon, a welcome home. But no. The sound never came. There was nothing but nothing.

Ava didn't want to think about it anymore. Maybe her double had died in the last battle with the Neballats. Maybe he had died in the attack on the safe house. Maybe he hadn't made it through his time either on Earth or here on Upsilia. So many things could happen in a life, so many things that a Cygirian child wouldn't know how to take care of by himself. Maybe he'd never even made it to one place or the other in that first emergency escape from Cygiria, a casualty of that mad rush to safety over twenty years ago.

Sometimes, that's what Ava believed because in all her five years in the Source, she'd never been able to find his energy, and she knew that she was likely going to spend this lifetime alone, her power incomplete. Her eventual connection with any other man would be half at best and thus, hardly worth the effort. She had to get over it. So that's why she needed to help with the building of Talalo. But what could she do? She wasn't really even sure what her power was, something so internal and strange that she hated to think about it.

"Your hands are so smooth," people would say. "Your

skin like a teenager's. How do you do it? You must never go outside."

Or worse was "How old are you, anyway?"

And then the inevitable "No way! Really. Wow. Good genes, I guess. You are so lucky!"

Ava was twenty-five but the questions about her age, her skin, her looks were apt. During the course of her short life, she was certain she had slipped back in age, losing years of skin damage, repairing her cells, going internally from twenty-five to what? Twenty? Nineteen? Her power was the dream of every woman or any person, really, a perpetually youthful glow that came not from potions or lasers or powders or good genes but from thought. What use was that to anyone but her? And what could her double, her twin do? Age himself? She'd be eighteen and he'd be eighty, May and December. Or January and December. Maybe New Year's Eve and nothing.

A sudden dry wind whipped her long blond hair around her face, blew her thin, white dress around her legs, and she blinked against the sand peppering her eyelids and cheeks. The sun began to beat down, hard in its afternoon slant, and she left the mound, walking to a wilika tree for its small piece of shade, its thin spindly branches surprisingly full of wide fan-shaped leaves. Once under it, she wiped her face and leaned against the rough bark.

After being awakened from the Source by the two men from Earth, she'd found herself mostly by herself, confused by everything once she landed at the safe house. Ava hadn't been able to really figure out how to get back into interacting with people not in the Source, staying in her quarters or walking the perimeter of the safe house world for hours at a time. She'd tried to find those she could talk with, but she didn't know how to move into a conversation, the rhythm and current of it like a cold, too deep river.

How to step in without slipping? How to swim without drowning? How to act normal when she felt anything but?

After the destruction of the safe house, she'd ended up with a group on Earth, and none of that had made sense to her, either. Earth seemed to be a vile, dirty, dangerous place. The people on Earth had no idea about Cygirians and their powers, so they'd had to hide their powers lest they were spotted. Not only that, but the air was dirty from the rudimentary machines the Earth people used to move from one place to another and their planet was in disrepair, the sight of the garbage and waste much like the images she had seen of the Neballats' planet before it folded in on itself and died.

So she was relieved to leave Earth, even if it meant coming back to Upsilia to face certain death from Neballat attack or Upsilian censor.

All she had wanted was to return to the Source where she understood the rules because there was really only one rule: everything is everything. Nothing is separate. Everything is connected. Out here, well, there were so many rules, she felt like she'd breathed in cotton, her head clogged and stuffed. Certainly, she'd fought back when she was called to, but since the last battle against the Neballats on Upsilia, she'd stayed at the temporary shelter in the desert. In the mornings and evenings, she helped prepare and serve food, sitting down when her work was completed, listening to stories about sand and buildings and powers and plans. At those moments, she felt connected to the project, to her people, to their battle against those who would destroy them. But in the mornings after breakfast was over and everyone left, she wondered what she was doing here. Why did she stay? How could she possibly think she was any help at all?

Sighing, Ava pushed back from the tree, stood straight, and decided to head back to the temporary shelter. At least she could be of some use there. Maybe she couldn't lift weighty things or start fires or melt steel. She couldn't create water or move earth. No matter how hard she tried, she would never be able to conduct electricity. But she could make a pretty damn good meat pie and sauté the hell out of simind squash. No one ever complained about the dark brew the people from Earth called coffee, all of them wanting it morning and night. And that, she thought, as she pushed through the sand, was something.

"Is this real? It can't be. It's impossible. What is this called?" a Cygirian named Stephanie asked her. "It is absolutely amazing."

Ava smiled, wiping her hands on her apron. This woman had just come to the temporary shelter this very morning, popping in to ask for a glass of water. And along with the water, Ava had given her a taste of her best recipe, a crispy pastry made of ripe abricas and cocats, fruits that didn't grow on Earth but were definitely appreciated by the workers here. Even those who had grown up on Upsilia remarked on it, and at least for a time, Ava felt like she was contributing. Food was tangible and of use. And dessert was most important, at least on a comfort level.

And with a scoop of what those from Earth called ice cream—the heat of the pastry melting it—the dish was enough to cause lines to form outside the shelter. And when Ava went out with the lunch cart, that's what everyone asked for.

"Based on all my Earth research, I'd call it a tart. A crisp? Maybe it's more of a pie. I don't know. I just know how to make it," Ava said, handing Stephanie another rich, juicy slice.

"I'd just call it heaven," Stephanie said. "It's probably the best thing I've had in forever. I don't know what the fruit is. Something like peach or plum or apricots. I'm not sure. But really, I don't care. All I want is more!"

Ava smiled. "Thank you. I'm glad you like it."

Stephanie looked at Ava as she ate, the woman's short spiky almost black hair framing her heart-shaped face. She wore work clothes, but in the desert work clothes were scant and thin: shorts, a small cotton shirt, ankle-high boots with thin socks. Ava almost felt like a nurse in her long white dress and thick white apron.

"So, um, I don't think we've ever met before. . . . You are?"

"Ava. Ava Arganos. At least Arganos is my Upsilian name. I don't know, well, who my parents were on Cygiria or what our family name was."

"I'm not sure too many of us do know who we are or were yet," Stephanie said. "I think we won't have the luxury of compiling family trees until we have a tree to call our own, you know what I mean?"

Ava nodded, realizing that back when she imagined she was simply a weird, freak Upsilian, she wouldn't have understood the connection between the words *luxury* and *family*. Now she did.

"You're right," she said. "Maybe it will be a while before any of us know who we really are."

Nodding, Stephanie took another bite. "You grew up here? On Upsilia?"

"Yes, but I spent five years in the Source."

Stephanie stared at her for a moment, shrugging. "Really? They must have put you in there when you were really young."

"Not too young," Ava said. "I was almost twenty."

"Hmmm," Stephanie murmured. She took another bite

of the tart but looked at Ava as she ate, staring enough at Ava's face that Ava turned away and picked up a couple of dirty pots and pans and put them in the sink. "Really."

"I was," Ava whispered to herself, knowing that even though the years were true, her skin was not twenty-five.

"Well, I still don't get the Source," Stephanie said. "I don't think I want to ever understand it. It seems like prison to me. A punishment."

"It isn't so bad," Ava said. "In fact, it's a lot easier than being out here. Some days, I think it was a blessing."

Putting down her fork, Stephanie stopped chewing. "Holy cow. You can't be serious. You can't actually want to be in there?"

Ava nodded and turned to put the pie back in the cooler. "I am serious. I do want to go back. All the time. . . ."

"How could you stand it? How could you bear to be separated . . . Do you—where's your twin? Your double? How could he ever accept you wanting to be there?"

Again, the question. The very same one everyone asked. Ava wondered if she should wear a sign that read "Twinless. Don't Ask Unless You Know Where He Is." Or "Without a Double. So Shut up About It," or what about "Doubleless. Have a Problem with It?"

She turned when she heard Stephanie laughing. "What?"

"Those thoughts came through loud and clear. I wouldn't have guessed you had such a good sense of humor. You seem so focused on fruit and flour. You are very serious, you know."

Ava shook her head, smiling into her blush. "I'm sorry. I usually keep my thoughts tamped down. But I just get that question a lot. I think I do need to have a sign up."

Stephanie took another bite of her pastry, licking the fork. She put the plate down on the table in front of her, *umm-*

ming her pleasure at the dessert. "So I guess the answer is no. You haven't found him."

Ava wiped the table, avoiding Stephanie's eyes. "Right. The answer is no. I haven't. But I guess I don't get why having a twin is the answer to everything. Maybe I won't have my mirror self, my other half. Maybe I won't ever get to find the balance for my power. But does that mean I'm doomed forever? That I can't lead a satisfying life? There's this idea that with your double everything is perfect. And I don't see why it has to be like that."

She put down the towel and looked at Stephanie. "Why does everyone imagine that your life is over if your twin is gone? I don't understand. I don't get it. I think I can do just fine by myself."

"Clearly," Stephanie went on, her smile turning into a laugh, "you haven't met my twin, Porter. He and I—well, our fit is a strange one. Not like some of my friends who seem to have found their perfect halves, the yin to their yang, the left to their right, the up to their down. There are no elders to tell us how to do this, so we've just been trying to figure out how to live together. He and I aren't like any other twin couple I know. Porter and I have, I guess, a different arrangement. But because we haven't all been together very long as a group, it's hard to know. I would imagine we aren't the only ones like this. I think there's a whole range that we will figure out one day when things calm down."

Ava flashed to a vision of two men looking her over—one blond, one darker—talking to her in a language that took a while for her to grasp. As their words came into clarity, she realized they had pulled her out of the Source. One of them was called Porter, all black hair, glittering black eyes, and pouty red lips. He was a beautiful man, but he held himself back, held himself away, using humor and sarcasm as protection.

"Porter," Ava repeated. "Does he have very dark hair? And a way of expressing himself that's a bit—that . . ."

"That shows he's a pain in the ass? A bit of a prig? A royal jerk if you will?" Stephanie said. "That would be my Porter. My one and only. The pain in the ass to my yin."

"He and his friend Garrick pulled me out of the Source," Ava said. "Rescued us all."

"You were in the pods there? In the mountains?"

Ava nodded. "Yes. And they woke me up and pulled me out."

"I was there that day, too. So weird to think about the pods. The Source," Stephanie said. "That was a strange, fast, dangerous day."

"Porter brought me out, took me out of there before the Neballats arrived," Ava said. "They saved me. He was brave. He—"

Stephanie lifted a hand, gave it a little wave. "Oh, I know. I get it. I'm not saying he doesn't have his brave moments. He's amazing during a crisis. So smart. It's just that he's not my—I mean we don't." Stephanie juggled her words, trying to find one that would work. "It's not the relationship of my dreams. Let me just say it that way. But I couldn't do this, any of it, without him."

"Even with the other way you feel?"

Stephanie shrugged. "Yeah, call me crazy. He's with me for life, I guess. In this way, in another way. And I wouldn't have it any different. But my point is, everyone doesn't have it perfect, even with a twin."

The two women looked at each other, and Ava realized that probably she'd been inflating the importance of her inability to find her twin, making it the wound she carried with her, like an arm in a sling, a crutch to aid a broken foot. Maybe it wasn't as important as she thought. Maybe people weren't really talking about her, pointing fingers, whispering how sad it was that she was alone. Even with Cygirian culture based upon the idea of twins, doubles, it was entirely possible for her to live a normal, happy life with only half of her powers. And it was also possible that she could find someone to love, eventually. Maybe a group would form on Upsilia for unmatched twins. A sad dating group that met every other week for stilted conversation and beverages.

Stephanie took her plate to the sink, rinsing it off. As she did, she shrugged.

"I think that we are all tied to this idea. It's who we are. It's our common dream. When we were rescued, when we found each other, we found that part of us that finally helped us make sense of everything. And it's true in a way." She stopped talking, seeming to find her words carefully. "We are only half in some respects without our twin, our double. I mean, literally. We can't utilize our powers fully without our partners. But the living thing? The enjoying thing? The doing what you want to do thing? I think we can be okay, no matter what. Twin or no twin."

As Ava watched Stephanie at the sink, she felt a sense of calm settle over her. She'd never heard any other Cygirian say these words, and she was grateful for them.

Stephanie dried the plate and turned back to Ava.

"So what *is* your power?" she asked. "If it is more than making succulent, delicious pastries, then I know you are indeed gifted."

"I can—" Ava began, but then the shelter door flap was pushed aside and Porter walked in, his black hair wild and upswept, his eyes intense and irritated. He frowned a bit at

Stephanie, and then turned to look at Ava, his face barely giving away the surprise Ava saw in his eyes when he recognized her. He nodded at her—so cool, Ava thought—and then turned back to Stephanie, putting a hand on his hip, his stance ironic.

"Imagine that. You found the one place in this enormous Upsilian desert where they serve pie," he said. "Are you all fueled up? Enough carbos to push that skinny rear end of yours back to work."

He almost smiled at Stephanie, though Ava could see it was hard for him to wipe the sarcasm off his lips.

"Yes, my dear jerk-off," Stephanie said. "I am all ready for work."

"Excellent," he said. "Because they need light over at the new structure. Like, now. As in minutes ago. And you and I are the prime candidates for such a crucial, mind-blowing task."

"Porter, aren't you going to say hello to Ava? I hear you have a little bit of history together."

At the word *history*, Porter seemed to blanch, standing up straight, his hand falling away from his hip. His mouth moved, forming words he couldn't seem to say aloud.

"She means about you and Garrick saving me from the pod. From the Neballats," Ava said, trying not to laugh. "In the mountains."

"That's where I know you from," Porter said, clearly relieved that he hadn't been caught in some kind of indiscretion. "How are you?"

"I'm fine. Doing really well," Ava said quickly, turning back to her work and away from her lie. She didn't want to get involved in another discussion of her missing double. She and Porter had already talked about this on the ship back to the safe house, so she hoped he wouldn't feel the need to bring it up again.

Porter nodded. "That's good. I'm glad you survived the safe house debacle. I haven't seen you since then, I guess. I thought maybe you'd left for Earth. Or you were out looking—"

Ava shook her head, hoping, praying he would stop talking. "No, I made it through. I was on Earth for a while, but now I'm here in the desert. Doing what I can. Which isn't really very much."

"So what did you say about electricity?" Stephanie asked, leading Porter down another conversational path. "Whose skinny ass do I need to kick?"

Ava knew that Stephanie was saving her from explaining her life and her lack of a twin, and she smiled at the woman. For the first time since Ava was put in the Source all those years before, she was making a friend. When had she last had a friend, someone to confide in? Back in school? Back in the small town she lived in outside Dhareilly? Ava realized that she could barely remember faces or names of any of her childhood playmates, images only vague, voices soft and unclear. Her life before the Source was like a dream, something she only had flashes of. There hadn't been anyone of import, not even her family. There wasn't anyone now, either. It was at times like this that she thought she'd left too much of herself in the Source. Maybe she really didn't want to be out here in the real world at all.

"The least you could do is offer me a piece of pie," Porter said to Ava. "After all, if you gave one to her—"

"Later," Stephanie said. She put her hands on Porter's shoulders, moving him slowly toward the shelter door. "We can come back and you can be nice. And if you are lucky,

Ava will slice you a piece of that absolutely stunning pastry. That is, if there's any left."

As Stephanie pushed him out the door, Porter turned back to Ava and gave her a real smile, his dark eyes shining.

"Oh, please," he said. "Make my life worth living. Give me Ava's baked goods."

If all it took was pastry, Ava thought, she'd be in heaven.

"Of course there will be tarts, pies, crisps," Ava said. "Even more. I promise. Come back."

"We will." Stephanie waved, pushed Porter out of the shelter, and Ava was alone again with her baking, the flour, butter, and salt ready for her to create something. At least she had this power. Ava picked up an abrica and started to peel it, focusing not on being alone but the smooth skin under her fingers, the curls of peel, the sharp orange tang in her nose.

Pastry, she thought. *Pie*. Maybe it was heaven enough.

That night, Ava tossed and turned in her cot, trying to ignore the quiet but suddenly intensely loud sleeping sounds of other Cygirians. Each breath she heard sounded like a snore, each snore like a foghorn, a loud warning from the shrouded shore. People tossed and turned like ships lost at sea.

At night, the loneliness she felt always grew stronger, like a hand reaching out to grab her, a hand that wanted to squeeze her tight. There was no one on this planet or on any other thinking about her. Her Upsilian parents had made it quite clear that they didn't want anything to do with her before she'd gone into the Source.

"It's best," her father had said as he stood by the doorway, his eyes averted from her. "You never really belonged here. You haven't been able to have a normal life. It's too dangerous for us for you to live here any longer. The government has told us what to do and we are going to do what they asked."

Her mother had just waved once—a quick, small movement—and turned to go back into the house, and the last sight Ava had seen of her childhood home was her mother's back and then the front door closing both her parents in the house, away from her. The vehicle she'd been put in was full of other Cygirians, all of them stunned into silence for the entire long ride to the mountains. What could they have said to each other? How would they have learned to talk about this? This abandonment. No, this giveaway, this throwaway. Like they were trash their families had put out on the curb for pickup.

The last word she remembered saying before going into the Source was "Good-bye." But she couldn't remember to whom she'd said it. Another Cygirian? Her parents? The person who had closed the pod door? Or was it the first word she'd said in the Source? Her hello to all that wasn't.

She turned on her side, pulled the blanket up on her shoulder, keeping away the always surprising desert night chill. Closing her eyes, she thought of the Source, trying to recapture the hypnotic sway of energy that had always buoyed her. When she had first gone into the swirling energy, she'd missed her body, wanting to feel things with her hands, needing to breathe in air, feel heat or cold on her skin. She wanted to run, to swing her long hair, to spin on her toes. After a while, though, she'd grown to accept and then crave the fluid stream she'd become, the way she could simply flow with everything and not have to exert any energy to be fully alive.

At times, she'd meet up with another energy. When she first went in, she sought out the souls of her Upsilian parents, the small part of them that remained in the Source. Before going in, Ava had no idea that no one came to a body with a whole soul, leaving a little bit behind, a small piece that was attached to the Source at all times. But once in, once floating in the red and orange energy, she understood that completely.

So she sought them out so she could ask them why they didn't want her, why they didn't fight for her. And before she heard the answer, Ava knew.

"We aren't strong enough," her mother's energy had said. "We just don't know how to live with the confusion. We will be thinking about how we let you go all of our lives. It will be our greatest failure, our greatest mistake."

"But you raised me," Ava had said. "Didn't that count for anything?"

"It will later," her father said, and then their energies seemed to drift, to sail away from Ava, most of her questions still unanswered. So she sailed away, too, letting time turn into nothing. Every so often, she'd thought she'd seen her twin, but then the shadow of energy she'd tried to grab on to flickered away. So Ava floated. For five years, she dreamed and her dream was real.

Breathing lightly as she lay on her side, Ava tried to find that dream feeling again, hoping that she could lull herself to sleep. Next to her, people breathed; outside, a night bird cawed, its heavy wings flapping. The desert air patted the shelter, insects buzzed against the fabric, skittering their fragile wings against the folds. The night moved on, aching with sudden and temporary cold. Ava slid down into her blanket, her mind drifting, moving slowly back to the Source.

She reaches out her hand, and feels something grab it. No, not something. Someone. And this someone's grasp is warm and strong and firm. She lets her fingers slide a little against his palm, feeling the smooth skin under hers. Smooth but also worked, as if he has been building something, calluses just below the start of each finger.

Ava wants to say something, to feel more than his hand. Maybe just a wrist. A forearm. But does she need to? She feels that she can already see his body, his skin a lovely gold, fine blond hair covering his arms. His neck is strong, his shoulders broad, the muscles powerful, strong, well used. The hair on his head is blond, too, and she can almost imagine reaching out to push a strand away from his face. His face . . . his face. She cannot see his face, though now the rest of him is available to her eyes, and how she wants to stare, to gape, to take in every muscle, every plane of muscle and bone and flesh. She can imagine what all of him would feel like under her hands, smoothness and hardness. He would taste like sun and salt and citrus.

He is absolutely beautiful, an almost heat pulsing from him, a feeling mellow and lovely and golden. He reminds her of a cat—no, a lion, his energy strong and contained and hidden. She wants to lean into him, take him in her arms, feel all of him against all of her. But that's not going to happen. Not in this dream and not ever. He's going to leave her. She can feel it. He's not going to be here for long.

No, *she thinks, trying to hold on.* No. Please don't leave. Don't leave me here alone. Don't make me have another day like this one.

But it's too late. He loosens his grasp, his fingers and then his palm sliding away from hers, his figure disappearing right in front of her.

"Come back!" she cries into her dream. "Don't leave!"

But he is leaving; he is already gone.

"Good-bye," she whispers, the dream fading even as his palm still tingles on hers.

Ava opened her eyes, blinking into what was real. The morning light was emerging from the west, the sleeping shelter full of a pewter gray, the air lighter, less cold. Finally, everyone in the shelter was quiet, no sleeping noises, no snores, only even, deep breaths. Outside, she could hear the first shufflings of movement, some people already getting started with the day.

She turned on her back, looked up at the ceiling, wiping away her tears. She hated him. No one should be able to give her so much pain. No one should be able to leave her again and again as he did each time in the dream. Maybe her twin wasn't dead, but he might as well be. Even in her fantasies, her imagination, he left her. He never sought her out in the Source, the one place he had to be. He didn't search her out here, in life, calling to her, needing her.

The light grew brighter—orange, gold—and Ava sat up in her cot, looking at the sleeping people all around her, some now starting to stir. She blinked, shook her head. Clutching her blanket, she knew she had to protect herself. She didn't want to feel the way she did in the dream, so needy, so desperate for his touch. Ava realized that she had to protect herself from what she needed most. Because she didn't have it, and it seemed she never would.

Throwing back the blanket, Ava swung her legs around, her feet on the smooth cool floor. She had to forget about him. She couldn't keep lugging around this terrible sadness. She had to ignore the want and need that showed up in her dreams. She had to push away the sorrow that always threatened to spill over. She was a strong, capable woman, who didn't need a man to make her whole. She didn't need her twin, her double, to make her life all right. It didn't matter that her power was incomplete as it served her no purpose or anyone else for that matter. All she had to do was control herself, keep her age clear, on target. She was twenty-five and she wouldn't use her power again.

Ava Arganos stood up and walked toward the showers at the end of the shelter, promising herself with each step that she would keep her want away. She would keep her need buried deep inside her, condensed into a solid rock no one could crack open. All her life, she'd been alone, lonely, away from others. She'd kept herself in the corner because there was no one she really wanted to sit with. And that was the way she wanted it to stay. No pain that way. No loss. No risk. That was the way that made sense. That was the safe way, the best way, the only way to live her life.

From this moment on, that's how she would live. This was what she would do.

She nodded at others who were moving, getting up, and with each firm step, she felt her resolve form around her like steel, like armor. Nothing coming in, nothing going out. Safe at last.

Chapter Two

Edan Mirav had to be careful. Very careful. If he let down his guard for one moment, if he somehow managed to forget and allowed himself to just be, he might trigger it. He might suddenly feel inside himself the acceleration of cells, the rush of blood speeding to his organs, the breakdown of collagen and muscle and bone. And before he had a chance to stop himself, he'd be older, his body going through years in just milliseconds. He wouldn't be able to tell how much older, either. Just older. Aging himself felt like sadness, like exhaustion, like a long climb up a longer hill, and he had no time for sadness or exhaustion or extra exertion now. Not when things were going forward so well. Not when they were on the cusp of rebuilding their world.

The day just beginning, Dhareilly glowing and silver in the bright morning sun, Edan knew he had to keep his focus about his power and about everything else. Today he and his group were meeting once again with the Upsilian Council, hammering out the agreement that would allow them to live here until either the Neballats were no longer a threat or the Cygirians could find a world, a place of their own. Edan didn't trust Upsilia, not after facing their censure and their punishment. Not that spending time in the Source turned out to be a punishment. There, he hadn't been able to age himself. There he had seen the images that were helping him pull together his world right now.

But the way Upsilia treated its own people was cautionary—their strict, punitive measures against any and all crimes—left little leeway for Cygirians to do wrong. And after having spent time with the Neballats on their version of a safe house, he knew that the Cygirians congregated here had to focus. They had to grow. They had to spend some time becoming the people they had once been, the people they were to become.

It was a good thing the Cygirians were building a compound out in the desert. It was a good thing most Cygirians hadn't spent time with the Neballats as he had. Edan hadn't wanted to be captured by the Neballats, but that short time with them had shown him a type of person, a type of people who took what they wanted without thinking of any of the consequences. And he had to protect the others from them.

Edan sat up, looked out the window of his room at Dhareilly, the city a sparkling silver sheet flowing toward the mountains. Beyond the mountains, in the desert, his people . . . Edan stopped his thought, shaking his head. *His people.* Where did he get such hubris? Though he'd somehow felt that he could help with the reforming of his culture, the finding of a place to live, he never felt more than just a sense of belonging. But there was the thought. *His people.* He smiled, stood up, letting the sunlight cover his body, the warmth penetrating him through skin, to muscle, making him feel languid and happy.

Stretching, he knew that he didn't mean to possess his people but claim them as his own, his tribe, his web of connection. They were his, and that word did not imply ownership. It implied belonging. He had a group of people. He had siblings, relatives, relationships, where before there had been none except those that had been imposed. And he felt that with this support, he would be able to help. He would be able to lead. But something was keeping him back, holding him still.

His twin.

Even with his new role in the negotiations with Upsilia, Edan felt incomplete. He knew this was a ridiculous feeling, one that he should be able to overcome. Over the millennia of Cygirian life, there must have been thousands and maybe millions of people who never found their twins. There were accidents, illnesses, and wars to consider, all tragedies changing the course of many relationships. Apparently, Cygiria never had access to the Source, so those answers weren't sought out, and when Edan was there, he hadn't had the foresight to search them out, either.

Edan closed his eyes and wondered what it would feel like to have that loving, knowing gaze upon him. His twin, his double, would know him in a way no one else ever would. How would it be, then, to live without that for an entire lifetime? Somewhere, there once had to be information on how to get by in such a circumstance, but all that knowledge was destroyed, either on Cygiria or during the destruction of the safe house.

But what was the answer? How was he supposed to live when there wasn't that one person who completely understood him? Who could meld into him? Who could know his thoughts before even he did? Who would love his body as he would hers? Who would match him with her power and make sense of what he could do? With her, Edan knew he could find equilibrium, balance, perfection.

At the safe house, he'd met a woman named Ruth, who was likewise twinless. Ruth had been raised on Earth, and out of their loneliness, they'd slept together a couple of times. While the experience had been pleasurable—Edan able to forget about his longing for minutes, sometimes hours as they made love and then slept together—it hadn't been enough, and Ruth had known it, too.

"We need to find them," was all she said the last time he saw her before the safe house was destroyed and they were all brought to either Earth or Upsilia. "We need to find them soon."

"But how, Ruth?" he wanted to ask now. "How? Where is she?"

There was the question, the one always on his mind. Where was his twin? All during his time in the Source, he'd searched for her. At times, he felt as though he'd glimpsed her, swirled through something that might be her energy. He'd call out, wanted to merge with her, take her into his center. But in all the long five years of his time there, he'd never learned anything about her. Not her location. Not her name.

When he arrived at the safe house, he'd asked everyone, consulting the pulled-together list they'd come up with, the one that detailed everyone's power. But there was no mention of someone being able to "unage" herself. When he met people recently come from Earth or Upsilia, he'd ask questions, searching for anyone who might know her. But nothing.

And all this thinking here, now, wasn't going to help him. All his hoping for his twin wasn't going to bring her to him.

Edan rubbed his cheeks, realizing he needed to scrape his beard off his face before the meeting. Sometimes when he cleaned himself up in the morning, he imagined that this would be the day that he'd find her. For a quick second, he'd smile at himself in the mirror and see the Edan that she would see. Going forth in his day, he'd quickly turn, look across a room, and there she would be, so beautiful, waiting for him. Happy to see him. Needing him.

Or even better, he would hear her thought and find her, touch her on the shoulder, and have her turn to him, smiling. Edan knew he would recognize her face anywhere. He just hadn't seen her yet.

And then finally together, they would be able to come to balance, keep their ages real. Or, Edan thought, smiling, maybe just a little bit younger. And who knew? This power might be transferred to others, enabling their entire people the chance to live longer lives.

Without her, though, no one would ever know.

Walking toward the bathroom, Edan sighed. He might have to forget about her. There wasn't time or space for mooning around, moping about his missing twin. In fact, he had a feeling that he should just let the search go. This life wasn't supposed to be only about finding this connection. His purpose wasn't just to discover his other half. Sometimes, things weren't supposed to work out, the Cygirian experience in the universe enough of an example of that. They'd lost two generations, a planet, and most of their culture. Edan knew he was lucky simply to be alive.

Turning on the water in the shower, he sighed, looked at himself in the mirror. The thought he'd had upon waking was the one he'd hold close. He would keep to the task, ensure that he didn't slip into old age before his time, and work on bringing Cygiria back to its full potential.

Steam rising around him and filling the small room, he watched his image in the mirror slowly disappear until he was nothing but a shadow, nothing but thought.

"No," Kate was saying, waving her hands. Edan was sitting next to her at a table with twelve other Cygirians, which included his two sisters, their twins, and others he trusted, fellow Cygirians who had survived the safe house destruction, who had fought, who wanted nothing more than to see their culture thrive once again. Across from them, the same number of Upsilians listened, their faces set in almost the exact shape of disapproval.

Edan had met Kate and her twin, Michael, shortly after his arrival at the safe house. Kate was strong and forceful, her upset with the Upsilians fierce since her first visit here and her introductions to the pods and the Source. Like many of the Cygirians, she refused to even think about traveling into the Source, despite the many good reports that had come back as people emerged from its swirling energy. While the Upsilians had put the "abandoned ones"—as they called the Cygirians—wholesale into the Source without asking permission, most who had been there were not angry about the experience. Confused perhaps, but not upset.

Edan's sister Claire and her twin, Darl, both had gone in and come back understanding things that they hadn't before and to no ill effect. Both of them sat next at the table, staring at Kate, obviously sending her messages, trying to calm her down. At one point, Claire turned to Edan and tried to give him a reassuring smile, a smile he'd carried in his heart and head his entire life. For a second, Edan flashed to the dream he'd carried in his memory like a talisman, the one with the two little girls and him on a spaceship, flying away from danger. Just like now, Claire was looking at him, waiting for an answer. Edan hoped he could give her one. He wished he could calm Kate down and, at some point, get her to listen to his ideas about the Source. But Kate would have none of it, refusing to be out of her body for a moment.

Frankly, Michael thought from his position two people

away from Edan, *I don't want to be out of her body for too long, either.*

Unaware that he'd let his thoughts loose into the meeting, Edan blushed but kept his face toward the Upsilian group. Kate went on.

"We will not be subject to your medieval—no, make that barbarian—rules about loitering. No 'Death Ray' on our streets. And, in fact, if I could, I'd force you to get rid of the damn thing entirely. It's heathen! It's violent—"

"We have some rules that we want in place in the desert," Edan said, stopping Kate, who was clearly about to go one hundred miles an hour on a highway of complaint.

The Upsilians were silent for a moment, all of them clearly communicating through thoughts that were off-limits to the Cygirians.

Edan continued. "We know that we are guests here on your planet, and for that we are grateful. And you have clearly suffered from the Neballat interest in us. From my time with a small group of Neballats, I know that their intention is to take what they want, with no regard for what or whom is in their way. They made sure that I carried that information home with me. So this time for you hasn't been easy, and you have been very generous with your gift of space in the desert."

"Why did they let you go?" an Upsilian asked. "Why did they bring you back here?"

"I'm not completely sure," Edan said. "The group that took me was trying to warn me. Trying to let me know their plans in order for us to develop protections. A strategy. But they have to protect themselves, too. They can't rebel because I don't think there are enough of them to overthrow those of their kind who are in power."

"How can you trust them?"

"I'm not sure," Edan said, standing up and then slowly walking around the table. As he moved, he could almost feel the argument he would make growing in him, coming from not his head, his thoughts, but everywhere inside him, his blood and bones and flesh.

He turned to face the Upsilians, looking at all their stiff, slightly scared faces. He'd seen the same look on Cygirians, everyone at every moment certain of hurt, failure, loss. Why were people always so afraid out here? Why was there always so much suffering and fear and worry and despair? In the Source, the answers to everything were just the answers, no emotion placed on them. The battles, the anger, the deaths that happened in life were somehow clear in the Source, the place where everything converged. Edan wanted to reassure the Upsilians that this meeting, this plan, was nothing more than a thread in the fabric of experience. But they wouldn't want to hear that now. They wanted order and clarity and clean, well-drawn lines between Upsilia and Cygiria, barriers and protections against the Neballats, freedom from eventual dealings with Earth. They wanted to help, but they wanted to help as long as it didn't effect them.

But they were effected already. It was too late. The Cygirian footprint was here, on Upsilia, forever.

Finding his thoughts and voice, Edan breathed in, nodding slightly.

"This situation will be temporary and it will be orderly and clear," he said. "We will keep our own government, keep our people in control. There will be no disruption to Upsilian life or to the Upsilian lifestyle."

"How can you be so sure of that, even with all the time that we've spent negotiating your stay?" An Upsilian woman named Romben picked up a folder that contained the agreements they'd forged between them. "You come here and tell us how to behave. You tell us what we can do on our own planet. You tell us what kind of punishment is appropriate when you do not even care to understand us. You bring your feelings, your beliefs, your desires and try to place them on us."

Edan felt Kate about to blurt out a retort and he sent her a plea for time to follow his line of thought. Behind him, Kate's mind settled, if only for a second.

"I grew up on Upsilia and understand the culture and people. I know about the rules, the desire for a quiet, orderly existence. I know how Upsilia values consistency, uniformity, peace. I also know that not all of Upsilia is in agreement. Why, even here in Dhareilly, there are groups of Upsilians fighting for change."

Romben shook her head, her lips pressed into tight disapproval.

Edan continued. "So this culture will change, eventually. Whether you want it to or not."

"Then why should we allow you to be here?" one of the men asked. "Yes, yes. We have the accord. The agreements. But if you cannot respect—"

Holding up a hand, Edan tried to breathe in understanding and out compromise. "I think you should also see that we cannot just take on wholesale your values, either. We who come from another culture, many of whom come from a different planet, solar system, galaxy. Give us time to adjust. Give us room to grow, to feel safe. And then we will fight away the Neballats. And then, with hope, with time, we will leave Upsilia for our own place."

"How can you guarantee that? We have harbored your people for decades. Nothing good has come of it. None of you have ever given back to our culture, made any lasting contribution."

"This is a new time for Cygirians. We are together in a way we have never been before. We have been almost exterminated, hunted down, killed. But we've learned something from you," Edan said. "You sent some of us to the Source. And that gift . . ."

As he said those words, Edan felt Kate's thoughts lurch, and he tried to calm her with his thoughts, hush her so that he could move on.

Just wait, he thought. *Listen.*

"And that gift," he continued, "has allowed us skills we never knew we had before. That's how we fought off the Neballats during the last battle. That's how we will be able to fight them off once and for all."

As he was speaking, Edan felt the gift that he'd had his entire life wash over him. This was the power he used when first talking with the Upsilians, hoping to convince them of the Cygirian need for space. Likewise, this was how he spoke to them when working on the future strategies against the Neballats. This was what he could do. This was what he'd always been able to do. He could talk with people and persuade them to his position. This wasn't his true power, the one he wished he could use to some good effect, but another skill altogether. He carried it with him all the time and had since he was a child and had wanted something from his adopted Upsilian mother.

"May I go outside and play?" he'd asked during a storm, needing to feel the exhilaration of weather, the whip of wind on his skin.

And instead of saying no to such a silly request, she'd always said yes. "Of course," his mother had said. "You must. How could you not?"

Now it was the same effect. *Look!* The Upsilian group seemed to have switched their focus, their minds, their ideas, their faces less tense and stressed and angry. They were nodding as he continued talking about sharing and trust and hope and change. They were seeing the two groups living together on one planet, seeing the benefits, forgetting the detriments. Without wanting to, really, they were coming with him on his discussion, following his words along like treasure.

Edan finished his talk and faced the group, standing behind the other Cygirians. As he did, he felt their strength, their powers, their energies flush through him. For a second, he wondered how any group of people had ever been able to do anything to them in the first place. Together, they should be able to do anything. Together like this finally, they would be able to get what they wanted.

Romben nodded, tucked the folder close to her chest, stood as did all the Upsilians.

Unflipping believable. You did it, Kate thought. *You are amazing.*

That's why we pay you the big bucks, Michael thought. *That's why you are the man.*

"We have been in agreement about your tenancy on Upsilia," Romben said. "And we will respect your wish to self-governance if you do the same with us. As long as Cygirians stay to the space allotted, you are not governed by our laws. But off the space, our laws persist, regardless of how you deem them. This is not for you to judge. But to obey."

Edan tensed as Kate's mind was suddenly filled with images of insane dictators, the crowds before them prostrate with fear or waving madly to stave off death or punishment. Streamers and banners flying wildly in a frightened wind, marking a party that didn't really exist. Then she saw jails crammed full of prisoners waving empty tin cups; she envisioned interrogation rooms with hooded people slumped on chairs. Her anger beat in her chest like her heart, and

Edan sent her calm. He sent her *now*. He sent her the hope that he had shown the Upsilians.

In tiny increments, she shut off the pictures and forced a thin, tiny smile.

Romben shot Kate a quick, harsh glance. "Does that not seem clear? Does that not seem like a fair compromise to you?"

For a moment, there was a pause. Edan waited for the support that would come, the bolstering of his group in thought and feeling. And there it was. Claire and Darl. Mila and Garrick. Odhran and Elizabeth. Kenneth and Whitney. Mark and Diane. Carl, who was another Cygirian who had not found his twin, his double. Even out there in the desert where the construction was going on, he could picture Jai and Risa, Porter and Stephanie, and all the others who were always sending him their strength, their confidence holding him, supporting him. Edan knew what he could say. What the right answer was for all of them.

"Yes," Edan said. "Yes, it does."

His words seemed to clear the room of discord, and then the Upsilians softened, almost smiled, their bodies slightly slumping into relaxation.

"Excellent," Romben said, lifting up her hand in the movement that was to Upsilia a handshake. "We have an accord."

"Yes, excellent," Edan said, lifting up his hand as well.

And with that, the Upsilian contingent walked out of the room, the doors opening and then closing behind them with a whoosh of electronics.

"Well," Garrick said as he sat back down. "I am really through with these meetings. They are worse than corporate retreats. Worse than sitting down with my former partners at the office. I think I need to go to the desert now and see if I can help Porter."

"You could help Porter with a lot of things, but electricity isn't one of them," Mila said. "First start with his manners."

Edan could almost see Porter in the room, the man rolling his eyes at the comment, putting a hand on his hip in complaint.

Darl and Claire came from the other end of the table, Claire smiling at Edan. In the short time that Edan had known Claire, she seemed to have bloomed despite the fighting with the Neballats and the tense situation here on Upsilia. Her pretty face reflected the happiness she felt with Darl, who was strong, funny, sharp, and happy. They were a good match, just like Garrick and Mila. And Edan knew that such happiness came not just from being matched with powers but from being connected in a deeper way. Being connected by love. Maybe they were drawn together by their twinness, their powers, but love kept them together. Kept them strong.

"Porter needs help with more than just manners. A good starting place, though," Darl said. "Move on to tact. Compassion. Caring. Concern."

Claire made a face of mock horror. "Really, Darl. Don't hold back your thoughts."

"You spend some quality time with Porter and then talk to me about holding back!" Darl said.

The group laughed, and as they did, Mila moved closer to Edan, putting her hand softly on his arm. She was glowing, now about eight, eight and a half—

"Eight months, three weeks, and two days," she said. "Can you tell I'm counting the very minutes until this baby is born?"

"It will be wonderful," Edan said, putting his hand lightly on his sister's rather large belly. He hadn't spent any time around pregnant women, but even he could see Mila was rather, well—

"I know, I know. I'm enormous. A whale. I was hoping I'd be one of those really cute pregnant women, but I'm as big as a house. And about as graceful. I'm an egg. A weeble. A drunken balloon. Put me on a string and let me float along in the Macy's Thanksgiving Day Parade."

Edan smiled at her, wishing he could convince her with words or thoughts of her beauty. Mila was literally glowing, her hair thick and dark gold, her skin slightly tanned from her time out in the desert. Her eyes were bright, happy, full of life. She *was* full of life. She was a miracle. This baby was a miracle. At this point, there were other pregnant Cygirians—many more babies on the way—but this particular child would be the first in the new generation, the firstborn of the ones rescued from Earth and Upsilia, the first to hopefully live in peace, safe from the Neballats, safe at last.

"You were amazing just now," she said. "I think things will go so much more smoothly with Upsilia. They've been holding out on this one issue from the very beginning. But now we will be able to govern ourselves in our own spot."

"What will be wonderful is when we have a place to call our own."

"We are almost there," Mila said. "Thanks to you."

"No," Edan said, wanting to tell Mila that it wasn't about him. It was about them—all of them—working together. This work they were doing together was the budding of a new Cygiria. But Mila seemed to hear his thoughts, shaking her head, her hair swinging.

"Look," she said. "You're going to have to accept it at

some point. You aren't just the average bear, okay? You are special. You have powers that go beyond what any of us can do. You're my brother and all, but you're something else, too."

Standing on her toes, she kissed his cheek, and then turned and walked back to Garrick. Edan waved to them both as they left the room, following behind the remaining Cygirians, who were headed back to their quarters.

Alone now in the large room, Edan looked out the window toward Dhareilly, the city shifting in color as the sun moved along its path. Mila was right. He wasn't the average bear—whatever the hell that meant—and he wished he could be. He'd like to have his twin at his side and go into life here like everyone else. Yes, they were all in a very unusual situation, fighting for their lives, but did he have to be the one to lead his people?

Edan ran his hand through his hair, shook his head, sighing. Couldn't he simply put his head down and help with the building and reconstruction of all that they had lost? He could go to meetings but not have to really be in charge. He wanted to just be one of the crowd. A part of the crowd. Not the center of it. Since he arrived at the safe house months before, he'd been pulled into the middle of the action and then he became the force that made the action.

And what would happen when the Neballats decided to come back?

Edan stopped breathing for a moment, the truth of it all inside him, his fear and indecision falling away. The Source had taught him that there was a purpose and a plan for everything. So maybe he didn't like the fact that he was alone without his twin and in charge of decisions he didn't feel completely capable of making. Maybe he didn't like the fact that he seemed to be in authority. The plain, clear truth was that he was. Edan needed to go with it, to roll along with the way life was unfolding. And somehow, Cygiria would prevail.

The sun was pushing over toward the East, the afternoon light now reflecting orange off the buildings, the busy city shining like a lit pumpkin. Things were settled here in Dhareilly, the Upsilian accord not complete. There was nothing left for Edan to do in this room or in this place. It was time to go to the desert.

Edan stood with Jai and Risa in front of a building that would eventually be housing. Rather than seeming exhausted by their weeks of work here, the first twins seemed exhilarated, alive, vital, both of them smiling as they watched the work going on around them on the structure. And there was quite a lot of work yet to do, Edan thought. The building was still under construction, being "skinned" with seemingly delicate glass. The completed section reflected back a glaring white sun, Edan grateful that two Cygirians had the power to somehow alter external temperature in limited areas. Without the change, the temperature had to be what? Ten degrees above body temperature, at least, no matter what measuring system one used. And it was dry, the wind everywhere else crackling like a dry sheet.

"This is quite a building," Edan said, his hand shielding his face from the light as he looked up. "And you say all this was done in less than a week?"

Jai nodded, his face tanned and shaved clean. "It's how well we've been able to marshal our talents. We are going to need a few more of these buildings, what with people still arriving daily. We've basically tapped out the living space in the city."

"I think our growing numbers are what caused them to try to stipulate their laws here. But once we are here," Risa said. "Out of sight, out of mind."

Edan nodded. That's what Upsilia did. Tucked things away in order to forget them. Put people in pods and hoped for the best.

Jai seemed to hear his thoughts, shrugging. "But we've had their help here, regardless of what they want to do with us elsewhere. In another few weeks, we will be able to move everyone in from the city. And thanks to your meeting yesterday, we won't have to worry about Upsilian law."

Risa nodded, her face serious. "No more death ray. No more forced Source time."

Jai put his hand on Edan's shoulder, his grip firm. Edan could feel the man's thanks, his gratitude, and Edan could only think that without Jai and Risa, none of them would be here now. Somehow these two had managed to find each other on Earth, escape the Neballats, and find the safe house. From this initial pair came the rest. Came Kate and Michael. Came them all. None of them would know what it was like to live as a collective body, as a people, as a tribe.

Looking around the construction site, Edan could almost see a true city, with streets and businesses and culture. Culture! What was Cygirian culture? Back when they had a planet, cities and states and countries, what did their people like to do with their free time, with their artistic endeavors? What did their music sound like? What were all the various expressions of life on Cygiria? Had any of this information been stored in the safe house? If so, he'd never seen it. Culture, he supposed, was a luxury Cygirians hadn't had time for lately.

"I know this looks promising," Jai said, his bright blond

hair blown back in the wind. "But we still have a great task ahead of us."

Risa nodded, turning to Edan. "I'm not sure why the Neballats have left us alone as long as they have. They seem to want what they want, and one defeat doesn't seem to be enough for them to go away and stay away."

"Maybe they aren't as strong as they once were," Edan said. "Does our informant have anything to say?"

Though he had never met him, Edan knew there was at least one Neballat who moved within the high ranks who supplied them with information. Claire had gone into the Source to unearth information from him that had helped them during their last battle.

"Not recently. It's been quiet," Jai said.

"Too quiet," Risa said. "It makes me nervous. Makes me—"

"We have time," Jai said, putting his hand on Risa's forearm, rubbing her gently, familiarly, enough that the slight and honest touch made Edan blush. "We have a little window here to get ourselves together."

Edan wondered why Jai had stopped Risa from talking, but when he tried to pick up an idea or two from their thoughts, he found they were both locked up tight. Clearly, they weren't sharing all that they knew.

But they were good, kind, careful leaders, who had gotten them all this far. And Edan had no reason to question anything they did.

"That's good to hear," Edan said. "So while we have this time, I want to help."

"But, Edan," Risa said. "You've helped us so much already. And there will always be negotiation work to do with the Upsilians. Maybe we are in a lull now, but I'm sure they'll want to continue the talks. As we grow here, so will the problems."

"Of course," Edan said. "I will always be ready to negotiate. But I can't just sit around. My power is of no use at all for anything, but I'm ready to do some real work. I've been cooped up in all those meetings for too long. And for at least a while, the time for talking is over."

"All right, then. You ready for some manual labor?" Risa asked, smiling. "Put-your-nose-to-the-grindstone kind of thing?"

"What?" Edan said. Whatever a grindstone was, it didn't seem like something he wanted to put his nose to. He had enough trouble not losing parts of himself inadvertently, parts he could not necessarily feel but those that he wasted by aging himself. What had he aged through inattention? His lungs? His stomach? His heart? He knew his heart was hurt, but that pain wasn't caused by age. But in any case, deliberately grinding off one's nose seemed ridiculous.

Jai shook his head, laughed. "It's a pretty stupid saying we have on Earth that just means hard work. Focus despite pain and hardship. Determination. So you better get busy, take the bull by the horns. Put your shoulder to the wheel, the ax to the chopping block. Just don't bite off more—"

"Frankly," Edan interrupted, "if the work means I don't have to listen to any more of this nonsense, I'm in."

As Jai and Risa laughed, flinging out a few more strange Earth idioms as they all turned once again to face the construction site.

Work, Edan thought as the cooled air lapped at him. Work he could feel. Things he could move and fix and create with his hands. That's what he needed. That's what he would do.

* * *

Somehow, the Cygirians with the temperature dip power had moved on because the hot, dry air held Edan in a firm grip. A death grip. A wet, sweaty, baking horrid death grip. Half of yesterday and all of today, Edan had worked with a crew that was pouring and then grading walkways between buildings. The machines spilled out the smooth, wet cement, and he and the crew made up of mostly Upsilians—a sort of slightly older than teenaged group from Dhareilly—graded the paths, moving on to the next spot as the walkways dried. Which didn't take long, that was for damn sure. The air smelled of rock and sand and heat, and for a moment, Edan wondered what he had been thinking.

Work? With his hands? In this heat?

The sun beat down on Edan's back, and he stood up for a second, taking off his gloves and then his shirt, wiping his neck with a towel he pulled from his back pants pocket.

"Hot day, huh?" one of the young men asked, a fellow named Siker. Siker sat on an unlandscaped patch of sand drinking from a bottle of water, his shaggy brown hair drenched with sweat. But the boy smiled, seeming to relish his task, this heat, the conversation.

"And then some," Edan said. "I only came out to the desert once when I was a boy. And I think I had the benefit of air-conditioning."

"It's pretty cool that they leave us alone out here," Siker said. "You know, go out to the desert to work like an animal and you get a free pass. No one telling you to move along. No curfew except for the fact there aren't enough damn lights here. No bar, either. But there are some hot— and I mean hot—chicks."

Edan shrugged. He knew he didn't want to talk about

Upsilian laws or hot chicks with this boy, who hadn't a clue that Edan negotiated with the Upsilian heads of government for the freedoms that existed in Talalo.

"I suppose," Edan said, moving his trowel across the smooth walkway.

"You're from here, right?" Siker asked.

"Raised, not born," Edan said.

"I knew it. I could tell. An abandoned one," Siker said. "You kind of have that spooky feel. You've been in that place. You know. The Source. I heard all about it, man. You got to tell me what it's like. Most of my friends don't even believe in it."

Edan stood up, wiped his forehead, looking at Siker, a thin, still growing young man with a wisp of a beard on his chin, the remnants of acne on his cheeks. Somewhere on his body, Edan was sure, were hidden tattoos, marks of Siker's independence.

"Who told you about the Source?"

"This chick I met one night. She had a foster sister—an abandoned one—when she was growing up. They, like, dragged her sister out of the house one day and she was gone. They told her parents about this 'containment' place. Where she would be all right and kind of like out of their hair for a while. But this chick did some digging around and found out about it. You know, what it's like in there."

Edan sighed, wondering how he could—or if he should— talk to Siker about the Source. It seemed like a punishment to Upsilians, but to him, it had been the greatest teaching tool. The only thing he hadn't learned in the Source was who or where his twin was. But other than that, he'd learned about the flow of life, the way everything was all connected. He and this boy were connected. Their interaction was somehow important to them both. But why? Out here, Edan didn't know the answers, only able to go with the moment that was presented to him.

"It gives you the ability to enjoy being alive here. This place—right here, right now—is the place where we learn what we need to, Siker. The Source has the answers, but we need to live the questions. Knowing why something happens doesn't always help us understand it. Living through it does."

Siker stared at him, his mouth open a little. Finally he breathed in, shook his head. "Living is hot, man. Living is a lot of work."

"Yes, it is," Edan said.

Siker nodded, his eyes wide. "Heavy. Way heavy, man."

Edan smiled, knowing that Siker was right. Living was heavy and hot, a lot of work, and sometimes lonely and mostly confusing. But the Source wasn't really living. Living was here, where Edan could feel every bone in his body, every muscle, every beat of his heart. Living was about this hard work, about learning what he needed to while in the flesh, while being pulled by gravity, while trying to make the miracle while contained in a wrapper, no ability to bust out a move through any field of energy, the way one could in the Source. Living was about discovering the mystery here, behind the veil.

But how to tell this to Siker? How to convey something that Edan himself wouldn't have known unless he'd been in the Source for all those years?

There was a movement behind him, and Edan turned his head, looking behind him at a group of five people moving along the dried pathways with a cart of food and water that seemed to float with them. As he watched, he breathed in a sweet aroma of fruit and butter, of other things savory and tasty and rich with flavor. The air tasted so good, his mouth began to water

"Damn, it's about time," Siker said. "I've been dying for some of that chick's food. It's, like, so good. Awesome. I mean the best stuff you've ever had. Makes working in this heat almost worthwhile."

Turning slightly to follow Siker's gaze, Edan found his eyes holding the figure of a woman. He blinked, wondering why he couldn't get her in focus. For some reason, he couldn't really see "woman" at first, only her blur, only her essence, like the way he could taste the food that was coming without even eating it.

He blinked again, trying to find a focus, feeling as if he were underwater or in a dream he couldn't wake up from. Slowly . . . slowly. There. There! He could bring her into view. But he didn't see her form. What he saw instead was color—white and gold and red. This twirl of color, this amazing vision of her hit his eyes, and he felt the impact of the sight in his head, throat, chest. For a moment, he imagined that he was paralyzed, his feet like lead, his body stiff. He wanted to move forward, but could not, nothing in him seeming to work at all.

"What's up, man?" Siker said. "Are you okay? Is it sunstroke or something? You need some water? Man? Are you going to make it? Should I like call someone?"

Edan took a breath to steady himself and tried to nod, but he was stuck in stillness.

"Dude?"

Again, Edan tried to nod, his chin moving a little.

"Okay, then. But you look like you've seen something totally freaky," Siker said, his voice trailing off as the woman, the cart, and the four other people came toward them. As they did, they handed out food, the smell growing more delicious as they approached.

"Hey," Siker said to the woman. "You have any of that, like, tart thing?"

Edan couldn't move, couldn't speak, watching as the woman came toward him. He wanted to call out her name, but he didn't know what her name was, though he thought the sound of it would feel good on his tongue. Her name would be as tasty as the food she was handing out, something soft and lovely and delicious. There would be heat and softness to it. And beyond her name, everything else would be wonderful, too. The citrus taste of her, the smell of the delicate skin behind her ear, the warm feel of her skin under his palms. She would whisper to him, her voice a lazy cat in his ear. He wasn't sure how he knew any of this, but he could almost feel the silky smoothness of her upper arm, the shimmering slope of her neck, the dip of her lower back. How could his hand know that? How could he know anything about her at all? How could he have sense memory of someone he had never touched?

"Man," Siker was saying from what felt like a million miles away. "Are you, like, hungry? You should get some of this."

The woman came closer, her blond hair a wave flowing behind her, her dark brown eyes taking him in. Edan knew her eyes, had seen her gaze before, as if she'd looked at him before, so serious, so calm. Her face was smooth, unlined, flawless, so clear and clean he wanted to reach out a hand and touch her. But at the same time, he almost wanted to hold up his hands to avoid her direct gaze, her eyes seeming to dig into him and beyond, into the desert behind him. She was seeing too much, taking him in as he was taking her in, and he managed to tamp down his thoughts, not wanting her to hear and know any more than she already must.

"Would you like something to eat?" she asked, her voice just as he imagined, smooth and low and assured. But there was something faraway about her, too, as if she'd thrown on some kind of protective covering, thoughts, feelings, and even air seeming to push past and around her.

Edan struggled to find his words, wondering if his tongue would move to form the fricatives, plosives, and bilabials that would make words that she might understand. If he didn't focus, he realized he might find himself grunting like an animal, a primordial, prehistoric beast.

"Please," he said, pushing the word out too fast. "Yes."

Her eyes still on him, she handed him a package, the food warm in its wrapper.

"I hope you'll like it," she said.

"Do I—do I know you?" Edan asked, gripping the food a little too hard in his hands, the soft contents underneath his fingers slightly squishing.

The woman stared at him with her same still look, and then shook her head. "I don't think so."

"Where are you from?" He was almost barking out his words, and she stepped back once, twice, staring at him as she did.

"Here," she said. "Just outside Dhareilly."

"Were you in the Source?"

She shook her head, her eyes narrowing. She put a hand on her hip, shrugged slightly, her mouth in a slim, irritated line. "Why are you asking me this?"

Edan wanted to put his hands on her shoulders and shake her. Where had she been? Why hadn't she shown up before this? Why now in the desert? How could she be here, now, finally? Where had she been all this time? How could their meeting be as silly as this? Now she shows up carting food around, unable to truly see him. Her twin, standing right in front of her.

But maybe he was wrong. Maybe he was just lonely and tired and desperate to discover her. Maybe he was suffering from heatstroke, dizzy from dehydration, needing nothing more than a cool shower to calm his nerves. Despite his limited vocabulary, Siker was right. Edan needed rest, food, and water. That's all.

"I—" Edan began, about to introduce himself, but then a group of workers rounded the corner from the other side of the building and approached the cart, laughing and eager to eat the delicious food, the smells wafting everywhere.

Distracted, she turned toward the approaching people, and Edan stepped back, trying to find his breath.

"Man?" Siker said. "Looks like you've got a major thing going on. Some kind of animal instinct. Some kind of tribal reaction. Like you are about to—"

"Eat," Edan said. He turned away slowly, wondering where he could go to run away from this feeling, this impulse, this need. He wasn't sure if he could, but he put one foot in front of the other and moved, heading back toward the temporary shelter Jai and Risa had allotted him earlier.

The hot desert air against his face, the sun at his back, Edan found it hard to breathe, hard to concentrate. He needed to go back to the city. Working here in the intense sun had been the wrong idea. He was dreaming up his twin out of the sand and shrub and wavery lines of heat. He was trying to find what he hadn't in all his years in the Source. How could he possibly guide his people to anything if he couldn't even recognize his twin? If he was imagining that a woman handing out pie was the woman he'd been waiting for his entire life, how could he ever be a responsible leader?

"Man?" Siker called out from behind him. "Where are you, like, going? There's more to lunch than this."

Edan held up a hand, unable to turn around, unable to answer Siker. He didn't know where he was going except away, except out of here.

That night alone in his shelter, the soft desert air finally holding a little softness, a little chill, Edan dreamed the dream he'd had his entire life. In his dream, he is sitting in the spaceship, his small back against the wall, his two sisters sitting with him. He didn't always know the little girls were his sisters, but now in the dream, he does.

"Where are we going?" Mila asks him, her eyes almost black in the dark ship.

"We're going to someplace safe," he says to her, knowing now as his childhood dream self says the words, they aren't true. They aren't going somewhere safe because there isn't a safe place in the entire universe. But in the dream, he's telling her what he's been told, telling her what will make her feel better.

Next to Mila, Claire—Sophia as he called her then—is humming to herself, her head leaning on Mila's shoulder. Edan turns to look at them, and for a moment, he is filled with contentment. This is all, this is enough. All he needs in the entire world are his siblings, and the dreaming Edan knows that he has them now. They are here with him on this planet. For this moment, they are safe.

He wants to wake up, to move into consciousness, but he turns his child eyes to the corner of the spaceship, something he has never done before. What is he looking for? What does he see?

Blinking into the vision, he notices a little girl sitting with another group of children. Even surrounded by them, she seems alone, isolated, unwilling to move toward them and be part of the group.

Who are you? Edan thinks to her.

As if hearing him, she shakes her head, looks down, tries to hide, pushing herself back into the shadows of his vision.

I won't hurt you, he thinks. *I want to be your friend.*

But the little girl doesn't want to be friends with him or with anyone. She doesn't want to look up. He can tell by the way she moves her body that she's trying to make herself as small as possible. If she had the power to do so, she'd fold herself into squares until she disappeared into a packet of nothing. She'd break herself into confetti and float into the cracks and slide away. She'd disappear into a flume of smoke, a wisp of time, a flare of electricity and sizzle away.

She's so little, so scared that the adult dreamer Edan wants to pick her up, press her against his shoulder and tell her it will be okay. All right. Just fine. But all he can do is watch the vision in front of him.

In the dream, the ship moves suddenly, shakes them all around as if they've been hit from outside by a weapon, the sound around them only explosion, the walls vibrating, the floor a river of movement under them. The children scream, take in breath, some cry out again. As this happens, the girl turns, looks directly at him, takes in his gaze, and gazes back. Edan feels his body take in air even as the dream goes on inside his mind, his imagination humming.

Her eyes. Her eyes are still the same. Dark. Sad. Thoughtful. Completely focused. Protected. Her eyes look at him the same way they looked at him today in the desert. The way they looked at him as he asked her questions about the Source.

The ship moves again, and the girl turns from him, slips behind a group of children, and then the dreamscape vibrates, turns gray, everything filling in dark.

With a tremendous push, Edan sat up, yanking himself out of sleep and the shards of the dream. He sat up in his cot, looking around, as if he could find the girl still, though the story had ended, time gone by. She had hidden herself in the dream, in life, and really, now. She hadn't been looking for him. She hadn't been searching for her twin. No, she'd been out in the desert passing out food to workers.

He pushed back the thin blankets, feeling the cool floor under his feet. Outside in the quiet night, creatures scurried past in the brush, making slight, rustling noises. A cricket or a frog scratched a bleaty song and then was silent. A light shone brightly for a second and then turned off in a hush of whispers.

His thoughts today had been true and right. He had known from the instant he had seen her, the truth clear. Despite his disbelief that he would ever recognize her, ever find her, he had, here in the desert. The woman handing out food—the woman who had stared at him as he asked her questions—was his twin.

Edan pushed open the door and looked out onto the field of shelters, roofs glinting in the glow of the moon. Behind the shelters, the new buildings shone chrome and glass even from where he stood. Soon, this would be a new Cygiria, a place for them all to recoup and regroup, and now Edan might have his twin with him. He finally might be able to use his power for something useful, something that wouldn't hurt himself or others.

His body felt full of heat and fire, his intense need to find her building up in him as he tried to figure out what to do.

How to find her? What step next? He couldn't go rushing through the camp searching for her now, calling out her name. He couldn't even think her name, forcing out the thought so hard and so clear that she would meet him in the middle of the settlement. Edan didn't even know her name, not thinking to ask that. Siker had called her "that chick." The one who made the best food. He couldn't run out calling for the food chick, either.

So he'd have to go back to work tomorrow, sweating in the sun making pathways, and wait. Wait for his twin, his double, to show up. Wait for his future to round the bend, her hair streaming behind her, everything about her gold and white and red.

Chapter Three

Something made Ava want to keep stirring, keep the wooden spoon moving around and around the enormous steel pot, clicking and swooshing through the savory stew. She stared at the cooking food, not really seeing it, though, letting the spin mesmerize her. That's about all she was good for anyway. Since yesterday, she'd had a hard time doing anything, much less preparing the lunch meal for the workers over at Building C. After her trip out there yesterday, she'd felt sick. No, not sick. Dizzy. Giddy. Sad. Tingly, like pins and needles everywhere. Like things crawling up her body, things she didn't want to look at but needed to flick away. Maybe all this feeling was caused by the sun beating down, the hot dry wind, or the sand pelting her skin like relentless bugs. She didn't know, and for some reason, she didn't want to think about it or discover what was bothering her so much. So she stirred the pot, watching the swirl of vegetables spin round and round and round, orange, red, green, white.

"Hey," someone said, and Ava jerked up, blinking, her heart thumping hard. She tried to swallow, but her throat felt dry. Strangely, she realized that she was about ready to run away, bolt out of the shelter, head back home. Home? There was no home. This, sadly, was home. There was nowhere to go but exactly where she was.

Ava breathed in, blinked again, and then felt better as she saw Stephanie standing in front of her, her hands on her hips, her dark eyes full of light.

"Hi," Ava said, her voice small.

"What are you up to?" Stephanie asked. "From the looks of that enormous caldron you've got there, that isn't a pie. And I hope it isn't some kind of potion."

Pulling the spoon out of the pot and putting it down on the table, Ava walked to a chair and sat down, wiping her forehead with the back of her hand. "No, it's stew. For lunch. Vegetable and grudion."

"Grudion," Stephanie said. "Isn't that something on a football field? Our one football expert, Darl, would know, but he and Claire are staying in Dhareilly, so I can't ask."

Ava knew that Stephanie was making fun of her, but she wasn't sure how. And actually the teasing felt good, took the edge off her bad feeling, almost made her want to laugh.

"I don't know the way to think it so you'll understand. Maybe there is no translation available. Like a small bird. Fat. Pretty tasty."

"Ah," Stephanie said. "A chicken. I bet it's like chicken. Everything tastes like chicken anyway."

Ava nodded, having had chicken on Earth. And pretty much, grudion did taste like chicken.

Stephanie sat down in a chair opposite Ava, and they both watched other kitchen helpers walk in and take their places behind the counter, putting on aprons, stacking supplies on the shelves. Soon there were pots and pans banging, laughs, short, quick conversation, water running.

"So what's going on with you?" Stephanie asked. "You seem a little, well, upset."

Ava turned to Stephanie and shook her head. "Something happened yesterday. And I think—I think I need to go."

"Go where?" Stephanie asked.

"Anywhere but here," Ava said. "I need to leave Talalo."

"Why? What happened? Was it something bad?"

Ava rubbed her forehead, sighing. "I don't know. I went out to do my normal lunch rounds and I got this feeling. A weird feeling. And there was this man—"

"What man?" Stephanie's eyes were wide, interested, sparkling even in the diffused light in the shelter.

"Just a worker. A man out paving walkways."

"Ava!" Stephanie said, leaning closer. "I know this is probably an insensitive question based on our conversation yesterday. But do you think—I mean, could it have been your twin?"

Ava knew the question would come even before Stephanie asked it, and even though Ava wasn't reading her friend's thoughts. The question always had come, and yet, this time, she wasn't truly sure of her answer. "He wasn't a Cygirian, I don't think. He was with a group of Upsilian workers."

"Did you ask? Did you talk to him? Did you find out anything?"

Ava nodded, feeling uncomfortable. She knew she should have paid more attention, ignoring the workers' requests for food. And when she turned back to the man, he was gone, only his younger coworker still there, eating a huge piece of pastry, smiling at her as if he'd taken a few too many hits of Gton, the drug rebellious Upsilian kids smoked. Even so, she could have asked him about the man, but instead, she'd walked away and done her job, just like she did every day.

"I did talk to him for a little bit, but then I had to do my job." Ava looked down at her hands, wishing she had the ability that she knew Garrick possessed. If she could go back in time, she'd try the whole meeting all over again. She'd look at the man and ask him who he was, ask him what his power was. But then again, if he'd been her twin, he would have known her. He would have said something. He *should* have said something! "But I don't really . . . I'm not interested."

"What? You aren't interested? What does that mean? How can you say that?" Stephanie said, and then she recovered herself, adding, "Okay. Okay. All right. I'm probably overreacting. But just as a point of curiosity, wouldn't you want to know your twin? Even if you feel complete and whole right now of yourself, wouldn't you want to meet the man who matched your power? Talk to him? See who he is, what he is like? I mean, even Porter wanted to meet me!"

Ava slumped against the back of the chair, trying to keep her ridiculous tears from leaving her eyes. Of course she wanted to meet him. And, of course, she didn't want to meet him at all, ever. Meeting him would mean that she had even more to lose in this world than she already did. Meeting him would make her complete and also put her right there on the teetering edge of loss. If she knew him, if she had him, then his absence would be even more painful than it was now.

"No, no, no," Stephanie said. "Holy cow. You can't think that way, Ava."

Ava started, not realizing she'd let her thoughts loose.

Stephanie reached over and put her hand on Ava's. "Look, it's all a risk. Life is a damn risk. We're here and anything could happen at any moment. The flipping Neballats could show up now and have a field day with us, destroy all the work that we've done here. But don't you think having that intense, amazing connection with a man, even if it is for a little while, would be worth it?"

Breathing in slowly, deeply, Ava thought about her new

friend's question. Was it worth it? Was living fully for a short time better than living okay forever? And truth be told, Ava wasn't sure that she'd been living "okay." Since she'd come out of the Source, the innocuous days had slipped into long flat weeks and then months. Okay was bland and lonely and still, and since coming out of the Source, she hadn't felt as much since seeing the man in the desert, looking into his dark eyes, feeling—feeling everything.

"You saw him while you were serving lunch, right?" Stephanie asked.

"Yes," Ava said. "He was there with the crew."

"Okay, so you go back. Today. And when you see him, you reach out and take his hand. That will show you what you need to know."

"Shouldn't I talk with him first? Shouldn't I make sure before I touch him?"

Standing, Stephanie put her hands on her hips and shook her head. "No. Don't talk. It's not like you are making much sense about this anyway. And the knowing you have of each other will come right through that first touch. It will all make sense, or it won't."

The word *no* flicked through Ava's brain. No to this idea. No to the touch. No to finding it all out. No to the way her life would change once she found her twin. No to the despair she would feel if he wasn't who she imagined he could be. No to the pain she would suffer if something happened to him.

Ava looked to the door, thinking that she could slip out and get a transport back to Dhareilly. She didn't have to stay here. She could be of some use elsewhere. Maybe she'd go try to find her Upsilian family, see if they'd take her back. Maybe she'd go with the teams looking for Cygirians on Earth.

"You can't run away from this," Stephanie said. "I mean, you could try, but I don't think you'd get very far. The truth has long arms."

"I could go," Ava said quietly. "I don't have to stay. I don't need to. No one will miss me."

Stephanie sighed. "Jeez, listen. I'll tell you what. I'll come with you. Porter, too. We will volunteer for lunch duty and we are going to help you ladle out stew. Trust me, we won't take no for an answer."

Ava swallowed, fear settling at the back of her throat. "Oh," was all she managed to say.

"And once I tell Porter this story, he won't rest. He's got this strange affection for narratives, the kind with an ending you can see. So don't try to run away. He'd just find you."

Ava felt irritation tingle through her body, retorts fomenting in her throat. She clenched her hands together, lowered her eyes. "Why is this so important to you? Why do you feel you need to help me with this? It doesn't mean anything to you if I find my twin."

"It does matter to me. A lot. Because this is who we are," Stephanie said. "We are halves of a whole. We are all made stronger if you two can find your power together. And it doesn't matter how the whole fits together. Like with Porter and me. We're a bit confusing. But I told you I wouldn't have it any other way. And if you run away from this opportunity, Ava, you will regret it. That I know."

Slowly, Ava stood, looking at Stephanie and then at the bubbling stew pot. In an hour, lunch would be ready. In a little more time, she would be standing in front of the man who might be her other half.

"That's right," Stephanie said. "That's exactly right."

* * *

The desert was a different place today, some sort of storm pattern hanging over the sky, holding down the horizon tight, the gray sky solid with unshed rain. The air felt lighter, softer, full of moisture that must have evaporated before it hit the ground. The creatures of the desert seemed to notice the change, not burrowing under the sand for protection as they usually did, tiny red lizards scuttling under the brush as Ava, Porter, and Stephanie passed by, birds cackling in the prickly Vs of cacti, snakes' S tracks undulating across the sand. The air was hot, but a periodic cool breeze waves kept Ava from sweating too much. And if there were one more degree in the air, she would be sweating because she was nervous, her body tingling, her breath at some undisclosed location in her body. It was a miracle she was even still alive.

What was she doing?

What you have to do, Stephanie thought.

Together, they and Ava's other kitchen staff members were walking alongside the food cart, the stew, sandwiches, salads, and desserts ready for the workers. Porter's eyebrows seemed permanently raised, but he hadn't said anything sarcastic since he'd walked into the shelter ready to accompany them.

Then, he'd put his hands on his hips and said, "I'm ready to be the matchmaker."

But when no one responded, Ava looking down at her hands, Stephanie rolling her eyes, Porter stopped speaking, saying nothing but staying close to her as they walked toward the buildings.

When they approached the first corner of the building, workers put down their tools and materials and approached them. Ava didn't see the man from the day before, and she looked up at the building that was almost now complete as were the pathways and landscaping that surrounded it. Other buildings nearby had gone up just as quickly, and soon Ava's work would no longer be required. This new Cygirian city, Talalo, would be complete, and her business would be about finding their rhythm, their culture, their lives.

"What's up for today?" a worker said, and Ava looked up at his question, recognizing him as the young man who loved her pastry from the day before. "Man, I know it's going to be something great. You are, like, one awesome cook."

Ava backed away a little, and Stephanie put a hand on her shoulder. "What? Is that him?" she asked, her voice soft at Ava's ear.

"No."

"What's the deal, then?" Both she and Porter looked at her.

Ava shook her head, breathed in, looked up at the worker who was taking a bowl of stew from one of the kitchen staff. Stephanie was right. Ava had to do this. She really had no choice. Running away wasn't an option. Not anymore.

She moved toward the young man, finding the words she needed to say. But they were clunky and hard to move on her tongue. She pressed her hands against her thighs, breathed in, and then found herself standing next to him.

"That man you were working with yesterday," she asked the young man, "is he here today?"

He looked up at her and smiled, blinked.

"The man you were working with yesterday? The tall one with the blond hair, brown eyes. Is he here?"

The man nodded and moved his hand in a little circle, indicated that he would speak after he was done chewing something he'd managed to gulp down before getting to the stew.

"Man," he said after a moment. "This food is so awesome."

"The man?" Stephanie asked, impatient, her arms crossed.

"You mean the dude who was in the Source? The kind of freaky guy. Not freaky. More like spooky—"

"He was in the Source," Ava repeated. Of course he had been. That's why he'd asked her. But as she stood there, trying to form another question for the young man, she thought about her time in the Source. She'd never seen the man from yesterday. Not in all that time.

"What's his name?" Stephanie asked, just as the young man took in another mouthful of stew. "Do you know who he is?"

Good damn Lord, Stephanie thought. *We'll never get him to talk with all this food around.*

"Uh," the man said. "Don't you want to know my name? I mean, it is polite to ask and all."

Though she wanted to scream at him, Ava nodded, wanting to hurry him along.

"I'm Siker," he said, smiling. "And you are the pie lady."

"My name is Ava," she said. "This is Stephanie and Porter."

Porter sighed, letting out the words that he had clearly been holding back. "All of this introduction is charming, Mr. Siker, but we would truly like to know who the man is you worked with. Surely you can supply us with that information. Surely it won't tax you too much?"

"Tax?"

Porter hacked out a half laugh, his eyes wide.

"What is his name?" Stephanie almost yelled, and even though Ava was nervous and scared and desperate to know her twin's name, she almost laughed at the shock on Siker's face.

"Uh, okay, hold on." Siker wiped his mouth with the back of his hand. "It's E something. Like, uh, like, uh . . . Evan. E

with a, like, kinda hard sound after it. You know. Like a V
or a K or an L."

"Evan?" Stephanie asked. "Ekan? Elan?"

Siker listened to her say the name and then shook his head.
"Nah, none of those. It's not Ekan for sure. How lame is
that?"

Siker looked at the three of them, pleased, it seemed, to
be at the center of attention.

"I will probably do something to you that is illegal if you
don't figure it out," Stephanie said, smiling so much that
Siker didn't sense the threat in her words. But Ava imagined
what Siker might look like if he got a whiff of her and
Porter's electricity.

"Right. Like, okay. I know it. It's Edan. His name is Edan.
But he, like, is so not here today. Left us shorthanded, the
jerk."

Ava was about to thank Siker, when she turned to Stephanie
and Porter who were staring at each other, clearly having a
conversation.

"What?" Ava asked. "Do you know him?"

Stephanie looked at her, blinking. "Yeah, we know him.
Of course we know him. Everyone knows him. Don't you?"

Ava stepped back, allowing Siker room to finish his meal.
"No. Why should I?"

"My dear girl," Porter said. "Have you been living in a
hole?"

Ava felt her skin prickle, and she swallowed. "I was in
the Source for a long time."

"But you came out of the Source. I know because I pulled
you out bodily. And then you were at the safe house. What—
where?" Porter seemed suddenly unable to find words, a
fact that relieved Ava. But his silence didn't last.

"Well," he said, his words filled with sighs and irritation.

"As we know, Edan was likewise in the Source. For a very long time. An excursion there doesn't seem to be much of an excuse these days, though everyone seems to be shamelessly trying to use it."

Stephanie put her hand on Porter's arm, pushing him away and moving closer to Ava. "You really haven't heard of Edan Mirav?"

"No, no, no," Ava said. "Never."

As she tried to figure out the confused look on Stephanie's face, Ava realized she really wanted to leave. She suddenly didn't want to hear anything that they had to say about this Edan Mirav. This whole situation was ridiculous. This experiment had failed. This wasn't working. She needed to get back to her kitchen and peel some fruit. She wanted to push her hands into bread dough or chop a whole bag of onions. She wanted to roast tomatoes and make a thick, delicious sauce, redolent with garlic and herbs. She wanted to slice figs and pears and arrange them in fruit fans on trays. But if she stayed in the kitchen, she would be close to where *he* was.

No, she needed to get back to the city, busy, ordered Dhareilly taking her mind off all this. There, she could try to negotiate the streets, the ordered rules about who could come and go and when, and find something useful to do. But that wouldn't work, either. Stephanie and Porter knew him. He would find her. Maybe she needed to go back into the Source where none of this out here seemed to matter.

Nothing made sense, and even though she was confused and upset, she could still see him: his warm, sandy skin, his strong arms, powerful chest, his hair blowing in front of his eyes. And he had looked at her, really looked at her, seen her.

But not clearly enough. Not clearly enough to come find her now.

Ava tried to turn away from them all, but Stephanie reached out and grabbed her wrist, her grasp firm but gentle.

"This is weird. I mean, well, he's," Stephanie began. "He's kind of . . . actually—"

"Flat out, he's our leader," Porter said. "He's the one who is going to lead us in the battle against the Neballats."

Ava felt her mouth open, her jaw grow slack. As she tried to find her breath, she noticed that Siker's mouth was open, too, and it wasn't necessarily a pretty sight, what with the lunch he was still consuming.

But this was ridiculous! How could this be?

"It can't be true," she said, shaking her head. "That's not possible."

"It is true, Ava," Stephanie said. "Really, it is."

"I don't believe it. What is he doing paving sidewalks?" she asked. "Why is he in the desert doing this kind of work instead of working with the Upsilian ambassador or something? Shouldn't he be figuring out battle plans against the Neballats or negotiating our rights?"

Stephanie looked at Porter and then shrugged, saying, "The last I knew, that's exactly what he was doing. He was in meetings with the Cygirian Council for weeks. I didn't know he was out here at all. No one told us."

"He probably wanted a break from the madding crowd," Porter said. "The rabble. The bourgeoisies. The groupies. The arduous decisions."

"So, like, why was, like, the leader of all you Cygirians hanging with me?" Siker said, licking his fingers. "Why's he here with us day laborers? The ones who barely escaped being thrown in jail or fried on the street? It's kind of a miracle I'm still alive, man."

Porter looked down at Siker and sighed before saying, "Yes, the miracle of your life is remarkable, my friend. But why Edan was here remains to be debated. Suffice it to say it's a big unknown."

Ava, Stephanie, and Porter stood still, all of them filled with questions that floated between them.

Why was he here?

What is he up to?

Where is he now?

Why didn't he say something to Ava? To me? To her?

The hot wind blew into Ava's face, kissing her with sandy lips. She stirred, breathed, tried to take in the unbelievable scene around her. Here she was, staring at a worker as he ate, trying to figure out why the leader of their entire people had been smoothing hot, wet pavement. There Stephanie and Porter were, standing next to her, their mouths slightly open, sand blowing everywhere. Ridiculous.

Ava shook her head, thinking, thinking, trying to find a thought that made sense. But nothing did. As they finished serving the workers, the kitchen staff began to move toward the other side of the building and more hungry customers. Without looking at Stephanie, Porter, or Siker, Ava followed them.

"What are you doing?" Stephanie asked.

"My job," Ava said, wishing—for the first time since meeting Stephanie—that her new friend would go away. She walked faster, hoping to leave them behind her.

"How can you run away?" Stephanie called out. "This isn't something you can ignore, Ava. And Edan's power. He needs you. He's lost years and years of himself. You are the only one who can help him. And we all need him. Cygiria needs Edan and the longer he goes without his twin, the older he will get. Don't you understand that?"

Ava kept walking, but then Stephanie's words seeped into her brain, and she looked down at her own soft smooth hand. She had always had this ability to keep herself young. It was never cause for alarm for her, one of the few solaces she'd had in her lonely life. She would have caught herself if she went back too far, never waking up as a child by accident. But the opposite! The ability to push yourself toward the end? To watch yourself prematurely age, to feel your insides somehow lose the ability to do what they needed to? Heart slowing, kidneys failing, arteries clogging.

What had happened inside Edan? What kind of help could she give him? What miracle of unaging would occur if they did ever chance to touch, hold hands, close their eyes, and change things?

Slowing her pace, Ava knew that all her time in the Source made death not so scary. When you died, you went there, to the place of all souls. It wasn't like life, but it was consciousness. What was more frightening was to live this life in pain, in hurt, the body betraying the soul by crumbling apart. And without her, Edan would slowly, accidentally, push himself sooner toward the Source.

"That's right," Porter said. "And you are the only one who has the ability to bring him back to his true age. Can you imagine what it must feel like to know that you've damaged yourself accidentally? Most of us drink or smoke or eat fried fatty foods by choice. But Edan is at the mercy of his own inattentiveness. You could fix it all. And while this might bring a wrinkle or two to your rosy skin, it would be worth it. For all of us."

Ava stopped, nodded, realizing that everything Stephanie and Porter said was true. If she and Edan were in fact twins, she did owe him this. She owed him the years he had spent without wanting to, back when his powers were unclear to him. Maybe he lost years still, in that time just before waking fully or when he wasn't concentrating, relaxing into the pull of years in his body.

She turned, facing her friends and the buildings in the background. "All right," she said. "Let's go find him."

Stephanie smiled, and Ava saw relief brush away all of Porter's sarcasm.

"Let me find Jai and Risa and find out where Edan is," Stephanie said quickly, moving fast now, worried, it would seem, that Ava was about to change her mind. "Then you can meet him. Then we can figure this all out."

"You don't know where he is?" Porter was restrained, careful, respectful, something Ava had never really seen him be before. "He is simply gone?"

Jai nodded, turning to Risa. "We had him settled, found him work, and then he just disappeared. Yesterday. We couldn't find him last night when we came to talk with him about future plans."

Ava looked at Jai and Risa, these two original twins from Earth, the first twins to find the safe house. The first to fight against the Neballats. The first to begin to understand Cygirian culture. They seemed almost to gleam, both tall and blond and dark eyed, radiating something so brilliant Ava wanted to step closer so she could peer at them. Of course she had seen them at the safe house, but she'd never had the opportunity to meet them, and now they were in charge of so much of the rebuilding of Cygiria. They were almost becoming Cygirian, even if Stephanie and Porter said it was Edan who was the leader.

These two, though, represented the struggle, the fight, the endurance that Cygiria needed to find its way. They were that important. Ava knew that talking to them was equal to talking with the Grand Council Head of Upsilia or the president of that big country on Earth, the one she'd stayed in. But here—right in front of her—Jai and Risa were in the kitchen, talking with Porter and Stephanie.

"Do you think something happened to him?" Stephanie asked. "Something bad?"

"No," Risa said. "Well, I don't know. But I didn't get a message or a feeling. He sent no thoughts our way. It seems he just wanted to leave."

Porter sighed, shook his head. "He doesn't understand."

"Understand what?" Jai said.

"His twin. Double. We found her."

At the same time, Jai and Risa turned to look at Ava, both of them breaking into smiles, their shine and brilliance trebling, sending a pulse that Ava could almost feel on her skin. She felt herself blush at their intense gaze, and she tried to keep her eyes level.

"I'm Ava Arganos," she said, holding out her hand, hoping that she wasn't shaking enough for them to notice.

Both Jai and Risa stood up, walking to her, shaking her hand one at a time. "He has been looking for you," Risa said. "He has been needing you."

"We've been needing you," Jai said. "You and Edan together are what we need so badly."

"So we simply must find our slippery friend, discover where he's slithered off to," Porter said. "And now. Pronto."

Risa shook her head, her long, smooth hair a wave of blond. "We've called out. We've done a group thought call and nothing. If he's heard us, he doesn't want to be reached."

Ava listened to them as they continued to talk. No one could reach him, but she was his twin. As the group tried to figure ways to find Edan, Ava let a slim sliver of thought leave her mind, push away from her, shoot out past the kitchen, the encampment, the construction site, the desert. Her thought circled the desert, a curl of an idea, a whip of consciousness.

Where are you? she thought.

Her breath hanging in her lungs, she waited, trying to keep what she was doing secret.

Where are you? I have discovered you. I am your twin. Your double. I want to find you. I don't want to run away from you anymore, so please let me know where you are. Let me find you.

For a tiny second, she heard something, felt something. The tiny blond hairs on her arm rose, her stomach twitched, her heart *beat-beat* against her ribs. There it was, a sound. A rustle, like the wind against a flicken bush in the desert, the dried leaves cackling out a cry. Like a lizard scrabbling into the sand. Like a snake sliding its serpentine S up a dune. One bird pecking a cactus, its wings shiny from the sun. But then there was no follow-up. Nothing.

Ava let the thought dissolve, her mind settling back into the kitchen and the conversation the others were engaged in.

"I think we are going to just have to wait for him to want to be found," Jai was saying. "He knows where we are and how much we need him. He's not irresponsible to our cause. But it seems he wants some time."

Ava knew there was nothing she could say to this. If Edan Mirav was who he was, he would understand his people's need for him. And maybe, his escape was doing what they all needed the most. It was also possible that his not wanting to see her, to meet her was part of the plan. If, as all her time in the Source suggested, there had to be a bigger plan, a master plan.

Stephanie seemed to catch that thought, and turned to Ava and shrugged before turning back to the group.

"Let's just let him do what he needs to," she said, putting a light hand on Ava's arm. "Let's just see what happens."

Everyone listened, still in thought for a moment, and then nodded. Porter seemed about to roll his eyes and then caught himself, but his mouth went back to its almost constant sarcastic smirk.

"I suppose Edan knows what he's doing. He's a big boy."

At that comment, the kitchen staff seemed to appear at once, moving the pots and pans as they always did, running the water, laughing. And then Ava and Stephanie were walking out of the kitchen shelter, into the desert afternoon, the sun beating down hard on them both.

"I know you're not convinced you want to meet him," Stephanie said. "But it will be worth it. So please stay. Please wait for him to come back."

Ava breathed in, feeling the heat in her mouth, her lungs, everything inside her aching from strain. But why? She had done no exercise, had run nowhere, hadn't been crying or wailing. But she felt Edan's absence like that exerted ache, like the aftermath of pneumonia, like the burn of a terrible scream. She hated it. She hated being at the mercy of a person she didn't know, her body and her mind affected.

"I'm sorry," Stephanie said. "I'd hoped he'd be here."

For a moment, Ava thought to say, "Me, too." But she wasn't sure if that statement was true. What was true? She didn't have an idea, but she nodded as if to agree.

"Just do what you always do," Stephanie said. "Go to work and make that to-die-for food. Feed the workers. Try to ignore that Siker idiot. And hang out with me a little bit. I'm not always attached to Porter. I mean, we could go grab a drink at that cantina we set up. Drink some of that amazing stuff the Upsilians brought in. I'm not sure what it's called, but it requires a great deal of sleep in a darkened room for twelve hours afterward."

"Shamma," Ava said. "I've never had any."

"It's about time, then, for some shamma," Stephanie said, just as Porter and Jai and Risa came out of the shelter. "It's about time for you to have a little fun."

As they all walked together toward the sleeping shelters, Ava looked out toward the desert, the outline of Dhareilly barely visible in the distance. The sun was casting its lowering light against the mountains that rimmed the desert, everything slowly turning orange and red and bronze. Then she looked at the buildings they were erecting, the city that would soon be theirs. She had to stay here. There really was no place else. Nowhere to go but here. And even if she set out to find Edan, where would she start? She knew nowhere to go, nowhere to look. This was home now. This was where she would wait.

Ava put her hand on Stephanie's shoulder, not saying a word. Stephanie understood, though, and smiled.

"You were right about one thing, Steph," Porter said. "Time for a drinkie-poo."

Ava giggled as Stephanie rolled her eyes.

"How is it that you are my twin? You are absolutely insane. A total nut bar," Stephanie said to Porter, but she took Ava's hand and together, they followed Porter toward the cantina.

The good news was that shamma tasted like treacle, sweet and lovely like burnt sugar, redolent of caramel and pecans. It went down like syrup, like soda, like the most delicious drink Ava had ever had. The bad news was that Ava had three glasses of it without much in her stomach but a few

stew vegetables. But it was such a relief to feel this way—
light and free and happy. All the long years of holding things
in, keeping herself together out here, away from the Source,
seemed to fall away. Everything felt expansive: her thoughts,
her body, her ability to love. How could she have ever wanted
to get away from Stephanie and Porter? She loved the conversation with them; she loved them. They bickered, they
laughed, they brought her into their twosome, making her
feel connected. How could this feeling end? And why should
it? She didn't want it to. She wanted to feel this happy all
the time.

The music whirled around her, the desert air warm and
soft. The laughter in the crowd was reassuring, comforting,
as if there were no Neballats. As if there was hope that they
would all live together one day, like this, laughing and
loving.

She hummed with pleasure, sipped the last drops of shamma
from her glass, licked her lips.

Before they left the cantina, Ava wanted to have one
more glass, but Stephanie pulled Ava to standing.

"What was I thinking?" Stephanie said. "I've created a
monster. No more shamma for you. Ever, I think. Back on
the wagon for you."

"Wagon?" Ava asked, her word sort of ending in a very
long *n* sound.

"You are such a stellar influence," Porter said, burping.
"What a role model."

"Excuse me, Mr. I Drank All Night," Stephanie said.
"Don't try to blame this all on me."

Ava couldn't quite make out the argument that followed,
but somehow she made it back to her shelter, Stephanie and
Porter carrying her to her cot, the world slowly spinning as
she fell asleep.

* * *

In her dream, she is in complete darkness, nothing in front of her but a light that blinks one-two, one-two. No, it's not a light but a star or a planet, heavy and white in the ochre sky. And the air. It's soft and light and warm, skiffing against her skin as she walks. As her eyes grow accustomed to the night, she can see the lumpy shapes of bushes, squat trees, rocks.

Ava is tired. She's been walking all night away from . . . away from? She turns back to look at a tiny group of lights on the horizon. She knows she can't go back there for a while. But why? Is it too dangerous? Too threatening? No, that's not it. Too confusing. There is something back at those lights that bothers her, so it's just best to leave. She doesn't have time to fix what is broken, so it's just best to leave and walk and walk and walk.

Even though it is she who is moving in the dream, Ava wants to stop her dream self to figure out what she is confused about. She wants to turn to herself, put her arm on her own shoulder and tell herself everything will be okay. But she also wants to tell herself to explain what exactly is going on. Ava needs to know what she is running away from. Yet there is no time to waste. She has to make it to her destination. But where is she headed? Ava feels her eyes find an object in front of her, the focus coming in slowly. Another rock. She walks around it, pushing through the cool sand toward a large shadow in front of her.

Where does this journey end? How far will she travel? What is she doing walking at night, without a light, feeling her way through the prickly terrain? A slight, sudden wind throws sand and what feels like leaves at her. She jumps, startled, afraid that some of the tiny things pelting her face might be bugs. Spiders. Scorpions. Moths with fuzzy antenna and dark black eyes.

Home, her dream self says. *I want to go home. I don't want to be here anymore.*

Home can't mean the small suburb she grew up in, that house that always seemed so empty and so cold. It wouldn't be her room, the place she closed herself away in every night to avoid seeing the lack of feeling in her adopted parents' eyes. And what else was home but that? It had been sad and lonely, but it's what she'd had.

The dream moon emerges from a bank of clouds, glowing silver and bright. A bat flies in a twisty twirl to her left. Fluttery insects and night creatures rustled around her, the darkness full of the life hidden during the heat of the day.

She turns, looks into the void, feels something grip her. A feeling, something twisted and black and hateful pulsing in her quickly and then leaving. She spins, looking for whatever had held her, but there is nothing but sand and sky and the eerie moon.

She breathes, looks down suddenly on the dream as if it were a movie, seeing herself walking away, the journey for this Ava not yet over. She wants to rejoin herself. Ava wants to know more about what home means, but as she stretches out to touch herself on the shoulder, the dream begins to stretch apart, to grow thin, to disappear, and she is left blinking into the darkness of the shelter.

Ava bolted upright, her heart and head pounding from too much shamma, her stomach a prickly pear of upset. She put a hand to her stomach and looked at the shelter, breathing hard, expecting something to be there. Expecting to have to explain something to someone. But it was simply her, her forthcoming hangover, and her sleeping shelter mates, the tent quiet and full of night.

She pushed off her blankets and slipped off her cot, rummaging in the drawers by her bed. She might have a headache right now; she might not be able to eat for a few days until her stomach forgave her. But she could carry water, and maybe some food to tide her over when her appetite returned. After having nothing from the time she returned from the Source, she was a master at traveling light. And no matter what, she was going into the desert. Right now.

Dressing quietly and in the dark, Ava knew she had no choice but to follow the path of her dream, walk the steps she had walked already because somewhere, at the end of the dream story, was home, the place that was her center. Somewhere at the end of the dream road was Edan Mirav.

Chapter Four

Edan's companion pulled his covering over his head, keeping his eyes shrouded. The rest of his body was likewise wrapped, his shoulders, torso, and legs covered against the night. At some point, Edan thought that the indecipherability of his companion's form almost made him invisible, imaginary, as though Edan were walking alone, this black swath of a figure only in his imagination.

But the man was there, his feet in the sand, his breathing audible. So Edan wasn't delusional; he was simply walking with a mystery.

Edan looked to the west, the sun not yet even a glimmer. But in a couple of hours, it would begin to rise from behind the mountains, and at that time, they would both have to find shelter. There was no Cygirian power out here, no way to keep the glaring sharp light off their skin, the heat from enveloping them like smoke. Edan had spent a day in the desert already, but as he walked, he wondered if maybe it had been longer. Maybe two days? Half a week? A week?

"It's growing warmer," his companion said, interrupting Edan's thoughts.

"Maybe it's a good time for you to go," Edan said. "You don't have to be here."

"I saw you alone in the desert, and thought, Why is he wandering? What is he looking for? He could use a little company," the man said. "Everyone can use a little help in times like these. You need help, don't you? You are likely very lost here in the darkness. You can't see what you are looking for."

"I don't really know what I am looking for," Edan said, half out of the desire to be alone, half out of truth. *What was he doing?*

The man seemed to nod, but it was difficult to really see what he was doing, the darkness and his clothes masking everything.

Edan sighed, and then took a swallow of his water. They had been walking for hours in the cool night, but now the sand glinted like diamonds in the coming dawn.

"Truly, you won't hurt my feelings if you go," Edan said. "I set off alone on purpose. And I am pretty sure that I can find my way."

"But you left to lose your way. To run away," the man said. "To escape what you must face."

"I know what we must face." Edan thought of Talalo, the city they were building out of the sand. He thought of the inevitable battle with the Neballats. He thought of the search he must make at some point for the woman, the one he was sure was his double. Once with her, he would be able to give his power fully to his people. None of this was avoidable. None of this he could run away from. But he could put it off, he could hide.

"You can't hide from your path." The man's voice was deep and clear.

Edan nodded. "I know. We—"

The man stopped, his gloved hand reaching out and touching Edan. "Not we. Not you and Cygiria. You."

Shrugging him off, Edan kept walking. "I know what I must face."

"So why do you keep going, my friend? Why do you leave behind the woman? And why don't you determine your powers with her? Why do you leave behind love?"

Edan shook his head, kept walking, wishing that his companion would simply disappear, as quickly as he had appeared just hours after Edan had set off from Talalo. Was it hours or was it days? Time had gotten a little confusing, the sun and moon and sun in a cycle he'd no longer been able to keep track of. Hot, cold; light, dark. But in any case, he hadn't asked for such companionship. Hadn't wanted anyone near him because he wanted to think. And he really didn't want to think about the woman. What were the chances that his twin, his double, his partner in power and perhaps in life had been right there in the desert? After all of his long years in the Source—the place where all things merged and flowed in one smooth energy stream—after all the searching for a mere trace of her, why would she suddenly just be there serving food? It was too ordinary, too ridiculous, too ludicrous. More than that, it was too good to be true, and Edan had felt something in himself shut off, turn away, need to go.

So here he was, but now he had this annoying companion for the journey. They walked, their legs in a metronome of strides, on and on and on, the journey never seeming to end.

"But what else would you be thinking of? How could you just shut out the surprise and wonder of her?" the man asked. "Even though there are bigger questions, you should be only of her. Yes, there are so many larger ideas to contemplate. But your twin? Your double? That is worth the thoughts."

Edan couldn't imagine what large ideas the man was re-

ferring to. What else was there to think about right now?
Things were settled with Upsilia. He and the council had ar-
ticulated the plan that would allow Cygirians to live on the
planet, the city was being built, and every day, more Cygirians were arriving, their numbers swelling. The only question, the only danger, was, as usual, the Neballats and their
intentions. But this was known, considered, inevitable.

"Ideas such as?" Edan said.

The man paused, his breath light and soft. Edan turned
to look at him as they both walked on. The man's face was
still covered, and between his clothing and the murky light,
Edan could only make out the dull glint of one bright eye.
The man's form, his body, appeared strong and tall; he was
able, it would seem, to walk a long time in the desert. A
long time, time Edan would be stuck with him.

"Well?" Edan asked.

The man laughed, the sound low and deep.

"Impatience!" he said. "All right, then. Ideas such as why
don't you take control of all of this? Such as why Cygiria
doesn't crush its enemy with its powers right now. It is possible. Think of all that Cygirians can do. The forces of nature, the power over life and death, of the very processes in
the body. The elements—fire, water, air, earth. Your enemy
wants you all for the powers that you have. Don't you ask
yourself why? Don't you realize that you could have it all
just like this, in seconds?"

The man snapped his fingers, the slight sound echoing in
the desert dawn.

"But this is not what we want. Not what I want. We
don't want to crush them. We want to be left alone."

The man stopped walking, turned to Edan, both eyes
white with reflected moon.

"How can you know you don't want to crush them? Can

you honestly tell me you have never wanted to take the Neballats—the remnants of their entire culture—and break them in two?"

Edan swallowed, trying to find a way into the man's thoughts. But they were locked down tight. And he realized he wasn't quite sure how the man got here with him, how he appeared at all. As in dreams, the segue between his arrival and now was fuzzy, unclear, even though this moment, the now, was in sharp focus.

What he was saying, though, was clear, made sense.

"We don't want to fight," Edan said. "We don't want to do anything but live our lives. We want to be able to just live out the day without worrying about the Neballats. We want to have children, create some context, figure out our culture." Edan stopped suddenly, realizing that he was breathing hard, his body full of desire for his people, for Cygiria, to have a place.

"But if they were gone, you could have all that right now. No worries, ever." The man seemed to laugh, the sound muffled by his face covering.

"We don't want to kill them. We don't want to destroy what little they have left."

"Oh no? Even after what they did to your parents, the generations before that? Even after the way they've chased you throughout the universe? Even after they've kept you from the life you could have lived with your twin?"

Edan thought of many sentences about living in harmony with others in the universe, ideas he truly believed in, but he realized that a new feeling was pooling in his chest, hot and full. The man was right. He wanted the Neballats gone, dead, away. He did hate them completely and without remorse. He hated them for all the death. For all the struggle. He hated that he'd been separated from whatever family he might have had. He hated that he wasn't sure who his twin was, that he had to search over the universe for her. He hated that whenever Cygiria managed to find a small toehold—the safe house, Upsilia—the Neballats were there ready to destroy it. As he thought, he crafted new sentences like daggers, sentences that would tell the man how he wanted the Neballats dead.

In his mind's eye, he imagined a house that he lived in, somewhere quiet, somewhere warm. And without wanting to put her there, Edan imagined that in the house was a woman, his twin, his double, the one who helped them both stay the age that they were supposed to be. A woman who loved him, who matched his strength, his temperament, his physical being. She understood him completely, knew his thoughts, his feelings, his needs just as he did hers. His mind filled in the blank and into this opening, Edan put the woman from the day before, her blond hair a whoosh of fire surrounding her, her eyes bright and wild. He could almost imagine her laughter, even though the day before, she'd seemed so serious, so silent, so solemn. But not in this dream. No, in this house there was laughter and joy. In the house were children—his and hers—children who would grow up without having to run, without having to be thrown into the Source, without having to hide no matter where they went. They would know their parents, they would find their twins. And their children would have the same comfort, the same knowledge that what they needed was right before them at all times.

"Yes," Edan whispered. "Yes. This is what I want. This is what we must all have. This is how we should live."

The man and he walked on, up a bit, toward the edge of a slight hill. Stopping, they both exhaled, the air actually crisp and cold enough that their breath looked like plumes of smoke.

The man cleared his throat, the sound somehow transparent, light. "The walk has been long," he said.

Edan nodded, realizing that his body felt fatigued, as if he had been walking for weeks instead of hours. "It has."

"How much longer will you walk? How far will you sojourn?"

Edan wanted to answer the man, but he didn't have anything to say. He wanted to walk as long as he needed to. He wanted to walk until this feeling left him. This longing. This ache.

"I'm not certain," he said.

"Then you must eat. You've long run out of food," the man said.

Looking down at the bag he had packed the day before, Edan realized that he was, in fact, out of food. At the thought of food, his stomach growled. Oh, what he would do with some of the stew the woman offered up yesterday at the construction site. Some of that pie. Everything she had made seemed so rich, so delicious, so tasty.

"A bowl of stew," the man said. "That would hit the spot, wouldn't it? Fill you right up."

The stew, and then the woman, Edan thought. Food for the body, food for the soul. He felt so empty, so bereft, so without anything holding him down on this planet.

"You could make it happen," the man said.

"What?" Edan heard the promise, the temptation, in the man's statement.

"Food. Nourishment. You could turn . . ." The man paused, lifting up his hand, indicating shrubs, rocks, sand, sky. ". . . anything into food. You have that power."

Edan laughed, the sound harsh in the silent desert. "I can't do anything like that. By myself, I have a power no one wants. If I could make food out of rocks, I'd never need to—I wouldn't have to . . . Look, I can't do that."

"Have you ever tried? You seem so compartmentalized. You can do this, a friend can do that. With your doubles, well, you can do more. But why so separate? Why is everything so individual? Why is your power so focused? Have you ever asked yourself any of these questions?"

Edan put his hands on his hips, keeping his face turned toward the vista. "It's not like that. If we could do whatever we wanted, we wouldn't have use for each other. Why live in pairs, in groups, in cities and towns? Why get together for any reason except for those of the body?"

"Do you really need anyone? Yes, yes, I know you think you need your twin. But who is here now?"

The man lifted his arms, turning around, seeming to search for those people who seemed to have abandoned Edan. "Well?"

"I didn't tell anyone I was leaving. If they had known—"

The man shut him down, his words fast, strong. "Are they here to help you now when you are hungry? Has anyone sent you nourishment? Have you heard one thing from one person since you left the site? You all can think to each other. And during your ordeal out here, who has sent reassurance, kindness, love? Who?"

Hurt panged through Edan's chest. No one even knew he was gone. No one had sent him a message, a kind thought. No one would care if he learned how to make food, turned his powers inward, thought only of himself. The empty space inside him that he always imagined his twin would fill banged against his heart.

"Nourishment," the man repeated. "Sustenance."

"I can have that? I can have what I need?" Edan imagined what a full heart would feel like, the warmth of an embrace, the sweet inhale of his lover's breath. But he couldn't conjure that. But there was food. Something for now. But could he do that? He could. He must.

"Right," the man said. "Exactly. Just what you need. Now. Think about it. Look to the rock. Make it turn into something useful. Something to keep you alive."

Edan felt the urge, the need, the rush of power fluming through his arms and legs. Maybe he would be alone on the sand, but he would stay alive! He would eat! He would take care of himself. And just as he was about to focus, to concentrate on the objects in front of him, he thought of the woman. There she was again, her solemn eyes on his, her hair a flow of gold. If she had been his double, she would have noticed his absence. In fact, she would have called out to him as he left the construction site. She would have followed him into the desert. She hadn't. No one had. His sisters weren't here, those little ones he had done his best to protect. He was alone. So why should he feed himself? What was the point?

"Exactly," the man said. "What is the point?"

"What?" Edan felt his breath stop.

"What's the point of any of it?"

For a moment, Edan was confused. Hadn't they just been talking about food and nourishment, things to keep Edan alive? Wasn't the man trying to teach him how to stay alive? But the man was right. Exactly right. What was the point of living on like this? In seconds, he could be gone, floating in the Source like a waft of smoke.

"You could end it all. Use your power to destroy yourself. Age yourself into death. I'll witness it. I'll mark your death for you. I will be the one to see your most powerful act."

This was the very thing that kept Edan tense. This was Edan's greatest fear, the thing he guarded himself against every day, holding himself back from pushing his body through the aging process. From the moment he realized what he could do, he'd had to guard against it, protect himself from age he had not yet lived through.

And yet—what a release and relief it would be to let it all go. To just let the power surge through him until it was all over.

"Or what about this?" The man walked to the edge of the hill. "Jump. Jump now. End it all. You can die in your prime, unaged, whole. Your decision. Your choice."

Edan wanted to argue, but he felt as though he were in a dream, the story line beyond his ability to revise.

"Jump?" he asked. "Jump from here?"

"If you were meant to die, you will. If you were meant to die, it will all make sense."

Swallowing down a sandy breath, Edan thought about his time in the Source. He didn't remember anything about killing himself. There was no message about that from any of the souls that he met. In fact, he'd not learned much about his death, but from the time he was a small boy, he'd always assumed that he'd accidentally kill himself. Maybe at seventy-five or eighty, he'd doze into a too deep sleep and let himself go, his body withering as he lapsed unconscious and then dead in his chair.

"Jump," the man said.

"I can't," Edan replied. "I won't."

"But if you are so powerful," the man said, "you will

keep yourself from hitting. You will suspend yourself in midjump. You won't be hurt at all. You can do that, too."

Edan walked closer to the point he could launch himself from and looked down. Maybe it was high enough to kill him upon impact; maybe it wasn't. But could he catch himself? Would he keep himself from dying? All his life, he'd worried about pushing himself to the edge of age, needing his twin to save himself from himself. But maybe he was sufficient. Maybe he didn't need anyone to save him. Maybe he could do everything all on his own.

"Exactly," the man said. "That's right. Give it a go."

Would falling feel like flying? Edan wondered. Like Convergence? Like traveling in a ship? Or would he feel the air against his cheeks, his arms, pushing his hair back? Would it feel like being born?

"Try it," the man said. "Why not?"

Why not? Edan thought. *Why not indeed?*

When he stepped closer to the edge and almost felt the air take hold of him and lift him high, he thought about Mila and Claire. There they were in his mind, the two little girls sitting next to him in his dream, the two little girls who were now women who loved him, cared about him. He cast a thought out to them, wanting them to know that he wasn't really leaving them. If he fell, he would always be there in the Source.

Then he thought of the woman, of her hair, of her calm, beautiful face. He wanted to touch her. Once. At least once before he died. From deep inside himself, he threw out a message.

I need you. I want you here. I want to live to touch you once.

"Exactly," the man said, pulling Edan back slightly from the edge. "Maybe this isn't the chance you want to take."

Edan nodded, still looking down. *Maybe not.*

"But think about this. What if this desert were all yours?" the man asked. "What if the Neballats were gone?"

"This is Upsilia," Edan said. "It can never be ours. We have simply negotiated a place and a short amount of time. Then we will have to leave."

"Really?" the man asked. "Are you so certain about this?"

Edan nodded, but as he did, something began to fill his vision. At first, the images were fuzzy, like dream images that disappear upon waking. But soon they clarified, became clear, took on forms. What was he seeing? It was a city. Their city. The city that was being erected in the desert, a new Cygirian capital.

Edan turned to view his companion, who pointed back to the vision. Looking where the man pointed, Edan saw that there wasn't just this one city, but towns spreading out from the city in circling rings. And he knew somehow that these towns were populated by Cygirians, by his people. There were generations of them here now, living and learning and growing. The view changed, turned bird's-eye, and he saw that all of Upsilia was Cygirian, all the people his, everywhere. All the city states—even those separated by the one vast ocean—were Cygirian.

"What happened? How did we take over like this? Where are the Upsilians? Where are the Neballats?"

The man breathed in, a hollow, aching sound. "You wished it. You made it happen. You made this place yours and yours alone. You have the power to do this, all of this. You could make it so."

Edan shook his head, laughed. "But that is not my power. That's not something I can do. And I don't want to."

"Really? You don't want all of this land for your people, all of you who were hunted down, murdered almost to extinction? You who were made lonely and alone? Left thinking that you were abnormal, unworthy of family or friendship? All of you the small remnant of your generation with no ancestors, no history, no culture?"

As Edan listened to the man's questions, he felt his anger growing. He felt what he had never felt before, not all these long months out of the Source, not when he was captured by the Neballats, listening to what they wanted from them—life, whole, functioning bodies, time. He didn't care about their story, their loss, the hope a few of them held that somehow they could all work together.

No, he didn't care about any of that. Not after what they did. Not after they burned and destroyed, killed and hunted and murdered.

Edan was filled with what felt like black light, hard and cruel and evil. He was tired of trying to smooth things over. He was exhausted by the wanting inside him for his twin, for a place to call home, to land and feel safe. All of this made him want to blast something from himself, a flume of hate and anger. He wanted to destroy something in order to make whatever remained his.

"Yes," the man whispered. "That's right. You can feel it inside you, can't you? You could have all of this right now. The entire planet. This entire world with its lovely cities and towns. You could make this happen. Pull all your people's energy to you and through you. Force Upsilia to their knees. Send all of them to the Source."

Edan held on to the man's words, listening with his bones and blood and flesh.

He *could* have it. Energy was a stream. One stream. This,

Edan knew to be true. He'd learned that lesson in the Source. One stream that could be directed anywhere to do anything.

Edan was almost panting. The man was right, he could do this, he could feel the ability coursing through him. It didn't matter that he'd never felt this power before. He was the conduit, he was the one who could take what Cygiria needed and rule this planet. By himself. Without a twin. Without anyone.

He felt as though he were growing, becoming larger with feeling, taking up all the space in the night sky. He was enormous, dark hued, full of every bad feeling every Cygirian had ever felt. Betrayal. Despair. Loneliness. Regret. Remorse. Fear. He was them. He was a god. He was Cygiria's god. He would rule, making what he wanted a reality with a thought, a flick of his brain.

"Yes," the man whispered. "Yes."

It would happen now, now, now, and Edan felt his entire self expand into want and need and fire. He would blow all this house down, once and for all. Take it all back.

No, came a small thought, a gnat of an idea that Edan swatted away. *I'm here now. You called me and I came to you.*

Pushing up into the sky, his body enormous, he felt the sky pull toward him, the land beneath him sink. He was the middle, the sun to everything everywhere.

Edan, another thought came. *Edan, don't listen to him.*

He felt his chest, his breath, his heart beating.

"You don't want to listen to that insipid voice," the man hissed. "You have too much to do. Too much to concern yourself with. Look again! Look out to what is yours."

Edan looked out from the vista, the Upsilian cities arrayed in front of him. Everywhere it was only about Cygiria, the people who had lost everything finally with everything. He would have everything. The man was correct. This was theirs, his.

No. This isn't what we want, the voice thought.

"How can she know what you want?" the man asked. "How can anybody but you see how important all of this is?"

It's me, Edan, the voice thought. *Your twin. Your double.*

"Don't listen," the man said, and Edan imagined that he saw the man moving below him, searching for the voice. "Focus on what is out here. Focus on what you can have."

I'm here now, the voice thought. *I am here for you. I can't let you do this.*

"She's trying to control you? She tell you what to do? You who are so powerful? Who can do all of this? Who can control everything?" the man said, his voice like the edge of something sharp, a knife, a razor, a blade.

Edan turned his head, his eyes drifting from the cityscape. Where was she?

I know you've been looking for me, the voice thought, suddenly sounding a little different, scared, upset. But she continued on. *I am here now. You don't need to listen to him anymore. We can go back to the city we are building. You know what we want. We can—*

And then the voice stopped. What had happened to her? Had she left him already? Again? Edan looked back out to the city, seeing the lights of the imagined Cygiria fading, twinkling into nothing. Just like that, the city was gone. Just like it had been when their planet had been destroyed all those years ago. A thriving life and then nothing. A complete, rich, beautiful culture and then nothing but ash.

The energy that had been building inside him began to dissipate, and he felt as though he'd taken a drug of some kind, his body exhausted, his mind confused. What had he been thinking? And with whom had he been conversing? Where was she now?

Edan looked around, the sky light and gray and soft, but he could not find his companion or the woman who had been thinking to him. His twin? His double was here? He had to find her.

He ran forward, stopped, looking at nothing but brush and scrub and miles of sand. Beyond the mountains, the sun was rising, the sky opening up into a V of orange.

What had his companion told him to do? Open up to all the power around him. It seemed to Edan that the man was talking about Convergence, but maybe it was more. Maybe it was something that he could do himself.

So he stopped moving, tried to still his breathing, closed his eyes. Everything. All by himself. He'd always been by himself, so this was not unfamiliar, but the power? How could he do that without help? Without the stability of a twin? His twin. Her, the voice, the one who needed him.

Edan shook away his questions and breathed in, opening up to the feelings of power inside him, feeling the flow of the universe begin to pour into him, through him, out of him, a cycle of energy exchange.

Come to me, he thought. *Come back to me. Talk to me again.*

He let loose, relaxed, became nothing more than the feeling of movement inside him. As in the Source, Edan felt his body turn from solid into particles, his essence flowing out in a swath of energy, every bit of it calling her back.

Come to me, he thought. *Now.*

He could hear the whoosh of atmosphere, the flow of all that was around him, and then he felt as though he could sense his twin, the woman, as well as his companion. But

beyond that, for a quick moment, he felt everyone on the planet. Their beating hearts, their breath, their minds. Everyone was connected. He could pull a little harder and have them here, together.

We don't need that now, the companion thought. *But here we are.*

Without opening his eyes, Edan breathed out, let go, the wave of energy subsiding within him.

Are you here? he thought, directing his question to his twin.

Yes, she thought. *Yes. I am here.*

For a quick second, Edan wished for another power. His sister Claire's power. All she had to do was think of someplace else and she was there, no matter where it was. Until she met her twin, Darl, she'd thought the power was useless because she found herself stuck in places from which it was difficult to get home. But Edan would like to be anywhere but here right now. Or if he had Mila's power, he could make the moment over already, letting a week or two pass by. The awkward weirdness of opening his eyes and seeing his twin would have passed without him even having to feel it, moving through time without living it. Even though Mila said that was exactly why she didn't use her power often, Edan would right now, wasting his life away or not.

My goodness. From all-encompassing power to cowardice? the man thought. *I am really in shock.*

Edan nodded, agreeing, opening his eyes slowly. He was a coward. Maybe that's why he spent so much of his time in the public eye, working, talking with the Upsilian Council, helping with plans and ideas. He didn't want to face himself, but here he was anyway. Right here, in the desert, the sun beginning to flood the world orange and yellow.

So he looked up. He blinked, and then he saw her. The woman from yesterday.

Slowly, he took her in. Her long blond hair, the way the early morning light turned it a lit gold. Her face, so pretty but her expression nervous, shy, or irritated? He couldn't tell, not knowing her enough to be sure. She stood apart from the man, her clothing—pants and top made of a light material—a more obvious choice for the desert than his, though it was dirty and worn, as if she and the man had climbed a mountain or two or three while Edan was contemplating total dominion. Actually, she seemed to have been on a journey long before reaching him, as she carried a bag in one hand and a pack of some kind on her back. In fact, she looked as though she'd been on quite a trek, her daylong hike more arduous than his.

But despite the grit and dirt and marks of her trip, she was an amazing vision. The slight morning breeze rippled the fabric, showing Edan the shape of her body, her long, smooth limbs, her slim waist, her breasts lovely even under the unformed clothing. He almost laughed out loud, seeing that how after almost turning into the destroyer, after thinking he could control the world and then coming back to his ordinary mind-set, he could still see that she was beautiful. Perfect.

"Are you sure it's a good thing to come back?" the man said. "After all, you could have this entire world. Right now, you could change your mind and take what you need. Think about what you could do for you and your people."

"I didn't want what you showed me," Edan answered, his eyes not leaving the woman as he spoke.

"I can see that," the man said.

Edan stepped forward, and the woman stepped back. A

tiny step. Barely anything, but Edan saw the movement and stopped himself.

"Do you remember? We met before," he said to her. "At the construction site. Yesterday. You were handing out lunch. We talked about the Source."

The woman blinked, shook her head, stepped back again. "Yesterday?"

Edan tried to ignore her reaction, even though he wondered why she wouldn't agree with him. "I was with a coworker. A man named Siker who liked your food—"

"Yesterday? What do you mean, yesterday?"

Edan breathed in, looked at the man who was still bundled up from head to foot despite the growing warmth, the sand already starting to radiate heat. In the long night of their walking, Edan hadn't seen his face or his body really, a ping of worry running through him. But before he could deal with the man, he had to figure out the woman's story.

"Yes, that's right. You—what is your name, anyway?"

For a second, he thought she wasn't going to tell him, her mouth opening slightly but no sound coming out. Finally, she sighed. "Ava. Ava Arganos."

Edan smiled. "Okay, Ava Arganos. I am Edan Mirav."

She nodded. "I know."

"You remember meeting me, yes?"

"Of course, but—"

"So we met. Maybe not yesterday. But the day before. This is a new day, after all. But you know what I mean."

She shook her head. "No, I don't know what you mean. Not at all."

"You are saying we haven't met? That you don't remember me?"

Ava looked down at her feet, kicking at sand before looking up, holding his gaze, saying softly, "No, that's not what I'm saying. We have met, yes. Right. What I'm saying, though, is that it wasn't yesterday or the day before or the day before that when we met. You've been gone for over a month. Forty days. Forty!"

For a moment, Edan didn't really hear her words, imagining that he was underwater, listening to someone talking way up at the surface, all of her syllables muffled and murky. Or it was like being in the Source, where it was possible to shut everything off, to float in the surge of energy, ignoring anything but the soft, warm feeling holding him in the swirl of everything.

But then he heard her comments, felt her words. Forty days. Forty days!

Turning slowly to the man, he waited, and his fully swathed companion shrugged.

"That's right. It's been quite the journey."

"It's true, then? I've been out here for over a month?" Edan asked.

"Yes," the man said.

"But why?" Edan asked. "Why have we been out here for so long? Why do I remember it as just a day or two?"

The man lifted his hands, slowly began to unfasten the button at his collar. "We needed to find out who you truly are. We couldn't go forward with our plan until we saw how you would react to the visions that I offered you. Tired, exhausted, depleted, we needed to see what options you would take. We needed to see who you were at the core."

His breath somewhere in his throat, Edan looked at the man who appeared to be taking off his coat and then at Ava, who was staring back at him. As Edan watched her, he noticed that she had a smudge of dirt on her right cheek, and just as he was going to step toward her so he could brush it away, she rubbed it off herself.

"Who are *we*?" she asked the man, just as Edan thought to ask the same. "Who are *you* to test him?"

The man slowly dropped his coat to the sand and then began to slowly unwind the black scarf that hid his neck and face.

"You really don't know who I am?" he asked, the unwound scarf revealing another one he began to take off as well. "You really can't figure that out? Who else would want to know more about you, Edan? Who has been trying to get to know you for a while now? Who has a vested interest?"

And as the man said the words, Edan knew. He'd been with them before. He knew how they could alter perceptions, create scenes that played out like life, panoramas vast and wide, as wide as a desert. He knew what they wanted and how they thought, their voices in his head for weeks. He knew now he had been gone from the construction site for far longer than a day and a half. Maybe Edan hadn't really even been here for all the forty days, locked up somewhere viewing a scene created by this man and his cohorts.

"I know what you are," Edan said. "But who are you?"

"My name is Luoc," he said simply. "I am with a group who wants change to come to us in a different way."

"What do you want with me?" Edan said.

"I don't get any of this. Who *are* you?" Ava said to Luoc, clearly not understanding what Edan did. She turned to face Edan. "Who is he?"

And then the second scarf came off, Luoc holding the ends in his gloved hands. Edan heard Ava's quick, sharp inhale of breath as the man stood before them, exposed. The man didn't need to show them anything more than his face because it was the Neballat faces that always struck Edan the most, the pale, invisible skin barely seeming to cover the wild traffic of veins and nerves and muscle underneath. There were the tendons reaching up from his neck, the eyes bulging in their shimmering sockets, the brain just barely covered by a translucent cap of skull. What was worse and what neither he nor Ava could see now was what was underneath Luoc's clothing, the organs beating, the blood pumping, the flickering way the people seemed to move. Edan could imagine it all, having seen their forms, their see-through arms, their impossibly transparent legs.

"Why?" Ava started, her sentence tumbling into the morning air. "Why did you . . . walk with Edan?"

Luoc stared at them both, his eyes brown and wet. He breathed in, the sound ragged and filmy. "Not all of us like the course of action we as a group have taken. We've been trying to find the one Cygirian who could convince those of us who would destroy you all. To prove that there is another course of action, another way of life. Now we are sure."

"And that's Edan?" Ava asked, her voice light, like a disappearing note. "He's just supposed to save you all? He is supposed to overcome everything and just help you out?"

Luoc shrugged and then smiled, a horrible thing to see as the muscles under the skin arched, and then he rewound the scarves and put on his coat, standing before Edan and Ava as he had moments before.

"Is that why you took me before?" Edan asked.

Luoc nodded, his eyes shaded behind the scarf.

"But you could simply destroy us," Ava said. "You could take what you want when you wanted it."

"No, you have it wrong," Luoc said. "Neither of you has any idea about what is possible. You could destroy us completely. Most of my people don't understand that. They see you as a means to an end. To fixing our ills."

The man opened his hands, seeming to look down at his body. "To making us whole again."

"Upsilia knew. That's why we were all put in the Source," Ava said. "That's why we weren't allowed to live at all."

While Edan thought the Source was life, the main current everyone swam in, he knew what she meant. What might have been an ordinary life was stopped. During his time there, he didn't really live. He developed no connections or family or friends. Just a bond between all of those put in the Source and the strong pull toward a double. All of the Cygirians who had been in the Source were marked by their time there, heavy with the knowledge they'd found, unencumbered by the web of relationships one should create in life. Edan knew this was true because those who had lived on Earth were different. Lighter.

Luoc put down his hands. "But, Edan, you must see now. You must understand what Cygiria could do to us. You are capable of doing anything you want. Our elders saw it, held that vision of terror in front of them and passed it down to us. But there are those of us who know you could stop it. Right now. Without a war. Without the cataclysm. And maybe, with some help for us."

"Help you?" Ava asked, her question toneless, flat.

"Yes," Luoc said. "Heal us."

Seconds passed, Edan staring at Luoc, the sunlight behind him turning white. Help. They all needed help. For years, these three groups of people had hurt each other, even Cygiria, who had refused to assist the Neballats for generations. The pattern could change. He could help it change.

Looking up at Luoc, Edan nodded, knowing that all he had felt and seen—in the Source, with the Neballats, and now, out in the desert—was right. But how to stop the Neballat war machine? How to curb the hate, the need, the desire? And how to convince his people? How to convince Ava?

The sun beat down in increasingly hot stabs of light. The sand was heating, smelling like dust. Edan turned to Ava, who was still staring at Luoc.

"This won't be easy. I have to teach the rest of the Cygirians what you have shown me," Edan said. "Without frightening Upsilia. Without alerting those of your people who would attack now."

Ava slowly turned, her face blank, open, surprised stared. "I think you are going to have to teach me, too." Looking back at Luoc, she shook her head. "I don't know why they deserve anything from us."

"Think of the Source, Ava. You know what it is like. Can't you feel how we are all connected, even here, now, standing just as we are? We are separate out here, distinct, but you know what is real. You know what is true."

He saw the shallow rise and fall of her rib cage as she breathed, took in what he said. She blinked, sighed, her exhale long.

"I don't know."

"I do. I do know," Edan said, moving closer to her as he spoke.

"I was hoping you would say that," Luoc said. "And I and my compatriots will work on our end. Together . . ."

He trailed off, his words falling to the sandy ground, his arms dangling at his sides. For the first time, Edan really saw a Neballat as a person, a creature with feelings and hopes and needs. He hadn't ever looked at them except as adversaries, but Luoc made things real. This wasn't a man trying to take something away, to conquer or press the entire Cygirian race into nothing. This was a man in need.

This was a man who would put himself at risk for his people. *His* people.

"Together we can change it all," Edan said to Luoc, feeling for the first time more powerful than his companion. He knew what he had to do. And the most important thing he had to do was befriend Ava, make her unafraid of him, show her who he really was without scaring her away. She had come all the way into the desert to find him. Even though she wasn't sure about his motives or his desires, she'd stuck by him, defended him against Luoc. And it was now up to him to make her stay by his side.

So without knowing if she would take it, he reached out his hand to Ava, closing his eyes as he waited for her response. With the breeze between his fingers, he imagined her slight grasp, almost able to feel the warm slide of her fingers against his. His eyes closed, he imagined her smile, her full lips, her almost amber eyes. In this imagination, he pictured her smile, her moving toward him, accepting him, accepting his ideas, accepting his arms around her. For that simple embrace, everything was possible. With that gesture, the future was wide open.

With his eyes closed, Edan Mirav imagined what might be.

Chapter Five

Standing next to Edan, the desert a hot carpet under her feet, Ava knew what she should do. There was no reason not to and every reason to take what was offered her. He was her double, her twin, the man she had dreamed about, wanted, yearned for. Here he was, the man she'd traveled for over a month to find, enduring cold nights, sweltering days, hunger, thirst, fear, anxiety, and dread. He was generous to everyone, even to his enemies. And now he was asking for something for himself. There was his hand, outstretched, waiting for her to reciprocate.

Ava wasn't sure she wanted to touch him. After all, he was the one who never found her in the Source. Who had stayed away all this time, kept himself separate from her. And once she did reach out and take his hand, well, life would just happen. She would give up being able to decide what she wanted to do, which was mostly be alone. Everything would be completely out of her control. She wouldn't be able to make decisions by herself, for herself. She would have to be with him all the time. Certainly, she had wanted to find him in the desert, help him if he needed her, but life was hopefully long.

Ava, Edan thought.

Shaking her head, she glanced over at Luoc, who had turned from them, walking down the slope of the hill toward the valley below.

"Where are you going?" she said as he moved out of sight. "What should we do?"

"You won't need me after this," Luoc called back. "Do what you need to do with your people. It will all become clear."

Ava.

For a second, Ava wanted to bolt forward to see where Luoc was going. But she knew when she got to the top of the hill, he'd be already somewhere far away, disappeared into the day, vanishing like smoke.

And likely, she was using Luoc to put off what she feared and craved the most: connection.

Ava.

So now there was no choice. Nothing left to do but hold on to her future, the rest of her life. She breathed in, closed her eyes, and reached out for Edan's hand, not knowing what would happen when they touched.

And then they did.

His fingers were smooth, strong, cooler than she imagined hers were, the desert so hot even at this early hour. They clasped each other's hands softly, letting their palms skate and slide and smooth together. From this small touch, Ava felt his heat, his energy, his passion, his love.

You, Edan thought. *You are my love.*

Slowly, she felt an energy building between them, something like electricity, like a current, though when she looked down toward their hands, there was nothing but their skin, their flesh, their gesture.

Flesh. Ava closed her eyes again, and let herself feel, knowing she had never, ever let herself feel before. Oh, she'd embraced people, shaken hands, patted shoulders, kissed cheeks, and lightly kissed lips. There were hugs of hello and good-bye, accidental touches in large crowds. But this? This hand-holding was warm and soft and calm, like a massage, like a dream, like floating down a river on a raft, the two of them in the sun, dry, happy, laughing. This handholding was like a promise that was kept, a task that was rewarded, a hope that was fulfilled. This handholding was what she had thought about on nights when she was cold or lonely or scared. This is what she dreamed about those nights in her parents' house, the nights before she had been put into the Source, the nights here in the desert, the animals moving around the shelter, the bats and owls brushing the tent with their night flights. And finally, as she journeyed toward this handholding she'd imagined it, hoped for it, barely able to believe that it was possible.

Edan squeezed her hand a little more tightly, and she felt energy crackle up through her wrist, into her elbow, her shoulder, her jaw, her skin like a net made of pearls. She sighed, breathed in, moved closer, feeling his shoulder touch hers. He was so hot, his skin like a blanket she wanted to wrap herself in, and seeming to hear her, he turned toward her, letting his free hand cup her shoulder, then move slowly up her neck to hold the back of her head. His fingers moved gently in her hair, and all of her skin reacted to that move-ment, gooseflesh on her kneecaps, thighs, arms.

Slowly, he took his hand from hers, his fingers trailing away softly from her grasp, his palm sliding up her arm, now every molecule of her skin coming alive after his touch. Ava tingled, felt her breath quicken, parts of her melt, soften.

His breath was near, warm and light, and then she felt his lips on her jawline, moving toward her ear. Somehow, her legs seemed to weaken, and she wondered if she would remain upright. So she put her arms around him, amazed at how solid he was, his body perfectly muscled, strong and fit and beautiful. He smelled like sunlight, like linen, like sand, and she wanted to stop everything for just a second so she could pull his essence into her, savor his smells, the feel of him against her.

I'm here, he thought. *I'm so here. And I'm not going any-where.*

Ava took in a breath, his lips now on her neck, his hand still cupping the back of her head. But he moved closer, his chest against hers, his strong thigh muscles against her own. His other hand slid down to the small of her back, his palm pressing her even closer. Stomach to stomach, she could feel him harden, knowing exactly what that meant even though she'd never been in an embrace like this before, never wanting anyone in this way.

His lips traveled up from her neck, and then he was so close she felt his eyelashes on her cheek. All she wanted was his lips, his kiss, his lips, his breath, his lips, his lips, his lips. So she moved to find him, and there he was, his mouth on hers.

Oh, she thought, or at least believed she thought. No words were making sense in her head, and she knew she wasn't thinking in words but feelings and impressions. And there were so many of them. Inside her was a river of warmth and yearning and tears and desire, all her longing, all her life somehow answered by this kiss that was soft and sweet and wonderful and gentle.

You are wonderful, Edan thought, his tongue now on hers. She opened her mouth a little wider, realizing she wanted more of him, more feeling, more taste and smell and touch.

Edan put his hands on both sides of her face so tenderly, she almost let her lips fall away from his. He was loving her.

Even though they were just kissing, he was making love to her with his hands and with that kiss. He was making love to her with his presence, with his attention, with his intent.

Her arms wrapped around his waist, and she knew that she wanted him, needing him in a way she'd never thought she'd need a man. Since leaving the Source, she'd imagined that at some point in her long life, she'd find a companion, a man to spend time with, to maybe laugh with and talk to and sleep with. Someone to keep her company, someone like her without a twin. It would be a fine life, an adequate life, a decent solution. But there wouldn't be this. This. *This.*

Ava kissed Edan back, let her hands travel up the flaring muscles until she reached his shoulders, felt herself pull her as close as she could, feeling both their hearts beat hard against their ribs. And then she felt it start, felt it begin. The tingle of current scared her, made her want to pull back and look at it, though she knew there was nothing the eye could see.

It's what we can do, Edan thought. *Let's allow it.*

Their mouths close but not kissing, Ava tried to find her breath. Their power to make the body age and unage. Their power that seemed to have no purpose. She couldn't move a steel girder or create water or electricity. She couldn't move back or forward in time or transport herself anywhere. Their power was an internal power, a stupid, ridiculous danger-ous power. So what would happen when their two energies connected?

Let's find out, Edan thought.

Ava nodded slightly and moved back into his embrace, feeling the tingle restart, reemerge between them, hot and alive and yellow. It seemed to have started in the space be-tween them, and then flowed into her, a current as warm as melted butter, soothing and lovely and known. A river made of the two of them, working through her body, her flesh and blood and bones and cells. She felt the energy circle her, move through every system, and then Edan's energy moved into hers, her own moving into him, each of them flooded completely with the other.

She held on to his shoulders as the energy slowly dissipated, and then she opened her eyes, looking up into his handsome face, his dark eyes on her, wide open despite the glare of the desert sun. He was smiling, wide and open and full of love.

Stepping back but not far enough away so that she couldn't hold his hand, she stared at him, examining him for clues that their merge had worked. Had it? What were the signs?

"Look closely," he said. "What do you see?"

Somehow, there was some slight change, maybe in his face, maybe in the way he held himself, maybe in the texture of his skin. Time was almost intangible at their ages, but she could see a difference around his eyes, by his mouth, the sudden erasure of tiny lines. And then thinking about it, she dropped his hand and brought her hands to her own face, suddenly afraid she would find herself full of folds and wrinkles, a wrinkled plume, sucked clear of juice. Or all soft and crinkly like one of the dogs her mother had when Ava was a child, small and round and almost tripping on its loose skin.

Edan laughed. "You look exactly the same."

Ava dropped her hands. "Are you sure?"

"Trust me," he said. "You do. You couldn't have unaged yourself that much all these years."

"I never could be sure," Ava said. "I didn't understand what I was doing when I realized my power."

"So what do you see when you look at me?" he asked,

still smiling, everything about him now hope. He was all about hope.

Ava swallowed, tears ready in her eyes, her throat, a weight on her chest that was not a burden but a relief.

"I see you. I see only you," she said, her voice tight, small. "I only want to see you. And it wouldn't matter what you looked like. It wouldn't have mattered if you had aged yourself beyond belief. You are who I want to see."

Edan pulled her close again, and the weight that was on her, in her, dissipated, the warm flow between them filling her again.

Kissing the top of her head, Edan sighed, pulled away a little, lifting a hand to his face. "I think in my life, I lost over ten years. Maybe more. And like you said, there wasn't a meter I could check. No internal meter available to me."

Ava moved close, bringing her hand to his cheek, feeling the beard under her fingers, moving up to his cheek, his forehead. "We are balanced now. We are where we should be. I can feel that. I know that."

Edan took her hand and brought it to his lips. "This power of ours. What do you think it is for?"

Ava sighed, leaned against his chest, heard the rhythmic pound of his heart. This was the question she'd asked herself her whole life. Who else could this serve? Maybe alone, she was lucky as she would be able to stave off the ravages of time and age and if she were a different person, hard, wild living. But with her partner, they'd be able to achieve equilibrium, a stasis of age, even and on target. What was the point?

"I don't—" she began, and then stopping herself, realizing that there was a new answer now. Luoc had showed Edan his power. Ava had felt Edan's expansion, his total acceptance that he could do anything, his ability to change everything. And if Edan had the power to do anything, everything, then so did they all. And if that was so, they were unstoppable. Power was power, no matter the way they exhibited it. All these centuries, millennia, Cygirians had thought they had one particular ability, when the truth was they were conduits for . . .

"The Source," Edan said. "And that's why the Upsilians and the Neballats are afraid of us. That's why we were put into the Source. That's why we've been hunted down."

"And that's why the Neballats want us. We could fix their planets and their bodies."

Edan moved his hands along the contours of her body, slowly, softly, shoulders, waist, hips. "We could make everything all right in minutes."

Breathing in his smell, Ava nodded against him. "So why don't we? Why don't we make everything all right?"

"Not everyone will want that to happen," Edan said. "The Neballats haven't made many friends amongst us. And there are more than a few people upset with Upsilia. My friend Kate is ready to start a revolution against them. Let me put it this way: we will have some talking to do."

"Luoc is in the Neballat minority," Ava said. "We might not have time to convince our people before those who want to attack us. There isn't a lot of time."

Ava felt a trickle of sweat run down her spine. The air was full of heat, the desert unfriendly now, a harsh ugly place, and, like most of Upsilia, it wanted them gone. Silent, Edan seemed to think, but when Ava tried to move into his mind, she couldn't.

"What are you thinking?" she asked. "Why are you hiding it from me?"

"Well," he said, "I'm thinking that there is something I'd

like to do before fixing the universe. Something that just can't wait, attacking Neballats or no."

"What might that be?" she asked, nerves crackling inside her, her breath moving into her throat.

"Oh, something," he said, holding her tight. "Something very nice."

"Something?" she said, feeling him press against her and take in a breath.

"Don't you think that's a little inappropriate?" Ava said, feeling the laughter and the truth under all her words. "I mean, stopping to do *something* might be viewed as selfish and silly when there are millions of people to save. Sort of like a strange interlude during a time when we need to fight? Wouldn't that be a little inconsistent and perhaps gratuitous?"

Edan sighed, held her tight, and as he did, she felt the waiting in them both, all the years of time that they'd decided there was no twin or double out there. She could see them both watching other people—hoping against hope that one stranger would finally emerge as him, her, *the* one—both then trying to come to terms with a life that would be lived alone or maybe with quiet companionship at best.

Waiting. That's all they'd done, even while living, even while acting. Waiting was like a silent partner, always there, always important but never enough. But now the waiting was over.

"Not that I really know what day it is or anything, but if we had Garrick's power, we'd be able to push back into later. We could carve out a few hours that no one would miss," Edan said. "We could take this hour we've had here in the desert and live it over and over again as many times as we wanted. We could spend weeks in this hour, months. Years even."

Ava smiled. "But the desert isn't a great place for, well . . ." She felt the heat rise in her face, and she was glad she was pressed against Edan's chest.

"Then if we had Claire's power, we could simply think ourselves to someplace wonderful. My tent, for instance. It's a single. No distracting roommates."

Ava blinked, looking at a lizard scuttle past her and Edan, its tail leaving a whip-shaped indent with each flicking step. What had Luoc said?

"You are capable of doing anything you want."

"We can," Ava said, pulling away and looking up at Edan. "We can do it."

"We can what?"

"Time. And place. It's what we are capable of."

And she sent him the memory of Luoc standing in front of them, telling them about Cygirian power. When that memory was over, Edan sent her a slice of the powerful feelings he'd felt on the crest of the hill. She almost staggered back, seeing the full extent of what they could do if they just chose it.

"You are right," he said. "Imagine what this will mean to all of us."

"Let's go to your tent," she whispered. "Let's take ourselves back an hour."

"Three," Edan said. "And maybe more if we want."

He pulled Ava to him again, and she let go of herself and her mind, finding his energy, finding the wave she used to float on when she was in the Source. For a moment, she thought she couldn't find it, couldn't allow herself to surge back into the feeling. It was so far away, so not of this life. The Source was a place they were not supposed to be in during life. It was a place for later, for rest, a place to be until the journey began again. No one—not Edan, not she—should know what it felt like.

We are just borrowing it, Edan thought. *We aren't staying in it. We aren't going to keep it here.*

Ava heard his thoughts, relaxed. It was just for a moment. It was just to remember how it felt. So she relaxed, breathing into the floaty pull of the energy all around her, even in this hot desert. She could still see the almost blinding white sand, the cacti, the creatures scuttling fast across the top layer of sand in order to avoid the beat of the sun. But then those images disappeared, and she was over the desert and no longer standing on it, traveling back toward the construction site. She imagined that she could almost hear the clank of machinery, the flat whiz of electricity, the yells of the workers around the buildings. The air was cooler, softer, the desert more palatable here, able to sustain life. As she thought, she felt Edan's energy move with hers, join with hers, their thoughts—like themselves—twinned and bound.

Together, they moved toward each other, interchanging atoms, heat, feeling, thoughts. Ava had no body, but she felt more than her body could possibly—the total joining with this man. Not joined in body and flesh but in everything that made them who they were. Energy and soul. Power and heat. Feeling and knowledge.

Down, down, down toward the site, the panorama becoming focused, clear, seen. And then there was even more cool air, tighter all around her, the sun no longer a slash across her shoulders, the hot wind no longer twisting sandy fingers through her hair.

"Open your eyes," Edan said.

Ava was afraid to, even though she knew where she was.

When she opened her eyes, she would be opening them into her new life, the life that started right now. The life that would leave her open to such pain. Yes, she'd never truly been happy, but now there was so much more to lose. So much more to miss.

Actually, you can't miss me until you've had me, Edan thought. *Open your eyes, love.*

She breathed in the word, took it into her being, felt it everywhere.

Love.

Ava held on to the sound of his thought, knowing that love was what had been missing. All her life, she'd known that love was possible, but it had always been taken away from her. Parents? Gone. Siblings? Gone. Life out in the open, the companionship of others like her? Gone. A safe house full of those she'd finally been able to find? Gone. She'd had to take solace in her own company, find comfort in her own thoughts, find peace in the repetition of cooking and baking. In those activities, everything was measured and predictable and known.

She'd learned to pull away and hold her feelings dear and close because doing otherwise was certainly too dangerous. The threat of what she just found with Edan disappearing ran through her now like a hot sad flame, but he spoke again.

"Open your eyes, Ava. Be with me. Be with me here."

Slowly, Ava opened her eyes, not really surprised to find herself in the yellowish light of a small tent. Not surprised to find herself in Edan's arms. Not surprised to find herself crying, tears she had held in for months, maybe years. Maybe forever.

"You were right. Here we are," he said, leaning down to kiss her, his mouth warm and wet and wonderful.

Ava wanted to ask him *when* they were, wondering if they'd also managed to push back time, giving them that hour they'd promised each other. But there was no time for that thought. There was only time for his mouth, his body, and her own.

She put her arms around his neck, pulling him close to her, feeling herself move and sense things, all her being acting in a way she'd never imagined it could. Not once in all the time before the Source or after had she ever moved against the body of another, and this body—this man—was her twin, her double, her perfect match, her even complement.

Perfect, Edan thought, gently pushing away her thin cotton coat. It fell to the floor and he let his hands move over her shoulders, her arms, running them back up to place his palms on her chest, his fingers at the clasps of her shirt.

Still kissing, they both opened their eyes, and Ava saw his question before he could even think or ask it.

Yes, she thought. *Yes.*

Slowly, he undid the clasps, the tingle from the warming air on her skin, her nipples rising. She could barely breathe, her whole body concentrating on his fingers, her shirt, and then it was off and on the floor like her coat.

Edan was looking at her face and then his eyes moved slowly, respectfully to her breasts. "You are so beautiful. More beautiful than I could ever have imagined. Than I ever did imagine."

He placed his hands on the top of her chest again, his fingers grazing her collarbone. Then he moved his hands, letting them drift over her breasts, his palms lightly touching her nipples. Then he cupped her breast, one in each hand, and bent down to kiss her, bringing one nipple into his mouth, his tongue on her.

What was she going to do? she wondered, her eyes closing, her breath light and fast. How was she going to be able to go on? This sensation was almost too much, enough, the best she had ever felt in her life.

There's more. I promise, he thought, sucking now, gently, tugging at her, and it was as if he wasn't just sucking her nipples—one and then moving slowly over to the other— but only places on her body, everywhere filling with warmth.

His hands now on her back, holding her up, one on either side of her spine, Ava let her head fall backward slightly, allowed herself to feel this feeling of him, allowed herself to let go as she never had been able to on Upsilia or in the safe house or anywhere, ever. Nothing had been safe, nothing had given her the slightest notion to let down her guard. Only Edan had been able to pull the fear away. Only Edan.

He let her nipple fall from his lips, kissing her sternum, moving up her body with his mouth until he was at the base of her neck, his breath fast.

"Let me take you to my bed," he said quietly. "Let me make love to you."

Ava opened her eyes, swallowed, pushing the bright blond hair away from his face with her fingers. The long forty days in the desert had left him golden brown, his hair the lightest color she'd ever seen on a man. And he looked exactly his age, a young man. A young man with a very old soul. He smiled.

"What are you looking at?" he asked.

"You," she said. "And I'd like to see a little more of you if that is a possibility."

Edan laughed, his arm around her as he moved her the few steps toward the bed. "If I have anything to say about it, you will very soon. But I must say, I'm glad to hear you ask."

Together, they stood in front of his cot, looking at each other. Ava wanted to smile, and she did briefly, but she was too nervous to keep it on her face for long, her mouth almost quivering when she tried to move it. Her breath was too quick, stuck somewhere in her throat. The rest of her body trembled and quaked and hummed, every nerve on red alert, ready for action.

His eyes on hers, Edan took off his shirt, pulling it away from his body, dropping it to the floor. Ava saw rather than felt the way her arms rose, her hands reached out, touching his chest, the light hair under her palms. He was strong and lean and beautiful and so smooth, she didn't want to stop touching him, loving his warmth under her hands, smelling his salt, his scent, something she couldn't name, but a smell that reminded her of citrus fruit, lemons, oranges.

Sliding her hands around his back, she pulled him close, their two bodies touching, skin to skin, his warmth and feel making her close her eyes; she was seconds, she thought, away from her knees buckling, from fainting, from toppling over in preecstasy. Edan wanting her, Edan needing her, his flesh on hers, his skin pressed into hers, was joy. Full, true joy.

I told you, there is more. So much more.

He held her tight, kissed her neck, let his hands slide down her back to the waistband of her pants, his hands pushing them away from her hips.

Her nerves aching, tingling, her body wanting Edan, needing him, she forced herself away from the embrace. She didn't know how she was going to do this, but she had no choice. Ava wanted him to see her—to be seen by him. He was her twin, her double, her match in power and in life, and this was where he would truly know who she was, despite her fears. He would see what no one had before. What she had shared with no one, ever.

Yes, Edan thought, watching her. *Yes*.

Ava breathed, nodded, and pushed away her pants, her panties, letting them pool at her feet before she stepped out of them and with every bit of strength she had, looked up into his gaze.

He was looking at her face, her eyes, and then, when he knew she'd seen that he looked at her, saw who she was inside, he let his gaze drop and take in all of her body.

As he did, Ava focused on a vein beating in his neck, the pulse quickening, his skin seeming to flush. But even as she kept her eyes on his pulse, she could almost see what he was seeing, her body warm and ready and waiting for him. His look lingered, touched her, caressed her skin, and she could barely take the anticipation, needing his hands on her and not just his mind.

Reaching out, she pulled on the tie that held his pants up, tugging gently, the knot unloosening, the waist opening, his pants sliding down his hips. Ava felt herself blush, but she couldn't take her eyes off him, knowing that he was excited, just as she was.

Edan looked up from her body, and smiled, pushing away his underwear, his pants, stepping out of them and moving to her. Ava reached down and touched him, letting her hand wrap around him. She wasn't exactly sure what to expect with that touch, but his softness, the smooth tip of his penis surprised her. He seemed so hard, so ready, but his skin was the smoothest she had ever felt. She let her hand move over the soft tip and then took him completely in her hand, his girth hard and warm in her palm.

She wondered if she would keep standing, her knees shaking. Just this holding of him alone was wonderful, amazing, feeling his desire for her, seeing it so evident. He wanted her. She was the one he wanted.

Yes, he thought. *I do. I want you. But I have to make sure you want me, too.*

I-I do, she thought, even her mind in a stammer.

Edan put one arm around her waist, pushing closer, his body hard against her belly, and then he let his other hand softly skim her skin, her waist, her ass, cupping her cheeks, pressing closer to her as he did. In that press, she could almost imagine what it would be like to join with him, that smooth, hard, long, warm maleness inside her. She could imagine it, the slide into her, the movement that would bring them both to a peak of something she'd only heard about.

Now. Please, she thought.

Not yet.

Please?

I need to make sure you are ready, he thought.

And then his hand was moving around her hip, touching her, his fingers finding her, rubbing small circles over her, slowly, slowly, his fingers finding the place that seemed to want him the most, need him the most.

Ava knew she wasn't holding on to anything anymore, so glad that Edan held her body. Her feet might even be off the ground, she was so lost in this sensation.

But then his fingers slid down, parting her lips, moving into wetness.

"Ah," he said, his sound almost a growl. *Yes.*

What? she thought, everything inside her seeming to moan.

You are ready, he thought, letting his fingers slip even deeper inside her. *All this juiciness is for me. All of this feeling is for me.*

She brought her hand to him, feeling again his softness, his hardness, a little wick of wetness at the top.

This is for me? she thought, her eyes closed.

Everything I have is for you. Always has been. I've just been waiting to find you.

Ava put her arms around his neck just as he lifted her up, moving her to the cot, laying her down. He was above her, holding himself up with his arms, his stomach muscles tight, his muscles flexed.

"Would you make love with me, Ava?" he asked.

She could not breathe. Would never breathe again. How could she answer that question she'd never imagined she'd hear? There was no other answer than yes, yes, yes, now, please.

"Say yes, then," Edan said. "Say yes for now and forever."

Yes, she thought.

"Say it out loud, Ava. Let me hear it."

"Yes," she said.

With her word, Edan lay down, his body against hers, his erection against her stomach, his lips on her lips. Hip to hip, stomach to stomach, mouth to mouth, Ava felt them both completely connected, moving already as if he were in her.

Please, she thought. *I want you. I don't know what I will do if I can't have you right now.*

I'm going to have you. We are going to have each other, he thought, bringing a hand down to her thigh, nudging her legs open so he could slowly move close to her, into her. She felt him between her legs, hard and hot, and she felt her body move in ways she didn't know she could. In just a moment, he would slide into her. She was nervous but ready, feeling her own wetness, her own desire, her own need. Her heart pounded against the cage of her ribs, and she pulled him close, feeling his breath, his heat, his want. Feeling his heart, his love.

She breathed him in, his smell of sun and heat and sand and lust. His smell known to her, perfect, the very thing she'd wanted to breathe in without knowing it. Everything fit, everything was right, and she felt her body anticipate his.

Finally, finally. Oh yes, was all her brain could muster, her thoughts a flowing stream and want and want and want.

For a second before she heard it, she felt the urge to bat away the call, the noise like a fly, a gnat, a mosquito. Then she thought she was being ridiculous because all there was right now was Edan. Everything Edan.

Ava? came the voice, and she opened her eyes, blinked, looked at Edan.

"What?" she whispered.

Edan lifted his head, his face drowsy with their sex and confusion. "*What* what?"

"You said *Ava.* You thought *Ava.* Didn't you?"

"No, I didn't," he said, lifting himself back up onto his elbows.

Ava pulled him back to her, wanting more of the want. Wanting him now. "Never mind. Forget about it. Shh. I—"

Ava? Are you here? Where are you?

No, she thought, closing down her mind, not wanting anyone to find her.

Pulling her face away from Edan's, she looked at him. "That isn't you?"

"No," he said, pulling away again, leaning on his arm. "Who is it? What does the person want?"

Ava? I think you are here. Where have you been? We have been so worried about you.

Ava sighed. "I don't know. I didn't alert anyone of my return, not to mention my departure."

Edan sighed, let a hand lightly stroke her shoulder, her breast. "So you've been missed. People have been out looking for weeks. I don't want this to stop, but you should find out who has sensed your return."

"No," she said, trying to pull him back to her, trying to find that moment again, the one where he was hard against her, ready to slide into her, giving her what she wanted so much. And it wasn't just his body she wanted but that amazing place they'd traveled to—and she wasn't thinking about the return to Talalo. It was the bubble of their need and want and hope and desire. The place where there were only the two of them. The place that only the two of them could go.

Edan pushed back his hair, shook his head. "This moment here, well, it's a luxury we really can't afford. We did push ourselves about an hour back in time, but we've been gone for days. I—I shouldn't . . . we need to talk with the council. We need to tell them what we can do. What Luoc showed us. What he told us."

"But what about us?" Ava asked, feeling the slight whine and neediness in her question. She wished she could take it back and shape another sentence, one that was strong and whole. Not weak and selfish and immature.

"Allowing yourself to need me is strong," Edan said. "I've felt what your life was like. It was like mine. And it's hard to want something—to admit it—when you are sure it will be taken away. Don't ever stop needing me."

Ava felt the heaviness of tears in her face, and breathed into them, keeping them behind her lids. She knew she couldn't get rid of this need if she wanted to. He'd opened her up, let everything she'd kept hidden out into the world. And the world was a place she needed to work in, be a part of with Edan. Together, they would help their people. Together, they would show all the Cygirians what they could do as a group.

She ran a finger along his ribs, finding the pattern of muscles under his soft, now perfectly aged skin. He was like a dream, a dream she hoped she would have again and again and again.

Ava? came the voice again. *Ava? I know you're there. I can feel you.*

Pushing herself up to sitting, Ava nodded. "You're right. I can't hide from this. And I think it's Stephanie calling me."

"You know Stephanie? Porter's twin?"

Ava smiled. "Yes. She came into the kitchen shelter one day. She's my friend. And she ate half a pie. I know Porter, too."

Edan turned, pushed himself off the cot, and stood, holding out his hand to her. "Everyone knows Porter. He's not someone easy to ignore. I don't think it can be avoided, even if you wanted to."

She took his hand, stood up, wondering how they got from that intense, passionate moment to this, one where they were looking for their clothes, ready to go back out to talk with other Cygirians about what to do with the Neballats. Talking about Porter. Porter!

"Are you sure we can't just stay here a moment longer?" she asked. "Can we push another hour back, an hour before Stephanie calls out to me?"

Edan put his shirt on the cot, and then turned to her, his hands on her shoulders. "I don't want just a moment for this, for us, for you," he said. "And I really know now that I want more than an hour. I want to take all the stolen hours we can and have it be as long as we need it to. I don't want to remember our first time together as something we rushed through. You are worth all my time, Ava. All the time I can give you."

And then he took her in his arms, his energy different now,

calmer, gentler, solid, desire only a faint aroma, something wafting slowly away. Despite all her anger and loneliness and fear of her supposed twin—the despair she'd carried forever—she knew this was the man with whom she'd spend the rest of her life. And he was the man that Cygiria needed right now, the one who would save them all.

In a brief flash, she had a vision, a thought, a glimpse of something she'd seen in the Source: an image of a life without struggle, without hiding, without fear of a force outside attacking. This would happen someplace safe, someplace theirs. In that vision would be the time that Edan spoke of. In that place would be their life.

Love, she thought to him, the word he'd used earlier, the word that changed everything.

Yes, he thought back. *Love.*

Chapter Six

Edan wasn't sure how he had been able to stop himself. After all this time of wanting and searching and needing her, he'd had his double, his twin, in his arms. There she had been underneath him, her arms holding him, her legs spread to take him in. Not just take him in. Want him inside her. And if he had moved into her right then, quickly, he wouldn't have been wrong. Ava had wanted their sex as much as he, and she'd been so ready, so wet, so welcoming.

He was hard now just thinking about it.

She was so beautiful he couldn't even look at her right now. He didn't even want to let his arm graze hers, imagining that he could see her with his skin. For without even looking at her, he could picture her long hair, the way it fanned out beneath her when she lay on the cot. He could smell her, take in something yellow and warm, a burst of sunflower, salt, sky. Edan could taste her warm brown skin, awash in lavender. His hands would find her softness, the shimmery skin of her thighs, the smooth landscape of her waist and chest and shoulders, the swoop of neck, the patch of warmth behind her ear. He couldn't sneak a look at her profile as she listened to Michael speak. If he saw her lips, he would think about her kiss. If he saw her throat, he would think about sliding a hand from that smooth place to her breast. If he thought about her breasts, well, then, he might as well leave and go back into the desert. Spending time with Luoc and his temptations would certainly take the edge off.

Why had he stopped? Why had he insisted that they get up, move back into their lives? Yes, there had been the call from Stephanie. And truly, how had he expected anything else? This tenuous time was hardly the time or place for lovemaking, and he'd managed to not forget everything and kiss Ava hard, take the magnificent gift she was willing to give him.

No, Edan had pulled them both off the cot and gotten dressed.

Probably, he was an idiot. Definitely, he was an idiot.

Because now he and Ava were in a quickly organized meeting in the largest temporary shelter, sitting with a group of Cygirians that included his youngest sister and her twin, Darl, Kate and Michael, Porter and Stephanie, Odhran and Elizabeth, Risa and Jai, the entire council, and others involved in the construction of Talalo. The only people of importance missing from the group were Mila and Garrick, both in Dhareilly with their newborn baby girl, Dasha.

"Don't you remember what happened when the Neballats attacked us by ship?" Ava asked the group. "When it seemed that both Upsilia and we were about to be destroyed?"

"Of course I remember. How could I not?" Claire said, looking at Darl and then back to Edan. For a swift second, Edan thought of his oldest memory, the one where he was sitting in the spaceship next to Mila and Claire, tiny little girls looking to him for strength. And now? Here was Claire, the smallest, the youngest, so strong in her words. She was no longer that little tiny girl, playing with her stuffed animal, crying for her mother.

"Mata, Pata," she'd cried out, her tears making her face slick and messy and slightly blurred. She leaned against Mila, grabbing her sister's shirt. "Mata!"

But now she wasn't resting her head on Mila's shoulders, waiting for an answer.

Edan breathed in briefly, knowing he couldn't let his concentration flag, but he wanted to see his niece for the first time, talk to Mila, let her know about what Luoc had shown him. He wanted Mila to know that her baby girl would be safe from the Neballats. Hoping that she was listening, he sent out a message.

It will be all right, he thought quickly and cleanly, keeping his thought isolated from Ava and everyone else. *We have a plan.*

I hope so, Mila's thought came back. *Dasha's just the first of many babies—there are so many more to be born. We need to know this generation will be safe.*

I promise, Edan thought. *They will all be safe.*

You've always said that. And you've always been right. Don't stop now.

I won't, he thought.

Edan? Mila thought.

What?

Dasha reminds me of us. The three of us. The whole ship of children. She's that vulnerable. That trusting. That needy.

Edan swallowed, the ship back with him once again in his imagination, the darkness, the stifling air, the hushed children's voices, the cries, the sudden jostling, the fear. They were all alone, without the parents who had put them on the ship, the matas, the patas. He could feel that ache now, the loss of them, the smell of flowers, something purple, when he thought of his mother. And then there was all the time with no sisters, no one who knew him, everything confusing until he was in the Source and could see a wider view, the bigger picture. But all his life, he'd felt he was still that little boy with the two small girls, hurtling to somewhere scary and unknown.

We will do better. We will find a solution that lasts, he thought, closing down the communication with Mila and turning his full attention back to the conversation. Ava was still answering Michael's questions about their time in the desert and Luoc, but none in the group seemed to understand the power that Ava was trying to explain, a power that they all had within them.

". . . and what we were able to do as a group," Ava said. "That you remember."

"I learned about it in the Source," Claire said. "It was like Convergence. All our powers together."

Edan allowed himself to turn to Ava, breathed out, focused on what lay before them all.

"Claire," he began. "We learned that we can do that with our twins. But there is so much more. We can harness our powers and do whatever it is we want to. Separately. Ourselves."

The entire group stopped moving, staring at Edan and then Ava.

"What are you saying, Edan?" Jai asked.

Tell them, Ava thought. *Don't worry if they don't understand.*

"Just what I said. We can do whatever it is we want to. Ava and I returned here from the desert on our own. We pushed back time an hour. These are not our powers, as you know. We simply put out our intention and it happened."

Again, there was the silence in among the group, the only noise coming from outside the tent, the air against the fabric walls, the distant whoop of workers at the site. For a quick second, Edan thought of Siker, the hot pavement, the relentless task of building. All of this could be over, he knew. All of it could be done.

Swallowing, he looked out to the crowd, feeling his heart beating a hot, heavy rhythm, feeling Ava's nervousness.

They don't believe us, she thought. *They don't want it to be true.*

Wait, he thought. *Just wait.*

"Don't you think we would have already figured out this ability?" asked Jai. "Don't you think at some point we've all tried to master another skill, another talent? There was none of this in the database at the safe house. Nothing, at least, that we could find."

Edan slowly stood, looking out at his family, his friends, his people. There they were, their eyes on them, their faces rapt, intent, keen. Since he came out of the Source—awakened to the new Cygirian life—he'd understood the way people looked at him, seen how they wanted answers, his answers. He'd never asked for this responsibility, but here it was. For a second, he remembered how it had felt to look out at the city that Luoc had promised him on the desert. So many promises. And one of them was all that power! All that potential for rule. For total control. And now, seeing this small group before him, Edan knew that he would never want that ultimate control and power. More than anything, he wanted to be a part of something, a member, a helper, a piece of the bigger puzzle. To get to that point, he had to convince them of what he knew.

As he looked at everyone, Edan realized that he felt something more intense than the power he'd felt on the desert hill. He felt Ava with him, by him, in him. Standing next to him like a shadow—no, standing next to him like light. She wasn't his dark reflection but his equal bright energy. Matching him thought for thought, power for power. Together, they were stronger than the sum of their parts, and together with all Cygiria, they would be invisible.

"We don't know who we are," Edan said. "We have only known of each other for a short time. And it's possible that our parents and grandparents and ancestors never knew the secrets of what we could do. And maybe, we have just come into it. But all of this is unknown. We are almost unknown to ourselves. Some of us have just met our twins, our doubles, our other halves. We've just come to the notion of being able to meld our powers with one other person. The information left to us at the safe house was quickly put together, minimal, not enough. How could we know all there is to know about our culture, especially if even those before us had no idea of the scope of our powers?"

There was a lull, a pause, a bell of thought after he spoke. Edan looked around the room, hoping they would understand. And then Claire looked at him, nodded.

"We did push away the Neballat ships," Claire said. "Who knew we could do that? Who knew that Convergence would work until we heard about it from those who came back from the Source? Each time we've tried something we could not do, we've been able to do it."

"Well, then," Porter said, "what is the point of this silly differentiation? Why do we think we can do only one thing? Why do we exhibit one behavior when all are simply at our fingertips? Why do we fall back time and time again to what we can do, what is known to us?"

"Many of us grew up on Earth hiding what we could do. Ashamed by it," Darl said. "We tried to hide it. I think opening up to more, to all of it might seem to go over the line."

"Maybe knowing we could do everything would have been too much for everyday life," Risa said. "Just living life with one power feels like too much sometimes. But knowing we can do anything we wanted might make people just sit down and do nothing."

The group seemed to think about this, listening to Risa's words.

"These are different times," Kate said. "We need all that we can do. Even if it turns out that we can't. We will have tried."

"Well, this certainly explains everything," Claire said.

"What pray tell are you talking about?" Porter asked.

"Why the Neballats have hunted us down as a people. It seemed for a while they were going after particular pairs, those who could help them regain their bodies and planet and life. But all along, they wanted of us. In one group, with one thought, we could fix everything for them. And they could keep a small number of us to do their bidding when necessary."

"Slaves," Kate said. "That's what our parents must have known. That's why they said no to the Neballats' demands. Why they fled Cygiria."

"Excuse me," Porter said. "If we are so damn amazing with all this exciting firepower, why have we been running from anyone? Why don't we just turn about and let them, as they say, have it?"

"They can control us," Risa said. "They can tamp down our powers. We haven't learned or don't know how to do everything, it would seem. Look what they did to our world, our parents, the millennia of life on our planet. They take us by twos, interrogate us, control our minds. To get what they wanted they destroyed the very thing they needed. They destroyed Cygiria. Our world."

"We will make a new one," Edan said, the words coming out of him from somewhere deep, like a line of a poem he'd memorized in school.

"A new one what?" Porter asked, this time no sarcasm in his voice.

Ava took his hand, her feelings a question he could hear as well as Porter's.

"A world," Edan said, his voice low and even. "We will make a new world. Another Cygiria."

When he'd said the words, he'd been looking beyond the group, but after his idea was floating out in the crowd, he looked down at those staring at him. No one said a word. All of them watched him unblinking, their mouths full of words they could not speak. Finally, the silence shifted.

"We will make a world," Darl said, the first to speak. "We will *make* a world? A planet? With atmosphere and a sun and moon and all that goes with planet-ness?"

"That should be easy. Done in a trice," Porter said. "In fact, after I'm done making a world, I will make a little key chain as a memento of the experience. Then I'd like to have a big garden salad and—"

"For God's sake, stop it," Kate said, turning to Porter, and then looking back at Edan. "What do you mean, Edan? How can we make a world?"

Before Edan could answer, Ava said, "By envisioning it. By imagining it. By believing it real."

"I think you are a little . . ." Porter trailed off, unable, it seemed, to find a sarcastic comeback that would fit.

Again the room was quiet. Edan looked at the group as they thought. Many of them had come of age on Earth, a place that did not understand, acknowledge, or accept

Cygirian powers. Many Cygirians had been "treated" for their powers by doctors and medications. On Upsilia, the Cygirians' abilities had been recognized and hidden, most of them put into the Source during late adolescence and early adulthood.

So they were a group of people who had just accepted their strengths and their power, the one thing they imagined they could do with their twins. But to tell them that anything they desired or imagined was possible was probably too much to bear.

I told them incorrectly, Edan thought to Ava. *I've made a mistake.*

How else could you have told them? Ava thought. *There is no other way but to tell them what is true.*

There has to be a way, he thought.

Show them. Let's show them, she thought. *Let's do what we did earlier. Or something. Something that will show.*

At her thought, Edan smiled, thinking not of their travel from the desert but their exploration in the tent.

Not that! Ava thought.

I know, love. It's just that I will never be able to stop thinking about that.

Pulling away from the images of Ava in his head, Edan cleared his throat. "There is no other way for us to prove to you what we learned out in the desert. So let Ava and me show you. Let us show you what we know."

Out in the crowd, Claire smiled, nodding, and there was a relief that Edan could feel, a trust that was already starting to build. The group began to murmur, talk, slowly come to standing.

"Show and tell," said Porter, standing up and putting his arm around Stephanie's shoulders. "I can't wait."

* * *

Outside, everything but this group of people standing around Edan and Ava was as it had always been. Construction continued, workers moving back and forth between buildings and projects, the sound of metal and machines and motors clanging into the thin desert air. Beyond Talalo, the desert stretched on all the way to the mountains, the Dhareilly a diamond at the foot.

But it was clear that the group was causing some attention, passing Cygirians stopping, asking questions, staying to watch. Slowly, more and more of them trickled in, thoughts reaching to them as they worked. Edan knew that the more of them who saw, who understand, the better for everyone, the faster they could begin to form a plan.

Edan and Ava hadn't had much time to compare notes, to decide what they were going to do. But since they had traveled through space and time and matter, that seemed a likely choice for this exercise, something they had already done.

I'd hate to screw up this time, Ava thought, reaching out and taking Edan's hand, hers cold, reflecting her nervousness.

I don't know if we can screw up. Being able to move through space won't be like creating a world, Edan thought. *So let's just do what we can and hope they can extrapolate.*

But will it show them what they need to see? Ava thought. *Will they understand it?*

Edan wondered what Cygirians couldn't understand. They'd been through so much with the Neballats that any power, any magic, any attack, and defense would likely seem possible.

Let's try, he thought, squeezing her hand and turning toward the group. *Let's just do what we can.*

"You know of Ava's and my power to age or unage ourselves," Edan said. "Ours is one that you cannot see and one that we do not want to use on our own or too often."

He saw Claire and Darl and others nod as he spoke. "But now we are going to use a power we did not think we had. This is a power that my youngest sister and her twin have, the ability to move through space with only a thought. This is the power we used to return here from the desert. This is what we have done with Convergence, but we can do it with each other only."

There was a pause, a slip of silence after he spoke. Claire was smiling broadly, her eyes bright with feeling, clearly happy that Edan and Ava were using her power, a power that just a few short months ago seemed a burden to her.

This going places runs in the family, Claire thought. *Seems that moving time around does, too.*

Apparently, Edan thought back. *We have finally learned to share.*

Still smiling, Claire nodded, and Edan looked down at his and Ava's clasped hands. How would he survive such connectedness? Such love?

By practicing all the time, Ava thought. *So let's get this over with!*

All right, he thought, looking up at the growing crowd.

"So we are going to go and return quickly," Edan said, pulling Ava toward him.

Ava looked at him, thinking, *Where are we going?*

To Dhareilly and back. Picture the government building, he thought.

The one made almost all of glass? she thought.

Yes.

I can already see it, she thought.

And when we arrive, we turn our thoughts back to this very place. Come back as soon as we can.

All right, she thought.

Without looking one more time at the assembled people before him, Edan closed his eyes, brought Ava as close to him as he could, feeling her thoughts merge and flow with his. And in that embrace, there it was, that flow and ebb of the Source, the melding of everything, the river of same thoughts, same feeling, same heat. Everything was fluid and red and orange and lively, he and Ava but a stream moving through a plain of energy.

Dhareilly, Edan thought, imagining the gleaming, clean streets, the rising steel buildings, the orderly flow of people in the streets. He saw the way the city looked on the horizon, the way the buildings grouped in the city center, and then imagined the shining glass structure of the government building, saw it with not only his eye but with Ava's eye, their vision one, their vision twinned.

Dhareilly, Ava thought, and with her same thought, there they were, on the street in front of the building, watching the passersby. For that one moment they were there, Edan felt himself tense, remembering the harsh rules that Upsilia placed upon its citizens. He and Ava were still, standing on the sidewalk unmoving, not focused, not businesslike, not intent on going somewhere fast. In this city, that stillness often meant death, and he held Ava tight, not wanting to deal with the Upsilian rules right now.

We don't have to stay. We don't have to deal with them, Ava thought. *Let's go back. Now.*

Edan closed his eyes, breathed in, and then with that same feeling and intent, that same warm vision of the desert and Talalo, they were back in the merge and stream of thoughts and then back in the desert again, the air dry and hot on his skin.

Edan opened his eyes to see the group staring at him, un-blinking, unmoving. And then Claire smiled at him again.

"You did it," she said.

Edan nodded, still holding Ava tightly against him.

"You were in Dhareilly," Porter said, his voice slow and calm. "Where in Dhareilly?"

"Yes," Ava said. "We were there. Right in front of the government building."

"Just like that. Without the whole group pushing together and thinking together. You were there." Porter's eyes were steady, calm, questioning.

"Yes," Edan said. "That's exactly correct."

"So we can do what we want with simply intent?" Michael asked. "We imagine it and we can do it."

As Michael spoke, Edan realized that this notion seemed absolutely too simple. To simply want something, to desire it, to think it, and then have it come about did seem ludicrous. Impossible. But it shouldn't. If everything was one thing—if all the energies of the universes were one flat plain of matter, no differentiation between anything at all—and if people were conduits of that matter's energy, then what they wanted manifested, what they wanted in the world, should be that easy to call forth. Somehow, the universe had made all of them. Here they were, born of other energies. Here were all the planets. All the creatures, florae, faunae, stars, moons, black holes. Why would moving through anything seem amazing after looking at creation itself?

"Michael," Edan said, "I don't pretend to understand it. I just know now that it is possible. I know now that we could probably . . ."

He stopped talking because he couldn't talk anymore. He had told them it was possible, but he'd never really imagined it before, the very idea only a concept, an abstraction. Yes, he had said that they would create a world, a new Cygiria, but had he himself really believed it? Shutting down his thoughts to the whole group, he brought forth the world that he had talked about, seen only once before in a dream, months ago. In his mind's eye, he could see a world forming out of darkness, out of nothingness, out of the blackness that threatened to swallow everything. As he watched the world, it spun into life, the atmosphere cradling the earth, plants and animals and humans thriving in the clean, pristine air. He had the vision. This was what they could make, could create. This was the world on which they would live.

No, Ava thought, her word full of wonder.

Yes, Edan thought, unable to breathe, the idea so full inside him. *Oh yes.*

He turned to Ava, knowing that the world was part of his dream and so was she. What was supposed to be happening was unfolding just as it should. She'd found him and together they were going to galvanize all Cygirians, use all their energies to make this place out of the nothingness. It was going to happen.

"If Ava and I can travel through space, we can make a world," Edan said. "But we will need all of our energies. We will need everyone to help."

"A world. I still don't see how moving through space can even begin to equal making a world," Kate said, her face full of wonder and perhaps a portion of doubt. "We will make a world to live on?"

There were some murmurs, questions floating toward Edan as he stood before them.

"You did do a nice show there going to Dhareilly and back. But don't you think," Porter began, "we might try with creating something a little smaller than a world first?

Maybe a doughnut or a baseball or a house or what about a town? Should we make our first project an entire world?"

Edan shrugged, knowing now that what he was about to say was true. "A doughnut, baseball, a house, a town, a world. All the same stuff. All matter. All things we can conjure. Together, we are stronger than we can imagine. Together, we have the power to create what we need to survive as a people. All we have to do is gather ourselves in force, gather to do this thing we've long been capable of."

There was a pause as Edan's words moved through the crowd, filling in the spaces where doubt had once been. They had all lived lives of hiding their powers, running from those who wanted to either capture or kill them, and to know that all along they'd had the power to defeat their enemies was likely too much to think about. What to do when the answer to everything presented itself, clear as water, clear as glass? How to say yes to what would save you? How to take yes for an answer?

"Well," said Jai, breathing in and putting his arm around Risa. "We will need to organize if this is going to happen. Pull people in from Dhareilly. Find the last of us on Earth."

Looking out at the group, Edan saw that they were all with him. Behind him. For him. And more importantly, he saw Ava was next to him, his partner, his equal, his twin. That fact alone made him realize that anything was possible.

"Let's make it happen," he said. "Let's finish this story once and for all."

Somehow, he and Ava were back in his tent. Night had fallen in the desert, the sky a deep steel gray. Night birds called in the distance, fusing with the sounds of people walking past the tent, heading for rest. The air was slowly taking on a flat sandy chill, but Edan wasn't cold, not even close. In fact, all evening while the rest of the Cygirians in Talalo learned of the plan to create a world, he'd felt that he was going to have to use his newly found talents to create an ocean to jump in. Just looking at Ava made him hot. Made him hard. He kept feeling her skin under his hands, even when Jai and Claire and Michael and Kate were speaking. Even when the Cygirians from Dhareilly began to arrive, everyone beginning to organize, to practice this new way of manipulating their talents.

Defeating the Neballats, creating a world, finally having a true place of their own was really second to his need for his twin. He knew this was selfish and slightly insane, but he couldn't stop it. Her body spoke to him, her voice and scent were like music he wanted to hear and swallow and feel. Edan wanted to swim in her taste, her feel, her embrace. He wanted to take her hair in his hands, running his palms over the smooth river of blond. He wanted to feel all of her against him, push inside her wetness. And he wanted her to feel him, touch him, know him in all ways, in this most important way.

But now that they were alone in his tent, looking at each other, silent, he suddenly felt confused, not knowing how to start, to pick up the thread of what they had begun after Luoc left them standing on the hill.

Why don't we go back to where we were this morning? she thought, slowly taking off her top, letting it fall to the floor. Edan stared at her, barely able to swallow, unable to take his eyes away from her beautiful breasts. He forced himself to look elsewhere, concentrating on the pulse on her neck, the fast *one-two* beat that showed her excitement as well.

Slowly, he reached up a hand, ran a finger along her jaw,

down her throat, resting his finger on that pulse, that quickening, that heat, her fire. Ava closed her eyes, and Edan moved his fingers lower, letting his palm smooth the soft skin of her chest, bringing up both his hands so he could cup her breasts.

With that perfect flesh in his hands, he wanted to fall to his knees, thank whatever power that was that connected Ava and him in this bond. She felt so lovely! This smooth, soft weight in his hands was like treasure, and he slowly touched her, feeling her hard nipples.

She tilted her head back, let out a quiet "Oh" with her voice and an *Oh!* with her mind. And then Edan moved closer to her, dropped his hands, put his arms around her, and kissed her.

This kiss was the beginning of the conversation, a story of tongue and taste and passion. She pressed him close, she opened up to take him in, holding the back of his neck and head with her hands. With each movement, she told him that she wanted him, that she was ready, and Edan knew that finally, with this love, with this woman, in this place, he was coming home.

Moving just slightly away from their embrace, his lips still on hers, Edan took off his shirt, his pants, letting them join the cotton swirl on the floor. He shuffled off her pants as well, letting his hands play on her lovely rear, the skin amazingly soft. As he touched her, he pressed against her, letting her feel how much he wanted her, careful not to move too much against her as he wondered if he could take the excitement of being so close. Never before had he felt this way, completely sexually aroused and one hundred percent in love with the woman he wanted to sleep with. And he couldn't wait anymore.

So without completely picking her up, he scooped her

into his arms and put her gently on the cot, lying down on his side next to her, allowing his hands to roam her body, her curves, her breasts, the smooth plain of her stomach, the warmth of her.

You feel so good, he thought, letting his fingers skim the fine surface of her skin.

You're making me feel that way, she thought. *You make me good.*

No, you come already packaged that way.

Edan smiled, bending down to kiss her, surprised by the firm way she pulled him closer, her arms around his shoulders.

You aren't the only one who wants this, she thought. *Not at all.*

Her thought made Edan want it all, the entire experience. All the feelings that he and she could have together, so he moved into her embrace, pressing himself against her, nudging her legs open slightly as he pulled from the kiss to move down to let his tongue swirl against her nipples.

Ava moaned, pushed herself against him, and he could feel she was wet and ready and wanting. But even if she was so ready for him, he knew that this was her first time so she needed all his attention, all the preparation.

Leaving a nipple free, hard and red and wet, he moved his head down her body, kissing her as he slowly wended toward the center of her, her stomach and belly and hips lovely and warm under his lips. He listened to her slight moans, her sighs, and almost smiled at the way her movements seemed to shrug him down to the exact spot he was heading for.

You'll like this, he thought, waiting for a response, but then he could sense that her mind was no longer thinking in words. Her thoughts weren't forming into questions or demands or ideas. She was only interfacing with the world in feelings and sounds, her body completely sensory, hungry, needing, wanting him.

He brought his mouth to her wetness, tasting her ocean, feeling the waves of her reaction to his tongue. Ava pushed up toward him, sighing, her thoughts still inchoate, inarticulate, full of passion. Continuing to move his lips and mouth on her, moving in the way that her hips were showing him how to, he felt her sound finally emerge as a thought, a word.

Yes, she thought, holding his head with her hands, her thighs pressed against his face.

"Oh yes," she cried out, and he felt her grow in his mouth, moving his tongue faster to her rhythm, loving the feel of her body trembling against him.

"Yes," he whispered against her as her body calmed, slowed, kissing her in a line, past her belly, her chest, her neck, her chin.

"Yes," he whispered against her lips, pressing himself against her. "Yes?"

Ava looked up at him with her umber eyes, and all he could see was her want of more. She nodded, and slowly, he pushed, feeling her body open, take him in. But she was so tight, her entire self clenched around him, and felt so good that he wondered if he would make it all the way inside her.

Breathe, she thought.

Of course. So simple. Breathing, a natural reflex. Breathing, just like being with Ava.

Breathe, she thought again, and he did, each breath a slow push, waiting for any resistance from her, any sign of pain, but there was none, no flinching, no resistance, no hurt, and then with a slight tug, he was in her, and she was holding him, and they were moving.

He felt like they were one lovely animal, running to safety. They were running and moving, and he was in her—Ava, his beloved double, his necessary twin. As they moved, he was his body and more than his body, floating and feeling, away from himself but more attached to every vein and nerve than ever before. He was in ecstasy inside himself and in ecstasy with Ava at the same time. There was more and everything, his mind cracking open to feeling, to love; his body letting go, filling her, as if he had waited his entire life to do so.

Yes.

Oh yes.

Chapter Seven

The moonlight disappeared behind clouds, inside the tent completely dark, and Ava liked it better this way, feeling even more protected as she lay in the small cot next to Edan. He had fallen asleep, and now she lay with her head on his chest, listening to his deep breathing, the *pound-pound* of his heart, feeling his taut chest muscles under her cheek.

She blinked into the gloom, snuggling closer, letting the blanket slightly obscure her vision. Ava knew she would never sleep tonight. Her body felt like a constellation of nerves, each point brightly lit, on fire, ready to go supernova. How had she lived all these years without him? How had she made it through her childhood, endured all the stares, the teasing, the feeling of aloneness? She thought about her twelve-, thirteen-, fourteen-year-old self staring out the window of her bedroom wondering why life was here at all. Nothing had seemed available to her other than this feeling of otherness.

But now everything was changed.

Ava wanted to go to that teenaged girl and hold her. She wanted to tell her to hold on, to wait. She wanted to tell her that she would be scared and alone some more—that she would go to a place where none of this mattered for a while. She wanted to let the girl know that in just a few years she would be lying next to a man she could love forever. But that girl next to the window wouldn't believe her. In fact, Ava wasn't sure she actually believed it was true now. It had happened! But how? How had this—this love she'd experienced here tonight—eluded her until this very day?

Shifting against him, she breathed in his sweet sun smell, rubbing her face against soft chest hair, running her hands along his smooth chest and belly. Swallowing, she realized that she was almost angry. But at what? At Edan for not trying to find her earlier? For walking away from her that day by the construction site? For wandering in the desert? Or was it because he'd shown her this love, this lovemaking, and now she knew exactly what it was that she had to lose? Even though it had only been one night, she knew that she would never be able to survive should she lose him. And it wasn't just about the sex, though the memory of how amazing he had felt inside her made a hot red flush spread over her face and chest. But no. That wasn't it. It was about the connection with his mind and soul. It was about the way he understood her, seeing into her thoughts, her past, her longing, her desires. It was the fact that he could see all of her and not walk away. He stayed. He wanted to stay. Not only did he not walk away, but he came closer. He asked for more. He had told her he was in this forever.

When she had been walking in the desert by night, sleeping by day, she wondered if she was crazy to follow this man. It had been hot even at twilight and lonely, even though she was always so often alone. But at least at the safe house and then Dhareilly and then Talalo, she'd had things to do, ways of keeping herself busy. Cooking had been the best occupier of her time, a constant meditation, repetitive, calming. Onion, pepper, squash. Slice, slice, slice. She hadn't had to think about herself or her missing twin every hour of the day. But her journey to find Edan in the desert had left her open to her own thoughts.

I'm not good enough to have a twin.

No one would want me as a twin.

If I find him, he won't recognize me.

If I find him, I won't want him.

It's easier to be alone.

I am alone.

I am alone.

I will always be alone.

And then came her inevitable chastising of herself, the anger at her victim mentality, her knowledge that she could live alone her entire life and be fine. She didn't need a twin to make her complete. While everyone longed for a mate, a partner, a true friend, soul mate, lover, she could do just fine all by herself. She was strong, capable, worthy, useful. She had talents and desires and drive that went beyond whatever was out there for her. Just look at how everyone loved her cooking and baking. People lined up for what she could make. She made friends because of her concoctions. This was something she could do and do well.

But then the sun would creep up on the morning horizon, and she would fall asleep only to wake up at sunset to start the walk and the thoughts all over again.

After days of the journey in the desert, she realized she was in another country. Not literally, but in her mind. She stopped seeing things as if she found Edan or if she didn't. All that mattered was the attempt she made to find him, the path she took to try to find the answers to the questions she'd always asked herself. The country was her body, her steps in the darkness, her steps toward the knowledge that would bring the light, bring clarity, bring peace, regardless of the answer.

But here she was, the answer next to her. The answer made her whole.

Edan stirred, pulling her close in his sleep. Here she was. Here she finally was, all the questions answered. He was her other half, the dark to her light. And together, they would work with all the Cygirians in the universe to create their own world, Neballats or no Neballats.

Closing her eyes, Ava kissed Edan's chest and pressed close, taking in his smell, his being, wanting as much of her skin to touch his as possible. There wasn't enough of him to feel, her hands moving across his skin, wanting all of him. She had years of touching to make up for, a lifetime, and she wouldn't let sleep keep her from getting what she needed, what she wanted. And she had everything she wanted. At last. Everything, for once, was absolutely perfect.

Whatever it was, it was slick and fast and stealthy. She felt its dark black arms slip around her like octopus tentacles, lift her from the cot as if she were buoyant, floating in water, helpless in an embrace she did not trust. She couldn't see, couldn't feel her body, could only think, but her thoughts were confused. She tried to feel for Edan, but her body seemed to be encased in cotton or foam or the thickest air. Ava was sure she was moving through air and maybe time and space, but the only clues came from her head, not her body. Her senses were deprived, and she wondered if she was actually in a dream.

If it's a dream, came the thought. *It's not a pleasant one. Not for you. Not yet.*

Who are you? she thought.

You know us well, the voice hissed through her ears, the sound a jagged saw in her brain. *And now you will learn to know us better. You will be our best friend. You will give us what we want, you and your beloved. You two will do for us what we cannot do ourselves.*

Edan? Ava again tried to move, to find him lying next to her, but she was immobilized, senseless, still. *Edan, where are you? What is happening to us? Who is talking to me?*

Don't think about him yet, the voice thought. *We need to work with him a little bit. Give him some help, so he can help us.*

Help? Ava thought. *What do you mean?*

It's the same help we are going to give you, a little device that will make things so much easier for us. We've used it to great results with your kind.

Ava felt her breath in her throat, the thick air making it hard for her to swallow. She wondered if she would choke, and blood flumed through her body, fear a hot, wide current inside her.

She knew. She knew where she was. She knew who had her. And she had seen what they had done to people, to her people, to Cygirians. Once she had watched the removal of the device she knew they were thinking of. And it wasn't a device. It was a thing. A horrible, awful, live thing.

I—she began.

Don't bother. Shhh. Just relax. Soon it will all be over. Just sleep. Sleep.

She wanted to twist out of her bonds, break free, escape. She wanted to run to the place where Edan was and save him from whatever it was the Neballats were going to do to him. But not only was she held tight and still; she was so tired. So sleepy, and she felt the small part of her that was conscious fade away, slip into the darkness they had carried her here on.

Edan, she thought, and then there was nothing but darkness.

The light was shining in her eyes, beating a stark ugly pulse into her brain. She tried to blink, she realized she couldn't, something holding her eyelids open. To her sides, she saw movement, and she wanted to turn her head, but she was immobilized, stuck in this supine position, staring into a light that made it too bright to see much of anything. She tried to close her eyes, but they seemed to be stuck open, pulled open, and she felt the tears stream down her temples, into her hair.

Then there was pain, something sharp and long and round, something that encircled her head. Ava wanted to cry out, but her voice was gone, her throat dry, her lungs empty. So pain became a thought, a way of being, a jagged cut of hurt that ran through her entire body.

She breathed in what hurt, what ached, what pulled, what tore. Everything was all that was wrong, what burned, what ripped at her head. As if in a dream, she found herself trapped in a small room full of images of knives and holes and things that were unnatural, impure, unclean, unwholesome. She thought of snakes and tubes and wires. Her thought was a scream she could not utter, the images were a nightmare she could not run away from, and she thought that her mouth must be opened, must be full of the no-sound, her refusal of what could not be refused.

But then, even as she imagined she saw what they were doing as they hovered over her, she felt herself relax, think about things that had no edges, things that wouldn't burn or poke or rent. All the painful images began to fade into a memory she couldn't even recall, and she saw something round and warm and lovely. It spun in a warm butter of sunlight, a perfect confection of life. Ava knew what it was. A planet. It was a planet, a blue, white, green, brown orb circling in her mind's eye, and it was a planet that would nurture and sustain and give. It was home. It was their home, the planet that they were going to create for themselves. Home for Cygir—

No, not for you. This is what we want, the voice thought. *This is the place we need. And you know how to make it for us. The one who showed you your power was not the only one who knew of your abilities. He was smart, but not, sadly, smart enough.*

And as the voice thought that, she saw how obvious, how clear it all was. Who else would need such a world? Who needed it more? They had waited for lifetimes for this world. Once, they had destroyed a planet precipitously, without enough consideration. So now they needed a new one, a better one, one that would allow them finally to live happy and whole lives. Who cared about their former mistake? Now it was time for Cygiria to finally give them what was needed.

It's your duty, the voice thought. *It's what you owe us.*

Of course that's what she would give them, Ava understood. This warm lovely place was exactly what they deserved. And she was going to help these people get what they needed. That was all she wanted to do. That's all she wanted, period.

She wanted to blink, felt something swimming somewhere inside her. What was it that she wanted to feel? She couldn't remember. But her conviction remained. She would help do what was asked of her. She would save them.

That's right, thought the voice. *That's exactly right.*

How should I begin? Ava thought, trying to sit up. *I need to start now.*

First, you need to sleep some more. And then you and your double will be shown how to proceed.

Double. Double. Ava felt her mind fold over something that was important. Or used to be important. What was it? She felt a longing, a rush of nerves and longing, but that sensation was almost instantly replaced by space, whiteness, an empty place.

My double, she thought.

Yes, and you will help us with our world. You will make it for us.

Ava nodded, and then the light grew dim, and she felt something release her body, her eyelids, her mind.

Sleep again, the voice thought. *And then we will start.*

Ava woke up and saw him. The man. Her man? She couldn't be certain. But it was Edan. They were both sitting at a table in a large empty room, looking at each other. She felt as though she should be doing something else, feeling something else, but when she grasped at the thought, the feeling, the action, it disappeared. Ideas popped into her mind and then burst into nothingness. She wanted to say something but found no words in her throat or on her tongue. There were sentences and phrases she knew but no longer understood how to articulate them.

So Ava did what she could. She smiled, as did he, and they kept sitting at the table.

Nothing happened for a long time, but Ava felt that nothing could continue to happen forever. Nothing seemed to be good. Nothing was comfortable and safe. Nothing was white and pure and clean. Nothing was known. But then again, when something happened, that would be just fine, too. Everything was fine. The people would come in and tell her what to do, and she would do it. Why wouldn't she do exactly what they asked? And why wouldn't she do it all with the man, with Edan? The two of them would find a way to make the world and then she could go back to spinning in this lovely blankness that filled her.

This feeling reminded her of another feeling, but Ava was unclear where or when she'd had that feeling before. She tried to think hard, to remember, but she winced, something circling her head like a noose. Everything was tightening, pressing close, in, fast, so she let go of the thought, sitting back straight in her chair, and the noose let go. Oh, that was better, so much better. That was almost nice. She almost felt good.

Breathing out, Ava looked up. Across from her, Edan was trying to say something, his mouth seeming to form words, his lips taut with purpose and effort.

"What?" he began to ask, his face contorted with some expression that looked like it hurt to produce. His hands were gripping the edge of the table, his knuckles white, his fingertips red.

"No," Ava said, not wanting to feel the noose again, the cinch of pain across her forehead. "No. Stop."

Edan looked up, his eyes watering. "No?"

She nodded. "No."

His chest moved with his deep breathing, his fight against the nothingness. "Why?"

"Because," Ava said simply, knowing somehow that particular word was the answer. Because. Because this was what was, is, had to be. This table, this empty room, the spinning orb in the butter-light sky. This. Only. This. For no reason but *because*.

Edan breathed out, nodded, put his head into his hands. Ava looked at him, knowing something else. She should feel other, differently, better. But then that thought let loose, too, and there was only and again the nothingness of the room, Edan's breathing, the constant threat of the noose.

After what felt like hours, maybe a day, a door appeared in the box of the room. And then the door opened, slowly, the black rectangle a gape like a surprised mouth in a pale face. Ava didn't blink, kept herself focused, watched as people who weren't people came in from the darkness. What were they, then? she wondered, seeing their terrible flesh under their terrible skin. Were they invisible? Transparent? Of course they were, she knew, watching the *beat-beat* of their hearts, the chugging flow of their blood, the swirl of digestion in their guts. Transparent. Almost entirely gone.

Not quite, came the voice. *The part that you don't like is still here.*

One of the people pointed to his head, and yes, there was his brain, a dark stain against his opaque skull. Ava couldn't take her eyes off it, wanting to see his thoughts, imagining that they would be moving through his brain like blood.

You will know what we want soon enough, the person thought, moving toward the table.

Ava turned to Edan, a flick of a thought telling her that he would help her against these invisible people. He would save her, but that notion floated away though the anxiety did not. As the person got closer, she wanted to hold on to something. She wanted—she wanted . . . She breathed, felt something stirring in her head, the pressure erasing her fear.

Yes, that's right. Calm yourself. We will show you what you need to do and where. It will all be so easy.

She and Edan were surrounded now, the table a ring of

see-through flesh. Ava breathed, stared at them, waited. That's what she was supposed to do. Wait and listen.

You will both do what you were planning, one of the people thought. Ava could not tell which of them was thinking, but it didn't matter. She stared at all of their dark eyes, wet black obsidian set in crepe papery lids.

You will be sent back to Upsilia, and you will gather your people. Together, you will create the world that you discussed—

How? Edan's thought pushed through into the room. *How?*

Ava turned her gaze to him, and saw how his question left him, the lines in his face relaxing, letting go of concern. In a second, he was staring up at the people again, and Ava looked back.

You will make the world to our specifications, given to you through thoughts we are going to give to you now. But this fact is not something you will share with the others.

The others. The others. Who were they? Ava had a remembrance of a woman, dark hair, dark eyes. Funny. Then there was the memory of clanging sounds, metal against metal, laughter, the smells of food. Food. Food she prepared.

She was about to smile, but the noose cinched, her forehead crushed by invisible bonds. The voice paused, seemed to chuckle, went on.

This will not be your world, but ours. And after we have it, we will let your people go free. You can do whatever you want. Create your own world. But first, you will give us ours.

Trying to take in his ideas as she let go of the memory of a kitchen—yes, a kitchen—she thought of the spinning world, the one they were going to make for themselves.

No, that's not quite the world we want. Here it is. Here is what we want. Just a few differences for us. Our preferences, as it were.

Thrust back in her seat, Ava closed her eyes, saw in the blackness all around her. She was sitting in the middle of it, suspended in the void, when she noticed something forming. What was it? It looked like the beginning of a migraine aura, wavery, pulsing, light beginning to crack it open. As it spun and glowed, she saw colors filling in the darkness, blue and white and brown. A brightness opened up behind it, cracking wide the darkness, and Ava blinked against it, holding up a hand to her eyes. She was witnessing a birth, a world coming into being, and even though she wasn't sure why, she felt tears prickle in her eyes. The noose cinched tight, she breathed, watched, her tears drying as she focused on what she was clearly supposed to.

The world spun, continents forming, a blue atmosphere hugging tight against the orb. And then she seemed to be thrust toward the world, pushed at amazing speed, her hair blowing behind her, her face pulled taut from force. She crashed through the atmosphere, hurtling close, close, closer to a continent, and then just as she began, she stopped, her heart pounding, her eyes wide.

Blinking finally, she looked around to a world that was like Upsilia in many ways, like the images she had seen of Earth. Land, trees, water, sky. A terrain not unknown to her.

But it's slightly different, the voice thought. *It's what we like, though your kind would be happy there as well. But this planet is a tad hotter, a little more arid, higher temperature. Of course, when your people are able to heal our bodies, we might want it a bit cooler. But for now, this world is what we crave.*

She wanted to stand, to protest, to scream. No, this wasn't what they deserved, these terrible people, these horrid beings.

Her quadriceps flexing, she tried to stand, lift herself into protest. But before she could do a thing, she felt the noose begin its constant punishment.

No, she thought. *You can't*—the noose cinched tight, squeezing away her thoughts, and Ava looked out to the world and knew that this was, in fact, exactly what these people needed. This lovely flat world, warm and dry and healthy. They'd been so displaced, so unhinged, so alone in space, a people without a planet. They'd lost their families and their friends. They'd been forced to travel throughout space without knowing where home was. Their bodies were destroyed, their minds really all that they had left. It made her so sad she couldn't hold her head up, the tears that had been there before reemerging.

The noose cinched.

Ava looked up, the surface of the planet still before her.

Yes, she thought. *This is your planet. This is what we will create for you.*

You and this man will do it, the person thought. *Together, you will create what we need.*

Turning, Ava realized that Edan was still next to her. Somehow, she'd forgotten he was there. He looked at her, nodded, and she knew that they would do this thing. They would go back and show all Cygirians how to make this world. And then they would give it to these people, who would go on to lead happy, whole lives. Somehow, this whole world would lead to whole bodies. They would be cured! They would be happy! They would always be thankful to the Cygirians. Good friends. Happy to share in their bounty, their fortune, their luck. It would be wonderful. It would be exactly as it should be.

That's right, the voice thought, soothing and low. *You are exactly right. We will be such very good friends.*

Ava knew that she wanted to reach out for Edan, hold him, but the idea of the noose around her head kept her looking forward at the planet, seeing everything she had to do. The only thing she had to do.

Later, without knowing how she arrived, Ava was back in the tent in Talalo. She stood, blinking, having trouble seeing anything but the planet the people had shown her. There was a cot, but really it was a continent. There was the flap leading outside to the desert, but really it was a teeming ocean. She looked around expecting to see Edan next to her, but all she could find was a shirt thrown across the cot. Outside. He was outside talking to the other Cygirians. But not telling them everything. That was the message the people had given them. That was what she and he had to keep secret until they could present the entire surprise of their help to the people.

"Ava?"

Ava almost jumped, breathing in sharply, a pain in her solar plexus.

"Ava?" A woman poked her head in the tent, smiling. "There you are! I haven't seen you since the meeting. I mean, I've been dying to talk to you."

Without waiting for Ava to say anything, the woman walked in, looking around. Something clicked in Ava's mind. What was it? A name. Yes, a name.

"Stephanie," she said quietly.

"What?" Stephanie asked, and then without waiting for Ava to answer, "Man, Edan doesn't keep much around him.

He travels light. No stuff. Not like Porter, who has to have all his particular little accoutrements, he calls them."

Stephanie laughed, turning to Ava as she did. But then she stopped, shrugged a little, kept talking. "Of course, Edan has you now, so what else could he need?"

Something Stephanie had said pulled at Ava, the noose loosening a bit, a feeling like laughter spreading through her. "You said you've been dying? Dying to talk?"

"Ha!" Stephanie laughed. "No. Not dying. Well, anyway, I'm not obviously going to die, except of boredom or pissed-offness maybe."

The noose tightened even farther as Ava felt her face move, the happiness that had begun to pool in her chest evaporating. "What's the matter?"

"Matter?" Stephanie said. "This whole thing is taking too long. Now Edan has some new ideas about the planet we are going to create. I mean, let's take a step back first and think about making a planet. How crazy is that? And do we really think that the Neballats are just going to let us make a planet without doing something to us? Like, what about taking it from us?"

"I've seen the planet," Ava said mechanically, the image of the world turning in front of her mind's eye. "I know it can be done."

Stephanie waved her hand. "Oh, all right. You and he are on the same page. I get it. You are officially into twinness. Step lock and all that."

"It will work," Ava said, the noose pulling the words from her. "It will be amazing. We will be so happy that we made it."

That's right, thought the voice, right into Ava's brain. *You are so right. That's the perfect thing to say.*

Stephanie looked at Ava, frowning slightly, her arms crossed.

"So when are we going to start? How long are these new specifications going to take?"

Get rid of her, the voice said. *Tell her what she wants to know.*

"Not too long," Ava said. "As soon as the remaining Cygirians arrive, we can begin."

All those Cygirians in one place, the voice seemed to hiss, the thought disappearing before Ava could truly catch it.

Stephanie sighed. "Fine. Something seems wrong about the whole thing, but no one seems to be too upset. So why should I be?"

"I don't think you should be upset," Ava said, the words marching out of her mouth like toy soldiers. "I think everything will be just fine."

Outside, they both heard the sounds of people headed toward the center of Talalo, the place where Edan and the other members of the council were explaining the discovery that Edan and Ava had made about their powers. Soon the planet would be made. Soon the people would be happy. Soon everyone would be happy.

True, so true, the voice whispered in her head.

"Okay, then," Stephanie said, looking as if she were going to ask Ava something else. There seemed to be whole stories that Stephanie wanted to hear, but she backed off. "Um, well, okay. I'll see you there."

Ava nodded, knowing that the voice would be grateful Stephanie was gone.

Stephanie turned and headed for the tent's flap, stopping suddenly, her hand on the canvas. "Ava?" she asked, looking back. "Are you all right? Did everything work out the way that you hoped it would? You know—I mean, with Edan and all?"

Get rid of her! the voice screamed.

Ava put a hand to her head, nodding. "I'm just a little tired, that's all. A little headache. I'll be fine. And things are good."

Stephanie shrugged, her face falling a little. "Well, you had kind of an ordeal in the desert. So get a little rest before the big show starts, okay?"

"Okay," Ava said. "Thanks."

Giving Ava a quick smile, Stephanie left, the tent flap falling closed. Ava sat down, but the noose tightened, the voice filling her mind.

Go to Edan. Start the process. Make the world. We need our world! Think of how miserable we are.

Yes, Ava thought. *I know how you suffer. I will go help. I will make your world.*

She stood up, breathed, moved toward the door. She would make the world and help Edan. Then she could somehow lose this feeling in her head.

The cinch pulled.

Then she could help the people. That's all she was supposed to do. That's all she was meant for.

Outside the tent, she took in the sight of Cygirians— thousands of them—moving toward the center of the construction site. All of them seemed so excited, so full of energy, a feeling Ava tried to grab on to, hold with both hands. But there was nothing but an even beat of deadness in her, a feeling of not being who she was.

The noose pulled.

From a distance, she could hear Edan's voice, hear his gentle instructions and explanations about the technique to harness their powers to do anything.

For a brief second, she remembered something, a wonderful feeling, a feeling that moved up her body like heat, like hands. A feeling that tasted like ripe fruit, like shamma, like candy. Closing her eyes, she wanted that feeling again, knew that it had something to do with Edan, his voice feeling her with longing. Her body seemed to waken, shimmer, glow, and the memory deepened before it suddenly stopped, shut down by the noose.

Later, the voice thought. *Later. Do what you need to do and later, everything will be yours.*

Ava opened her eyes. She would do what the voice told her. And then she would wait for everything.

Chapter Eight

Edan had a memory, a vision of looking down at a city-scape thinking it was his. For a moment, he remembered that feeling of possession, the rush of knowing that he could control everyone who lived below him. At that moment of greatest vision, he understood that he would be king, emperor, god. And now, looking at the thousands of Cygirians milling around him, something told him that he could be in control of all of them, too. No, that he was.

You make the rules, the voice thought, the sound a whip in his brain. *You tell them what to do and how to do it. Remember what we told you. Remember what we showed you.*

Edan nodded, thinking of the spinning world, the world he would make for the people who had saved him. The ones who would make sure that all would be well once the Cygirians had made the world. These people would be their friends, their helpers, their compatriots.

Yes, the voice whispered. *Right. We are your friends.*

"Edan," Jai said, walking over to him. "We are almost fully amassed. Everyone has been trained. I don't think it will be much longer before we can begin."

Edan turned to Jai, blinking, wondering why he felt so strangely pulled. Part of him had something to say to Jai, an idea, a sentence just on his tongue. It was so important that he tell his friend these things now. The words *help* and *no* and *stop* pricked his mouth like needles, but then the band of pain around his forehead pulsed.

"Good," Edan said instead of any of the other words. "Excellent."

Jai stared at him, and Edan turned away, looking out at the crowd. There were his sisters Mila and Claire, both of them looking toward him, smiling. Mila held Dasha against her shoulder, moving slowly in a way that reminded Edan of another mother, another time. In a quick burst of time, a memory popped into his head, a woman smelling of something sweet, a flower, a fruit. A man's voice in the background, his laughter. A baby's squeal. A familiar room, warm, full of things that Edan recognized. Toys and books and games. A fire burning in a stone fireplace. Smells of food fill the air. An ache pulled in Edan's chest and then evaporated before he understood what the memory meant.

"You are sure about this," Jai said, his question more of a statement. "I know that Porter isn't as serious as he could be, but do you think he has a point? We should start with something smaller and work our way up to a planet?"

Edan wanted to tell Jai that he was sure he had to help the people, those poor people who would not survive without this planet. There was no time to waste. They needed a home so dearly, their lives sad and lonely and wandering, their bodies destroyed, translucent, prey to the very atmosphere itself.

And as he was about to tell all of this to Jai, pain burst in his head and he just nodded, finally whispering, "Yes."

Again, Jai stared at him, and then he shrugged, shaking his head. "I don't really understand any of this the way you seem to. But I know what I saw you and Ava do. I know that with all of us here, we can create anything, really. It just seems so daunting."

Like a parrot, Edan felt his words come out rote and ordered. "It's all intention. We can harness our energy. It will be simple."

"Simple. That I truly find hard to believe," Porter said, walking up to them both. "However, based on your heretofore stellar reputation, I am willing to try."

Edan felt another feeling pulling at his throat, his face tingling, but then the pain pulsed in his head.

"Good," he said, and he walked away from Jai and Porter, finding a place to stand on the edge of the platform, looking out to the crowd of Cygirians. He had never seen so many of his people in one place, and he blinked at the numbers, stunned. He turned, wanting to find Ava at his side. She should see this sight. She was his . . . his what? His mind opened into blankness, and he turned back to the crowd.

So many of us, he thought. *We need—we need a pl—*

First ours, the voice hissed. *And then yours. All in good time. Everyone will have what he or she needs.*

Yes. Yes. All in good time, good time, Edan thought, feeling someone move next to him. He turned, and there was Ava. She looked back at him, seeming to want to say something, her eyes full of story he could not read. As he looked at her face, her long hair, her arms, he had a sensation that came not through thoughts but through his body, a prickle of flesh, excitement that dug deep into him, a feeling of bone and blood and spine. But then, like everything now, he lost the feelings, his body quieting, moving into blankness. Edan tried to grasp onto the sensation before it left, keep it close, keep it alive in himself, but it was too late, and he stared at her, seeing that she, too, was distressed. He wanted to ask her what was wrong, but just as the question worked its way to his mouth, he forgot it.

All is well, the voice thought. *The woman is here. You are strong. You can do what you need to do together.*

His head seemed to shift, the pain encircling him so thoroughly and so well, it was like a hat he was familiar with and couldn't take off. Pain was like a horrid person with an annoying instrument, banging sound in his ear. Pain beat a rhythm, pain beat a song, and Edan wanted to do nothing—nothing—but make the world for the people and throw down the pain. He breathed, once, twice, and again, the pain slowed, held back, sat in its corner.

But at least she was here. Ava. She could help him. They had powers that could be harnessed to do anything. Taking her hand, he channeled his voice through their combined strength, out into the crowd, loud and full and deep.

"Cygirians," he said, the sound of him echoing against the newly constructed buildings. "We are about to embark on something wonderful."

The crowd murmured, and the wave of thought almost threw Edan to the ground.

A place for ourselves.

Finally.

We will be free.

We will be safe.

We will be home.

We will never be lost again.

And with the thoughts came the images, some of which he knew well: the spaceship, the way it hurtled through time and place, leaving them with parents who did not really expect them—some of whom did not really want the child thrust into their arms with thanks and a push of power that would make them forget the encounter, remembering only the child. Their child. Their brand-new child. With the thoughts came the loneliness and the longing for something none of them could really remember, the dream of the spaceship their only reminder of home.

How they all wanted home. How they all needed it, and if the ache in his forehead would stop, Edan knew he'd be wanting that same thing now, this instant.

Cygiria would have to wait. He wanted to hold up his hands high and tell them that this would not be their world, not yet, but when he started to move, the pain stood up, walked toward the center of the ring, ready to punch him into unconsciousness.

All right! he thought, letting his hands go still.

Tell them how to begin. Tell them how to build the world. Our world. And then we will all be the best of friends. We will all live together so peacefully, and it will then be your turn to make yourselves a world. Think of it! Everything as it should be.

Edan swallowed, blinked, turning to Ava, knowing he should hold her hand. Seeming to hear him, she took his hand, her fingers warm. With Ava's help, his voice loud and full and deep, Edan continued. "We are about to change our lives forever. This is the answer to our parents' distress, our parents' deaths, the death of our culture and way of life. This is what they would have wanted for us."

Edan turned to look again at his sisters Mila and Claire, their twins Garrick and Darl, Jai and Risa, Kate and Michael, Stephanie and Porter, the entire council, and then he looked forward toward the swelling group of Cygirians before him. All around him was the evidence of their ability to work together, Talalo proof of their ability to work together. If he could only tell them! They would understand. If they knew about the people who needed them, they would give help. Why wouldn't they? Why couldn't he just tell them?

The pain throbbed, beat on his skull with meaty punches.

"Are you all right?" Jai asked. "You look a little pale."

Edan wanted to fall to his knees, rip his scalp off, tear the pain away with his bare hands. If only he didn't have all this pain. If only he could think without the voice in his head. But it was the voice that held him up, kept him on his feet, pulled his mind back to the creation of the planet. He needed the voice. He needed the voice to live.

Don't stop now! the voice thought. *Do what you need to do to get this over with.*

Edan nodded, opening his eyes, and going forward with his speech despite the low dull ache behind his ears. "You have all been trained. I will send out the images, and then we will concentrate our thoughts on what we are making, directing all our powers to the world that you hold in your mind's eye. When it is done, we will slowly break away from each other, let go, allow the creation to exist."

Even as he spoke, the words so optimistic, he felt something dark creep around the edges of his words, grab hold of all his optimism, and begin to choke it dead. What was wrong? What was going to happen?

Jai was at his side again, putting his hand on Edan's shoulder. "Are you ready?"

His voice was full of concern, and Edan knew there was something he should tell Jai, something that would explain everything.

Create, the voice thought. *Start it! Save us all.*

Breathing in, Edan reached out for Ava again, pulling her close. As her mind met his, he realized that he hadn't felt her mind in what? Hours? Days? And then he realized that no one's thoughts had crept into his. He'd been alone this morning with the ache and the throb and his confusion. As she melded with him, he knew that she had the same pain, the same ache, the same voice. What was happening to them? Why couldn't he do or say or feel what he wanted? Why couldn't he just take Ava into his arms and make all of this stop for a second?

The world, she thought. *Let's make it. Then it will be over. Then we can go on. Then everyone will be happy and safe.*

Yes, the voice thought. *See how right she is? Listen to her.*

Of all the things he could remember, he knew that he trusted Ava completely. She was the one thing in his mind that seemed true now, the idea and knowledge of her not fraught with hurt.

Edan nodded, closed his eyes, and thought of the blankness the people had shown him, the part of space that needed a world, that could support a world. Ava joined him in thinking about that blankness, and it was as if they were both there watching it swirl, the eddies of space a river within the dark.

Then as they watched, he pushed the image forward, and he felt it as Jai caught it, added his power, his strength. And then Risa joined in, as did Mila, Garrick, Claire, and Darl. One after the other, the Cygirians caught hold of the image, pulled Edan's thoughts into their minds, made it real, made it clear. Then the swirl took an outer, rounder shape, the blank dark void turning into a sphere that spun to life, whirling in the exact part of space that the people had told him a world would work best.

Life, the voice whispered. *Give us back our lives. Give us a place to finally live as we are supposed to.*

So Edan pushed out life, and the sphere began to take on color as it morphed from thought into reality. The blue of water first, aqua and navy and cornflower and cobalt. From the water then sprang the earth colors, blacks and browns and grays, the glacial silver of granite, the caramel of sand, the deserts that the people wanted, the hot, dry air that would support their lives best. Next the white of atmosphere, the clouds whipping around the sphere in reaction to the water, air to breathe, the air the people needed.

Yes, the voice hissed. *Yes.*

Wait, came a question. *Who are "the people"? What are you thinking about? Edan? Who are the people?*

Edan wanted to answer the question, but he felt the tug and pull around his head, and didn't answer back, moving forward with his thought. He focused next on the greens, the massive forests to sustain the atmosphere, the plants and trees and shrubs and grasses that would sustain any life on that planet.

As the florae sprang into being, trees towering over the terrain, flowers emerging—fertile, bursting with seeds, withering, reseeding, emerging again—Edan almost fell back at the strength of the Cygirian power. All this thought in a single stream could create all this, this planet that was alive and whole in his mind. It was there. It was a real thing, and Cygiria made it for the people.

Our lives, right? Us? Not the people. We people? Edan?

His head feeling like it would explode, Edan forced himself to press on. There was nothing but this planet. It was the only thing that mattered. He needed to finish it. He needed to make it perfect for the people, the poor people who lived virtually without bodies, without skin. They had no planet, no home to live on. They were counting on him.

Onward, onward. His head was a bell that wouldn't stop ringing. He couldn't stop thinking, each new idea a slam of the heaviest iron against more iron. He saw creatures pull themselves out of the water, struggle onto land, morph into air breathers, losing their fins and flippers. They multiplied, some of them branching off, becoming other creatures, animals that flew, that swam, that ran, that slithered. The planet was complete. There was water, land, air. There was space enough for all the people; there were animals and creatures, trees and plants. Every needed thing, from large to almost invisible, a perfect ecosystem. It was Eden. It was . . .

Our home, right? Edan, this planet is for us, isn't it? Who are the people? Who have you been thinking about? What is happening?

His head was going to fall off, explode. His spine ached, felt like it was starting to crumble, one vertebra at a time dissolving into the pain that was his entire body. He felt the scream start at the base of his skull and crawl up over his head, pulling itself over him like a raging baby.

Wrenching free of the vision, from the connection with the other Cygirians, from even Ava, he opened his eyes wide, saw nothing but white, felt nothing but the grip of something evil, and then the scream came from deep inside him, came out loud, became the only thing that he heard, until he heard nothing at all.

Edan wasn't sure what was happening. Everything was movement—tugging and ripping and pulling. And there was movement outside him, too, some huge hum underneath him, large turns and twists that threw him against something hard before he was rolled back onto something softer. And the sounds, hushed voices that turned to yells and screams and then hushed again. But after the movement ceased, slowed, after the tugging and ripping and pulling ended, he realized he was in no more pain. He realized that Ava was nowhere near him.

Ava! he thought, casting his mind out all around him. *Ava!*

But Ava was not there to answer him.

"Where?" he began, but his voice had no sound.

Where? he thought, but no one was there to answer him, the movements starting again, pushing him back and forth.

Where am I? he thought, but again, there was no answer from anyone.

Edan was alone, the thousands of Cygirians that had earlier been in front of him gone. The world they had created from specks of nothingness was gone, too. The world that he had envisioned and helped create for the people. The people. The people?

Oh no. No.

Edan wished he could open his eyes, wished he could make sound, needing the scream that had taken him over earlier. The people he had created the planet for, the people who had cajoled him into the plan—but how?—were the Neballats.

How? he thought. *Oh, how?*

He found his hand, moved it, grabbed on to the edge of whatever he was lying on, and held tight against the force of the movement, and waited. If he survived this confusion, this violent movement, soon he would have an answer. Soon he would find Ava. Soon he would find a way to fix the wrong he had created. He had to. So he held on.

The movements rocked him, and he let them lull him into sleep, the only place, he understood, he would find any peace until this thing was over.

"Edan?" someone asked him. "Edan?"

The person calling to him wasn't Ava. But the voice was familiar, and for a second he had the memory of a voice so much like this one. There was the same lulling lilt, but then, in the memory, there was also the smell of lavender, soap, warm towels. He had a word on his tongue, a word he knew to be ridiculous, but he wanted to say it, wanted to feel what it was like to say the word *mother* and mean it.

Mata.

But his true mother was dead, killed by—killed by the Neballats, the ones who had just tricked him into betraying his people. And then like his parents' generation, he and his friends and family would be dead. Just like that, a whole tribe pushed to extinction.

"Edan?"

The voice was a woman's, and he breathed, tried to find a way to open his eyes. He felt as though they were stuck together, as if he were in a dream from which he could not wake, his subconscious strong and sticky.

He tried his lips, wetted them with his tongue. "Yes."

"You're going to be okay," she said. "It was—it seemed like you might not make it. But you are fine."

He licked his lips again, struggled to see. "Ava?"

The woman did not speak for a moment, and Edan caught her thought, a feeling really. And the feeling said *loss*.

"Where is she?" he asked, his heart starting to lurch in his chest, his breath shallow. He forced his eyes open to see that it was Mila sitting next to him, leaning over the edge of a cot.

"We are under attack," she said. "Things didn't go well."

What Mila did not say hung between them. *Things did not go as you said they would. You lied to us. You made promises that you did not keep.*

How would he ever be able to explain?

"Where is she?" Edan asked again, sitting up in bed, almost hitting his head on the bunk above him. He looked around, realizing he was on an Upsilian spaceship. "She was standing right next to me. Right there. I can remember that at least."

He put his hand to his head, the pain he'd felt flickering like a ghost. "What—what was it?"

"A simulator," Mila said. "It's a form of mind control through pain. Those 'people' you kept thinking about put one in Garrick and sent him back to Earth. He almost ended up killing my mother because of it. So I know what they can do. I've seen it a couple of times. You can't blame yourself for what happened."

"Were you the one asking the questions as we created the planet?" he asked.

"Yes," Mila said, nodding. "I could hear you on two tracks, and I should have tried to stop everything. But it might have been too late."

"Where is she?" he asked, even as he wanted to ask Mila who else he could blame.

Mila breathed in, sat back, her dark eyes steady on his. "The second we were done—the second the planet was created—they attacked. You'd passed out, and Ava wandered away. She must have a simulator implanted as well. In the confusion, I didn't see where she went. We barely made it off the planet."

Watching his sister, he heard what she was thinking even as her words came toward him.

I don't know if we've made it yet.

"They are after us," he said. "They know where we are."

Mila stood, her hands on her hips. "They've always known where we are. When haven't they known, even when we were embedded in homes, supposedly safe among strangers? They found us, spied on us, waited for us. And now that they have what they want, we are no longer needed. They have a planet. We made them a planet."

"I started it. I envisioned a planet for them!" Edan shook his head, wondering how he could get that truth out of his mind. But it was real, true, a fact. And he owned it.

"Edan," Mila said. "You weren't acting on your own—"

Edan held up a hand. "It's true. I did it. And now they have a place to live. They destroyed our world, and we handed one over to them like some kind of gift. And now . . ."

She looked at him, her face open, taking him in. "It's not your fault. No one blames you."

"Who else can we blame?" Edan said. "I'm supposed to be this wonderful leader, this bright hope, and I do the very thing that brings about our final demise. I *am* to blame. No one else."

He swung his legs over the edge of the bunk and started to stand, ignoring his dizziness, the dull throb in his temples.

"Where are you going?"

"I'm going to the world we made. I'm going to destroy either it or them."

Standing, Mila put her hands on his shoulders, her eyes dark. "No."

"I have no choice," he said. "I started this, and I have to finish it."

"You can't," she said. "It took thousands of Cygirians to create the planet. How can you imagine you can destroy it all by yourself?"

He gently moved her hands away, standing up. In his imagination, he saw the world exploding into the dark space all around it. The life they had worked so hard to create snuffed out in an instant.

"I don't know." He moved toward the pile of his clothing on a bench.

"What about Ava?" Mila asked. "Don't you think that she wouldn't want you to do this? Don't you think she'd have something to say?"

Sliding on his pants and then taking off the thin cotton tunic, he nodded. "Yes, I know she'd have something to say. But I'm doing this for her. For you. For Claire. For all of us. I have to fix this. And then I'll find Ava. I swear I will find her, if it's the last thing I do. I will bring her to a world that we can all live on. She and I will be together. That's what has to be. That's all I know."

As he said the words, he felt Ava, felt her energy, her heat, her skin. He breathed in her memory, holding her deep in his lungs. She was a part of him. Without her, he wasn't whole, wouldn't function.

As he dressed, he heard Mila stand up and walk toward him. "You aren't going alone."

In an instant, he turned, his whole body reacting to the implication in her voice. "No," he said. "Don't even think about it. I can't put you at risk again. You can't endanger yourself now."

But Mila was not impressed. "I'm at risk now, Edan. We are being attacked as we speak."

Edan wanted to smile, but at a time like this, the reaction seemed ridiculous. Even now, he realized that the craft was moving at high speed, buffeted by the Neballat attack.

Mila kept her gaze on him, steady and sure. "We've been through this before. We left Cygiria together, Edan. You, me, and Claire. We were tiny children, but we were together. I remember Claire playing with her animal. Florsey, she called it. I remember you talking about Mata and Pata, how they would come and get us one day. I can even remember the smell of our mother, something like flowers. Lavender. Vanilla. But mostly, I remember the three of us, hurtling toward some adventure we never knew we'd have. Toward the lives we'd have that would always be confusing until we understood. I remember the spaceship, the feeling of being safe when I was with the two of you."

"Mila," Edan said, buttoning his shirt. "No. You have Garrick now. Dasha. Claire has Darl."

"And you have Ava. But this is about before. Before we found our twins. Before I was a mother. Before we were orphans. This is about us, the three of us, tiny children on a spaceship heading toward the complete unknown. And I know that Claire will want to go, too. This is something we have to do together. This will be the completion of our journey. This will be the chapter that closes the old book, finishes the story altogether."

Edan looked down at his shoes, the image of that long-ago spaceship in his mind, as it had always been, dark and purple and swirling, voices of the other children all around them. And there were the little girls next to him, both of them so important, that the memory is nothing but them— nothing without them. They were three, and they were separated, but they would be together now. Mila was right. They needed to finish out this part of the tale together. They would take the small chance that they had and try.

If we don't fix this, he thought. *There will be no place for us, for our twins, for our children. For the life that we all want.*

I know, Mila thought. And she held out her hand, reached for him, and together, in their minds, they called for their sister.

Edan and Mila were able to find her, even though the ships were not in contact, even though the attack was still upon them, even though Claire and Darl were in another quadrant. She burst into the room out of the air, using her power, her hair wild, a small bruise blooming under her right eye like a purple flower.

"What happened to you?" Edan asked, walking toward her, putting a thumb gently to her cheek. "Are you all right?"

Claire shook her head, ignoring his question. "What are we going to do?"

He watched her for a second, this fiery blond woman, her dark eyes wide and glittering. She and Mila were warriors, this battle the one they'd been waiting for their entire lives. He let his hand drop from Claire's face.

"We are going to the world," Edan said. "And we are going to destroy it."

Without having to hear the explanation or the need for such an action, Claire nodded, held out her hands. "We'll go my way," she said. "Even though I know we can all do everything now."

Edan took his youngest sister's hand and then Mila's, looking in that instant at both his sisters. There they were standing before him, two beautiful, dark-eyed women, women who looked like him, women from the same parents, the same house, the same life. He wondered what their childhood would have been like had they been raised on Cygiria, their parents and grandparents and even great-grandparents still alive. They would have gone to the same school, played in the backyard of their house, fought and loved and laughed. They would have watched each other grow up, their bodies morphing from babyhood to adulthood in steps they would have all been witness to. They would have taken care of their parents, held each other's children, lived on the same world, its terrain known and understood.

Somehow, all of them would have found their doubles,

their twins. Garrick, Darl, and Ava would have come to them, more easily than they had in this life. There would be no rescue from the Neballats or visitation on Earth or long explanations and disbelief. There would have been searching, but nothing like what they'd experienced. They would have grown up knowing that they had a fit with another, were matched perfectly with a person who would meet them right there, in the middle, a perfect energy exchange. Everything would have been so much easier.

But now—his sisters' warm hands in his own—Edan knew they were going to have another life, another experience, one that might end in the next hours or one that might go on for a different kind of lifetime. They would never have picked this life. Not ever. But it was what they had and it was here, now, in front of them.

Mila and Claire seemed to hear him, nodding, their faces so serious, so focused, that again he saw the little girls looking up at him as they traveled to safety, the huge maw of space all around them.

Now, he thought. *Let's go to the world. Let's end this thing now.*

All right, Mila thought.

Yes, thought Claire.

And in a slice of a second—the perfect, new world an image in all their minds—they were gone.

"Wow," Mila said, and Edan opened his eyes to what she was talking about. For a quick instant, he was able to forget why they were on this planet because of what was all around him, what pushed wildly into his senses.

Edan blinked into the crisp blueness of the sky, the air that was soft and fresh and true. He pulled in a huge lungful, staggered by what this air tasted like. There was nothing in the air but the air itself. This was what a new world smelled like, tasted like, the air around him only and completely perfect.

"It's so green," Claire said, letting go of Edan's hand and turning to look behind her.

She was right. Edan had never seen greens so vivid—the landscape verdant, lush, arrayed in a panorama of sage, lime, a green so dark it was like midnight. The three of them were standing in a clearing, surrounded by what looked like huge maple, elm, and oak trees, the leaves the size of dinner plates. Under their feet was soft, green grass, wildflowers, and clover, and at the edges of the clearing, Edan saw the small hurried hops of rabbits. All around them was the melody of birdsong, the scratchy hum of crickets, the calls of other creatures from their homes in the trees and shrubs.

On the horizon was the line of mountains, snowcapped, gleaming in the sunlight.

Somewhere, huge, whole oceans churned with fish and sea creatures, the water unpolluted, clear and full of life. Every part of the terrain was as it should be, nothing but what was natural happening. Creatures ate other creatures, life and death happening in the typical pattern. But there were no toxins or pollutants souring the land or sky.

The only thing that would make this world more perfect was Ava, his twin by his side.

"Eden," Mila said.

Edan turned to her, thinking she'd called his name. She shook her head and smiled.

"It's an Earth story, one a lot of people believe in. It's the place that the first people on Earth lived. God made the planet for them. A man first of course, and then the woman out of his rib. But then both of them were able to live in, well, this perfection. They had all the land and all the creatures under their dominion."

She swept her arm and then let it fall to her side, clearly amazed.

"What happened in the story?" Edan asked.

"What always happens with perfection. It's ruined. By an idea," Mila said.

Claire shrugged. "They got kicked out for bad behavior, and millennia of pain ensued for women because in the story, the woman gets the rap for giving the idea to the man. And though the first man and first woman would have done anything to return to Eden, they could never find their way back in. The place was guarded by angels with fire or something. But everyone's always trying to find it. And every religion has its Eden, its Nirvana, its Utopia, its golden age. And here we are. We get to see it. We are standing in the middle of perfection right now."

"Until we destroy it," Mila said. "Until we destroy Eden. With an idea."

Walking toward the edge of the clearing, Edan felt his heart beat faster, something like tears form in his eyes. The plan seemed so clear when he'd stood with his sisters in the spaceship. But now? He looked up to the tree line, the leaves and branches moving in the slight, soft breeze. How could they destroy this? This was a planet created by Cygirians, born out of a fused energy. A miracle.

"Don't we have to?" Claire asked. "Isn't this the only way to get out from under the Neballats?"

Edan closed his eyes. He wanted to find another idea in his mind, the one that would not force them to crack and split apart this wonderful world. He wanted that second idea, which the woman in Eden was unable to find. Maybe all she had needed was more time. He wanted to find the choice, the alternative, but he saw nothing but nothing, this part of space full of nothing but space itself.

"Yes," he said quietly. *Yes. It's what we have to do.*

And he reached out for his sisters' hands, feeling them take his hands, feeling their energy course together.

Chapter Nine

First there had been people, pain, and the presence of the man, Edan, the one she wanted then and wanted still. They had been talking to a group, envisioning the world they were going to make for the people, but then there had been flashes of light, screams, people tugging at her, throwing her to the ground, explosions pushing everything off-kilter. She'd felt heat, the almost burn of fire, and then nothing. Nothing.

Ava had floated for a long time, her mind suddenly clear, focused, sharp, even though she was unsure where she was. The ache that had been with her for what seemed forever was gone, just like that, a miracle cure. The noose had been loosened, freed, dropping away from around her. She'd felt as though she'd been behind a curtain, a wall, a partition from life, but the curtain had opened, the wall crumbled, the partition pushed down.

Now she continued to float, but she was able to open her eyes, and she saw where she was. Back again. Back in the Source.

She knew that if she was in the Source, her body was somewhere. And she knew now that the "people" that she and Edan had been trying to help were the Neballats. They'd done something to them to make Edan and her convince everyone to make a world—not for the Cygirians but for themselves. So she was likely a prisoner somewhere, maybe on the brink of death. She was unconscious in a Neballat prison on a Neballat ship. Maybe she was dead, returned to the Source until she would be reborn. And that meant she would not have Edan again in this lifetime.

At least she'd had him once. At least there had been that gift in that life.

Ava closed her eyes against the streaming wonder of the Source, feeling the ache in her body at his loss. She felt emptied, open, raw. It was the loss she'd imagined even while in his arms, knowing that wholeness had to be temporary. It had been easier to not have love, to not feel the vibrant alive connection she had with him. She wouldn't know what it was to lose it then. She wouldn't feel as she did now, adrift, alone, unanchored to anything.

Ava breathed in the heat and energy of the Source, and slowly she spun, allowing herself to meld with the flow of it all. Now she knew she should never have left this place. The Upsilians should have hidden them better, keeping them away from those Cygirians who thought they were rescuing them. Who did they think they were? What had they known about living? Who needed to live in the real world, where things hurt? Where there was so much loss? Being born into the real world meant losing everything, even one's own life. Why bother? Why not just stay here and float? What was the point of going back and trying to hold things together? Nothing held together, the center flawed, ready to crack at any moment.

Because, came the thought. The voice that brought it was soft and clear. *Because there is no other place to live so fully.*

Ava turned, opened her eyes again, looked toward the origin of the thought. *Who are you?*

One who lost everything, the voice thought. *One who lost all the world and more. One who lost her entire family, and yet, I would go back to experience it all again.*

Ava shook her head. *So why would you want to live there? What is the point? Why go through it all for what? To die? To end up here after all of it? To have to consider losing everything forever?*

She closed her eyes again, willing the voice to leave her alone. She wanted to float and spin and only exist until she was called to go back. She knew she had no choice but to go back at some point, but she wanted the space between lives to last forever. Here, she could have bits of that real life but none of the loss. She would find Edan's energy—she could find any one she wanted to. But loss was muted here. So was hate and war and strife. There were answers here. Clarity. And years, maybe millennia, of not having to care. Ava wanted to lie safe in the streams of energy until the very last moment.

Ava, the voice thought. *Ava, you know there is one reason to go back. One very important reason. The best reason of all.*

As the voice moved through Ava's thoughts, she felt Edan as if he were there twisting in the energy next to her. She felt his heat and light. It was as if just under her hand was his skin, warm to the touch, muscles just underneath. Edan. His voice. Edan. His smile. Edan. The way he looked at her, knowing her. The only person who ever had.

Yes, the voice thought. *Edan. My son.*

Ava opened her eyes, the orange and red streaming past in a vibrant, constant river. She concentrated, looked closely into the flumes of energy, and before her was a mass of darker, purple energy. Solid, intense, present. Comforting and real.

You are Edan's mother? Ava thought.

Yes, she thought. *My name is Isla. Or was in life. The last life.*

You put them on the spaceship, Ava thought. *You had to leave them all. How can you say going back there is better than being here?*

Isla didn't respond through thought, but Ava felt it anyway. She imagined the ship that they had all been on, the dark place, the scary place without their parents. But what had it been like to be one of the adults who'd had to let go, give away the small people most precious? There was so much pain in that instant of feeling, such a rent in that moment of holding out a child and letting him or her go forever. Three children carted onto a spaceship, Isla knowing she would never see them again, knowing that never seeing them again would save their lives.

Yes, Isla thought. *And I would do it again. It was the right thing. It was the only thing.*

You walked into pain. You opened your arms to pain. Why would you ever want to do that?

There was a pause in their thoughts, a flume of Source pushing between them, a current that Ava imagined she could ride away on. But she wanted the answer to this question. She needed to stay for these words.

Isla seemed to float a little, hover over Ava.

Sometimes, Isla thought, *that is what living is all about. Without the pain, there is no joy. You wouldn't know how to measure it. You wouldn't be able to recognize it for what it is.*

Isla's energy pulsed, and Ava let herself float in that

thought. She'd had enough pain in her life to know that Edan brought her joy, pure, whole joy. The difference between the entirety of her life and the past few days with Edan had shown her the stark difference.

But he and I did something wrong, Ava thought. *We made the world for the Neballats. I'm not sure why. We made more pain. And then I was here.*

The Neballats had a controlling device in you that made you do their bidding. You and Edan fought against it. It was not you and he who made the decision to make that world at all.

Ava considered Isla's ideas, remembering the pounding hurt, the way her head felt tightened in a noose every time she questioned her own behavior. She flashed back to a quick slash of pain, hurt, and a dull throb.

Was it still inside her? Was it still working? Or was she dead?

You are not dead, Isla answered. *Your full energy is not before me.*

But why am I able to think here with no pain, with no restrictions, no controls?

In the Source, none of the things that bind us on land work. You are your essence, your energy, your true being. And this is where you can decide.

The Source seemed awash in a sudden flow of greens and blues, the energy cool and quick and clean. Ava thought of oceans and swimming, bobbing contentedly for hours in the lovely feel of this place, one wave after another washing over her.

Ava?

What? she thought, her response lazy. She wanted Isla to let her think and spin and float.

You can decide.

Decide what?

To go back or to stay.

It's my choice? Ava thought. *I can decide? I can determine?*

You have free will. You have it here, in the Source. And you have it in life. You can make your life what you want it to be.

How? Ava thought. *Tell me how.*

She waited for Isla to answer, to tell her what to do. Isla would know. Isla would give her the information she needed. Isla was the mother of her beloved, and she wouldn't lie to Ava. But as Ava turned toward the spot where Isla's purple glow had been, she saw only reds and oranges again, a paisley of heat, like a shadow that slowly vanished, like smoke in an empty room.

She was alone. And it was her decision. It was hers.

Sighing, Ava felt the need to weep building inside her, a drum of water in the space where her heart would be. Life hurt. Life was lonely and dangerous. People had been trying to subdue her since she was barely a toddler, the Neballats wanting her dead, the Upsilians wanting her silent. Her own adopted family had ignored her, allowing her to be basically made unconscious for years. Out of sight, out of mind. People were mean and hurtful. And there wasn't enough time, everything so short. Look at Isla. Look what little time she'd had with her three children.

But Isla was right. The joy. There had been joy in Edan's presence, in his arms, his body in hers, his mouth kissing her, his words like the deepest caress. And there was more than his touch, but there was the way he saw her, looked at her. His gaze was sure, real, total. He had known her before they'd even met, understood her, their energies exactly the same. She had never connected with anyone else so truly. Truth. He was her truth.

Spinning slowly, feeling Edan all around her, Ava knew what she had to do. She had no choice.

When she awoke, it was in darkness. But even in the strange still black place, Ava sat up, bringing her legs to hang off the edge of what must be a counter or bed or cot. She brought her hand to her head and knew that the thing that Isla had told her about was still inside her. Even as she recognized its presence, she felt it tighten, pulling her thoughts back, yoking her into submission.

No.

There was no voice to accompany the pressure this time, no voice coaxing her into submission. So against the pressure that built inside her head, Ava thought of the world that she, Edan, and the other Cygirians had created. She saw the world in her mind's eye, but then she found what she was truly grasping for—the power of all the energy that they had created together. If she could be part of creating a world, she could certainly get rid of this controlling thing inside her, even as it yoked her still. A thing in her head was nothing compared to the amazing, alive, spinning world. Porter had wanted to start with something smaller, so she knew she could go backward—make a world, save herself from the controlling thing clawing at her mind.

Bring the world to her thoughts again, she focused only on it, the spinning colors, the life that teemed on the land and in the water. She thought of all the life that could be lived there, millennia full of creatures and people, life upon life upon life.

As Ava thought of the world, of the Cygirian power flowing into one collected, living space, the image changed to Edan, his form in front of her, all of him seeming to radiate heat and power, light shining from his eyes, his fingertips, his mouth, his heart. The hot, white pulse of him flowed back to her, made her strong, made her as powerful as all the Cygirians combined.

Turning that force, that full, powerful feel toward herself, Ava imagined the thing inside her, something she thought of as long and black and strong. She saw it suddenly still, stop, freeze, tighten not to control but out of a lack of power. As she thought harder, she saw its horrible sleek body slowly cracked open, break, flail against the last moments of its existence. Ava thought harder, keeping the beam of her intention on the image that eventually was nothing more than a flat cutout of its former self. No power. No energy. No control at all.

No form. No thing. Nothing.

Opening her eyes, Ava was still in the dark, but she felt clean, felt whole. The dark, oppressive sensation she'd had for what seemed like forever was gone. She touched her forehead, half imagining to find a scar or wound, but she was whole and free of the thing and its power.

But now what?

Tentatively putting her foot down, finding the floor beneath her, she relaxed when she found it dry and warm and clean. Slowly, she put the other foot down, and as she stood up, she realized that her eyes were adjusting to the darkness. Turning right, she saw what looked like a line of whitish yellow. Light. A way out.

She thought of her new friend Stephanie, the woman turning to smirk at Ava, her hands on her hips. "Girlfriend, what is the problem? Why are you waiting? You need to get the hell out of here. Walk through the door. Just get out!"

Ava knew that was the right advice. She needed to get out, but what would she be walking in to? Who was outside the door? Friend or foe?

But then she thought of the Source. She thought of the very energy that had helped her destroy the creature or thing inside her. She wondered why she kept forgetting about what she could do now, as if the truth of her newfound ability was only episodic or a miracle of some kind, not something she could use over and over again.

Again, she thought of the world made by thought. Why would she have to stay in this box in the dark, alone and scared and unsure? All she had to do was think her way back to Edan, back to where her people were. Her people. Her people?

Ava blinked into the dark. For the first time in her life, she realized that she felt as though she had people. People to whom she belonged, people who belonged to her. Maybe now it was just Edan and Stephanie and perhaps some of the people she'd worked with in the kitchen. For so long, she'd felt that it was only what she could do that was valued. She could work—she could chop and slice and roll and knead and sauté—but herself, her being, was unimportant.

Ava did not feel that way anymore. She was part of a bigger stream of energy. She, Ava, was more than she had ever been.

Outside, she heard something, the movement of bodies, something falling, steps outside the crack of light that shone from under the door. There was no time but now. She had to get away, go back where she belonged.

Closing her eyes again, Ava thought first of Edan, seeing him as she had seen him earlier, his eyes lit from within, his arms open. Then she pictured Stephanie and even Porter, the both of them turning to look at her as they stood in the kitchen, surprise and delight in their faces as they tasted her pastries. And then it was the view she had even under the influence of the creature in her brain, the field full of Cygirians thinking the same life-giving thought, the world something they all touched, all held in their imaginations.

Outside the room, the noises grew louder.

Ava was sure she heard footsteps, commands, the rustle of clothing, the jangle of something metal.

There, she thought. *Him. That. There. That feeling. That place. I want to go now.*

And though her eyes were closed, though the room was dark, she knew she was moving, heading through matter and space and perhaps even time, back to the place she had come from, back to the place she needed to be.

"Ava?" someone was saying. "Ava! Are you all right?"

First finding her body—noting that her legs were on something flat and cool, her arms and hands on her chest—Ava opened her eyes slowly into a darkened room. For an instant, she imagined that she hadn't made it out of the room she'd been in at all, her heart pounding in her chest, her mind trying to find the thought that she'd hoped would carry her away.

But then she breathed in, focused, and realized that it was Stephanie looking down at her.

"Ava?" Stephanie said. "What—How?"

Turning her head a little, Ava saw that Porter was in the room as well, and that the room wasn't a room at all. But a cabin of a spaceship. And she was moving through space, the roar of the giant motors almost deafening. In fact, now she understood that Stephanie had been yelling at her, and that Stephanie and Porter and the others who were standing by him looked distressed, their faces smudged, some marked with bloodstains, some leaning against the metal walls, exhausted.

Ava was looking at war victims. She was looking at loss.

"What has happened?" Ava asked, sitting up, bracing herself with one hand on the wall of the ship.

"That is what we've been asking ourselves," Porter said, no trace of sarcasm in his voice, his black eyes hard and still. "We thought we were creating a world for ourselves, but then it turns out the Neballats had other notions."

"And now they are trying to finish what they started over twenty years ago," Stephanie said. "And I hate to say it, but I think they might finally get what they want."

Stephanie turned to face the cabin and the Cygirians crowding it. "I have to say that it doesn't look good. And please, Porter, for all that's good and whole in you, don't tell me that's an understatement."

Porter didn't look at Stephanie but moved closer to Ava. "How did you get here? And from whence did you come?"

Ava shook her head. "I don't know where I was. I didn't wait to see. But it wasn't a ship, I know that. Or, at least, it wasn't one of ours."

"And?" Porter said, his voice clipped, harsh.

"Porter!" Stephanie said. "Knock it off."

"I want to know if we can even trust her," he said, his voice a snake of hiss. "She and Edan seemed to have gone over to the dark side, and I don't think it's wise to just let her pop back in here as if there's nothing untoward going on."

Bringing a hand to her head, Ava felt for the tug and ache that had been there with the creature in her head. But there was only the memory, nothing real left at all.

"I had something inside me, something in my mind. I think it was black and long. Almost like it was alive, with a voice."

Stephanie and Porter looked at each other. "A Simulator. You were being controlled?"

"Every time I thought something true, tried to break free, it pulled me back into the plan. Make the world. Make it now! Make it the way the Neballats wanted it. I guess Edan had one in him as well. I don't know. I don't know where . . ." She trailed off, her breath hard to find in her chest.

Stephanie sat down next to her, pulling her close. "It's not your fault. Those things are horrible. Disgusting. I—"

"How did you get free of it?" Porter asked.

"Porter! For God's sake."

"I want to know," he continued. "How do we know she doesn't have it in her still? No one has ever just taken one out."

"I understand," Ava said. "I wouldn't trust me, either. But I was able to think it gone."

"Excuse me?" Porter said. "Pray run that by me again."

"I used the same power that we were using to create the world for the Neballats. I knew that if I could help make a world, I could do this. Didn't Edan show us all that we can do anything? So I just thought it gone. And then it was."

No one said anything, but there was a murmur in the room, a wave of disbelief.

"And we can do that. We keep forgetting. We limit ourselves every time by thinking we only have this or that power. We remember and do something together, like Convergence." Ava looked at the people around her, willing them to believe her. Everything depended upon it.

Porter crossed his arms, looked down at her. Finally, he shook his head. "When I first saw Convergence work, I thought it was impossible. I didn't really believe it, but there I was, participating in it. And then there is the world we made. Not that I have actually been to it to do a thorough exploration. But I know we did it. I know we made it. So anything should be possible. You're right, Ava. You are."

Ava relaxed, exhaled, turned to Stephanie, who nodded.

"I think so, too," Stephanie said, turning to face the rest of them. "We can think it."

"Well, damn it, I want to think us away from the Neballats," one of the women in the room said, her voice urgent. "I want to think us somewhere safe in space."

As the woman spoke, Ava thought of space, and felt a stab, a weep of loss, a pain. The world. The world they had made.

Edan, she called out through her thoughts. *Are you there? Are you on the world? Where are you?*

There was no answer, the pathway leading to Edan dwindling, dropping off into nothing. But there was a hum of light and a push of heat that seemed to course through Ava's entire body, her nerves and veins highways of fire. She could see the world's core, a cylinder of molten earth, red and lively, pushing slowly, slowly to the surface, which was starting to heat up, grass singeing, water boiling.

What was he doing? she wondered, trying to figure what the lava had to do with Edan or any of their situations right now.

As people spoke, voices fast and strong and scared, Ava realized that the molten core of the world was heating, moving, pressing slowly for the surface. In minutes, it would flow up and out, destroying everything in its path.

"We need to go to the world," Ava whispered. "Now."

"What?" Stephanie asked.

"The world. We need to go to the world."

"Don't you think that would be a little counterproductive?" Porter asked. "After all, isn't that the very place the Neballats want for their own? Won't that make their lives a little too easy? A place to live and just the right people to kill all in one easy package?"

Ava shook her head, the fire still inside her. "We need to save the world."

"I always wanted to do that. Save the world," Porter said. "Think green. Plant trees. Compost. Paper instead of plastic. Recycling. You know reduce, renew, reuse."

"Will you shut it?" Stephanie said, whapping Porter on the shoulder with her palm. "Ava, what do you mean?"

"They are there," she said. "There isn't much time."

"Who is there?"

"Edan and his sisters." Ava paused, knowing what Edan, Claire, and Mila were doing on the planet, what they were about to enact. "They are going to destroy it so no one can have it."

"How fabulously Solomon of them," Porter said.

"We need to go there in this ship and stop them," Ava said, standing up, putting her hand on Stephanie's arm.

"Tell them to change course, Porter," Stephanie said. "Tell them where we need to go."

"No, that will take too much time," Ava said. "And you're forgetting again, too. We can go now. We have to do it the way we can do it. Using the powers we were born with."

Stephanie's black eyes seemed to flash light, the light that was bubbling inside the world. "What should we do?"

"Help me think us there."

Stephanie took Porter's hand. Porter moved to allow other Cygirians forward. Ava moved closer to the group, all of them pressing in tight. Someone shot a thought to the people in charge of the ship, and Ava felt them connect to the group standing around her.

Edan? Ava called out with her mind, trying one more time to get his attention. *Edan?*

In the quiet of the room, in the quiet of the universe, there was no reply. Only the world, spinning on its new axis, only the world, bubbling from within.

So Ava focused on the planet, seeing it as she had during its creation. And as she conjured it forth, she sent the thought out to the room, feeling all of them grab on to it and take it farther. The image grew clearer, sharper, the atmosphere on the planet wispy white, a whorl of clouds wrapped around the sapphire seas, the continents dark and full of all the life they'd created.

There, she thought. *Go.*

Even as she held on to the image, Ava felt time and space and matter open up again—a feeling she was almost getting used to—and push them all through toward the planet, toward Edan, toward the life they were going to have. This story, she knew, was not over. Not yet, not now.

And then, when the image faded, the energy of the group pulled back into individual bodies, Ava opened her eyes, and out of one of the windows there was the world that had come from a collective imagination.

"Terra firma," Porter whispered. "Home."

"They can't destroy it," Stephanie said, and for a second, Ava didn't know if she was referring to Edan or the Neballats.

"They won't. No one will," Ava said, and she changed the picture in her mind to Edan, held on to his smile, and in an instant, she was gone.

Chapter Ten

At some point, somewhere, somehow, Edan lost the shape of himself. He had no borders, no flesh, no skin, no sense of self. He could only feel his body as a connection to the energy that was coursing between himself and his two sisters. Everything inside him, everything outside him, rumbled and hummed and seemed to boil. Heat. Coals. Fire. A wave of swirling flames. There was wind and wildness everywhere, the burn and hiss of the inside of the world, the heat of beginnings, the fire of endings.

He wanted to say something to Mila and Claire, tell them one more time how he'd always felt about them, but he was out of words. There was no more time. There was only this explosion just waiting to happen.

Stop.

Edan wondered if he imagined the sound, the thought, the idea. The word was a lone cry piercing the universe with a whisper. He must have made up the sound. He had to have done so. His sisters wanted this to happen as well, wanting the war to end, for Cygirians to find peace. And there was no one but them on the planet, the Neballats off trying to kill the ones who could take this final prize from them.

Stop.

He felt the energy inside himself slow a bit, the earth under his feet stilling for a moment. Stop. Stop. Who would tell him to stop? Why would he stop this? No one should have this world now. It was a mistake, born from mind control and greed. They needed to take it away from the Neballats and fight back, keep this from ever happening again. And maybe then they could make their own world someday, much later, when it was finally safe.

Then the lone cry became a chorus, stronger, more insistent. *Stop.*

The sound was like a brick wall, his body hitting the hard surface. He wanted to step back, but there was nothing really pushing at him.

Mila? he thought. *Claire?*

What? Mila's thoughts sounded unsure, troubled, confused.

Something wants us to stop this.

Something? Claire thought. *Or someone?*

Edan didn't know, but the chorus of sound was still in his ear, a throbbing, thumping refrain. *Stop. Stop. Stop.*

We have to stop, Edan thought.

What if it's the Neballats again? Claire thought.

They would do anything to keep us from destroying the planet, Mila thought.

Edan knew that his sisters were right, but the voices coming at him seemed right, seemed true, seemed almost like Ava.

Ava? Claire thought. *Is Ava telling you to stop?*

Ava? Edan called out. *Ava, is that you?*

He waited, his heart pounding, his hands gripping his sisters', but she did not respond. But instead, the chorus of cries became louder, harsher.

I hear it, too, Mila thought.

Oh, Edan, we can't do this anymore. It's them. It's them.

It's us!

Casting his mind into the thoughts that came to him, the individual voices crying for them to stop the boil of the very ground they were standing on, he saw Cygiria, that old world spinning in remembrance of the world that they'd had. A reminder of the world they had, right now, under their feet.

Stop was right. Stop was now.

Together, holding each other tightly, Edan felt the energy push back, fight against their desire to stop it. Wave after wave of hot, orange heat seemed to gush from their small circle. Inside himself, Edan felt the heat, too, as if his body were a volcano, as if his innards were molten.

Water, he thought. Arctic tundra. The cool gleam of cold glinting off river ice, quick clean cracks running where a current used to. The grayest sky, steely and forbidding. A world of white, the air crisp and harsh and pure, too cold to breathe in, so cold it stabbed. Nothing growing. Nothing alive at all. No green, just frozen ground for miles and miles.

Slowly, his sisters' hands in his, Edan felt the press of earth, the lift of soil lessen, slow, recede. The molten flow in the earth, in him, slipped back into solidity, firmness, being. The air cooled, the colors changed, the smell of grass and water and damp leaves wafted around them. Land. Earth. Soil. Sea. Air. Trees and creatures. There was heat and fire, too, but where it belonged, where it was necessary, where it was useful to the planet. Now instead of burn and char, everything around them was alive.

Edan opened his eyes, looking at his sisters. They were windblown, swept wild by what they had almost done, their eyes bright, both of them so beautiful in the orange afternoon light.

"It's over?" Claire asked. "We stopped it?"

"Yes," Edan said. "Now we have to fight the Neballats in another way."

"What way?" Mila said, dropping Edan's and Claire's hands and putting her hands on her hips as she looked around them, the place as lovely as it had been.

"So where are they? Where are the people who were calling to us?" she asked, looking around. "Where—"

But then she didn't have to ask anymore because there they were, the ones who called to them. Stephanie was there. And Porter. And more continued to arrive, all those who had somehow heard what Edan, Mila, and Claire were doing. Garrick. Darl. Jai. Risa. And . . . and?

Ava, she thought, moving through the crowd, walking to him, her hair blowing behind her in the soft wonderful world, the air a blanket that held them all close. Her eyes captured his gaze, her body so strong and forceful, arms lithe and slim and strong. It was as if she were the first woman walking to him, and he the first man waiting for her.

Edan knew that before the first man and woman were kicked out of Eden in the story Claire had told them, everything had been just like this: they were perfect in themselves in a perfect world. So it wasn't just a myth; it was a story they would change, rewrite, give a happy ending.

Ava, he thought. And then he was with her, holding her in his arms again. Edan pressed her to him, feeling as though he'd never had the chance to do this before, as if he'd never have the chance to do it again.

Yes, you will, she thought. *Now and later and forever.*

So close, he thought, his mouth on her neck, her jaw, her chin, her lips, tasting her, not caring about anyone seeing this embrace, not even thinking about those around him.

So close what?

So close to losing you, he thought, feeling her breasts

press so softly against him. That pressure, that feel, that touch reminded him of the time they'd had together, when he moved into her body, her self, her flesh that unknown, pristine, perfect world. Like this world. Perfect.

I don't think we can lose each other, Edan. Whether we are on this world or Upsilia or Earth. Whether we are alive or not. We are together here, and we will be together later. I know that now more than ever.

He pulled back a little, looked into her dark eyes. She was smiling, filled with what seemed to be light, everything about her open and willing and hopeful.

I really don't want to take the chance of not being alive. It's just not something I want to aim for right now. Let's try to figure out how to stay here, he thought.

Ava smiled, her eyes on him, truly seeing him. *I want to be here, now.*

You are so beautiful, he thought. *More beautiful than anything ever created by anyone.*

And she smiled at him. In her smile was everything he'd ever wanted to see in his life. Recognition. Hope. Trust. Love. Beauty. Oh, beauty.

"Do I need to say it?" Porter said, interrupting Edan's thoughts.

Edan looked up, blinking. "Excuse me? Say what?"

Porter smirked. "It's an old Earth term. When two people are all over each other perhaps a tad inappropriately, some annoying soul will usually say 'Get a room.'"

Edan looked at Ava, who shrugged and then looked at Porter. "I have no understanding of the term, but it is clear that you are the annoying soul," she said.

"Exactly. Very well stated," said Stephanie. "However, as much as I dislike saying it, my dear Porter does have a point, and . . ."

Breathing out, Edan put his arm around Ava's shoulders and nodded. "I know. We have to prepare for the Neballats."

"We do," Stephanie said, motioning to the group clustered around Jai and Risa. "But now we can do so much more. It's all about protecting this world—"

"Instead of destroying it," Edan finished for her.

"Yes," Stephanie said. "We can live here. This is ours. For us. And we need to fight for it."

Against him, Ava was warm. Looking up, he saw the sky was bright and free and clear. Their world. Here he was with his family, his love, his friends, and a world created by them all. They did not have to keep it from the Neballats. They did not have to break it up so no one could have it. They simply had to keep it for themselves. To fight for it. To make it their own.

"All right," he said, and with his arm around his double, his twin, his true and only love, he moved into the crowd of Cygirians, who opened up and pulled them in as one.

The sky looked like a plate of metal. Edan would see a glimmer of blue, and then another Neballat ship would materialize, drawn here for the same need. To destroy them all.

They barely had the chance to prepare, to discuss what so many of them now knew to do. With intention, they could do anything, and now they intended to rid themselves once and for all of the Neballats.

"Kick their ridiculous, transparent asses," Porter said, without his usual flip tone.

"That's being generous," Darl said, holding Claire's hand. "Ridiculous is not the word I would use. Most of the words I can't use in polite company."

And in seconds, the Neballats would be gone. Standing with his arm around Ava, her soft presence something Edan knew he could never be without again, Edan saw the battle in his mind. It wouldn't even really be a battle. With thought, the Cygirians would finally do what the Neballats had feared for centuries, millennia, even. With thought, these ships hovering overhead would be nothing but atoms falling without threat to this new world. A rain of particles so fine they would never hit the ground, blowing free in the sky. And that would be that. A whole race, gone with a flash, just like that.

There would be no flame, no explosion, no cacophony or din or even tremors. Just wide-open sky and peace, as if all the persecution, kidnapping, terror, murder, death, and destruction had only been a dream.

Now, Jai thought, his words a ring of action and memory and need. *Now*.

The thought began slowly, a tiny blip of idea, a rumble of memory. Edan had just been stopped from destroying the planet, so he imagined that was what was holding him back, changing his thoughts, making him tentative. They'd stopped him from unleashing that destruction, so he imagined his impulse was thwarted.

Ava clutched his hand even with her eyes closed, scared, because what was before them, what was in the complete Cygirian vision was just as Edan had visualized himself. Total destruction of the ships, the people, the race.

And yet, he could not move any further into the thought. Edan pulled back, feeling only Ava next to him, her thoughts pulling away as well, until both of them were cocooned in their own pod of words and ideas.

I can't do it, he thought. *It feels wrong.*

They did kill our parents, Ava thought. *And that . . . that was horrible. I know.*

Edan didn't understand what she knew, but he needed to let her know what his plan was.

We give them another world. We make another world, for them. And then we negotiate a peace. A truce. A way of coexisting.

Within the small pod of their conversation, within the circle of Cygirian power, Edan felt the energy rise, lifting up and over them, toward the sky, toward the ships.

Can we trust them? she thought. *They have never acted right by us. Not once.*

What about Luoc? Edan thought, remembering all that the man had shown him. He wasn't like the others. *And there are more like him. People who have resisted our destruction. People who have tried to help all along.*

Maybe he was sent to teach us so all the rest could unfold, Ava thought, but her thought wavered with indecision, uncertainty.

We have a world, we negotiate, we both live different lives. Maybe we learn to communicate with each other, or maybe we don't. But no more killing.

He could almost feel her shrug, but he didn't have time to convince her more fully. The energy was rising, and the Neballats must have noticed because overhead, Edan thought he could hear the sounds of explosions, engines, but nothing was getting past the rising energy, which had become a shield deflecting weapons.

It's not an easy argument. Our culture was almost destroyed, Edan thought. *Maybe it was. You and I and everyone here will never know what it's like to be fully Cygirian. Where is our total history? Our songs? Our games? Our clothes, our art, our theater? We only have one child among us, one Cygirian child, Dasha. Even if we hate the Neballats, should we do back to them what was done to us? Does any culture deserve to be completely destroyed? Do we have that right?*

Now Edan could feel Ava move toward him, her answer in her slight touch, her hip pressing next to his. It had only been a very few days in his life that Edan had had Ava with him, and now, even now, he wondered how he'd managed to survive the time without her. She was so steady, so strong, backing him up, at his side, ready to believe him.

No, she thought. *We don't have that right. No one does. No person, no group.*

Let's stop this, then, he thought.

We need the shield, but we can also make the world. We can do both. We can do it all. We know that now.

Edan knew they could do anything. These past few days had shown him that.

Call to them, Ava thought. *They will listen to you. They will understand what you will tell them.*

Squeezing her hand, pulling her closer, Edan let go slightly of the building energy in his mind. He still worked toward pressing it up, toward the Neballat ships, but he opened up a conduit in the flow and stream of connection between him and all the Cygirians and called out.

My people, we can't do this to them.

Nothing came back right away, so he sent out the image of the world, the new world for the Neballats. It was as beautiful as the world they stood on, but a treasure, a gift, a peace offering.

This is what we need to do, he thought. *We need to create, not destroy. We need to give, not kill. I know that now, finally, more than ever.*

And then there was something like a hush, a lull, a wrinkle in the power pushing skyward.

Explain? came the question, a group question, a question bigger than any one person. *Tell us.*

So Edan let them see what he and Ava had discussed. The

world for the Neballats, a world of their own. Some kind of peace between the two groups, some kind of healing for the people who had tried to destroy them. But the past didn't matter. Only the present. Only this act of building rather than tearing down.

And like Ava, the group worried about retaliation, deceit, retribution. To that response, Edan sent out only the peace he knew he would feel if he could end this thing, make it stop. The feeling was centered in the slowly spinning world, the perfect circular orbit calming, beautiful, whole. And the feeling radiated out, warmed the sky above it, even warmed the calm, empty depth of space. Moved all the way to him, here on this planet. Flushed him, reminded him of another world, the world of Ava, her body, her touch, her smile. This was life. This was what made him know that life was the only answer. He had to show them all.

We can't do this thing, he thought. *It's not ours to do. We are not the creator of the energy we can control. Knowing what we know, we should not make life and death decisions for anyone.*

There was a pause. A space opened up in the intensity of their energy push.

They will kill us. They will hunt us down again and again. They won't stop until we are all dead.

The thoughts came fast, hard, driven by fear, apprehension, revenge, anger.

Then we have to let them. We can't have this destruction in our souls. It's not what we want, what we need.

But what about us? Our lives? Our children, our future? They are probably still holding some of our people. Who knows what has happened to them?

Edan thought of the Source, the place that had held him gently for years. He wanted to remind those who had been there that this outside life—this fighting and battling and raging and fleeing—was made to develop their souls, deepen them all into who they truly were. It was so hard to be real in this life where things hurt, where there was confusion and suffering. But sometimes, there was joy. The feeling of truly being alive. Of being that soul who flickered in the orange and red waves of energy in the Source. When he looked at Ava, he was in the Source. When he realized that he could create rather than destroy, he was in the Source. Now, right now, he felt the wisps of energy lick his body, and he was in that flow, the Source a feeling of potential within him.

We can't do this thing, was all he could send to them. *We aren't this way. This is not who we are, who we want to be.*

Edan let go, the thoughts leaving him, moving into the group. He had told them all he knew, all he could think. At this point, it was up to Cygiria to determine their history as a people, as a group. So he breathed, felt Ava close to him, and waited.

The movement was so small at first that Edan wondered if he had actually felt it. The shield remained a strong force above them, the Neballat weapons repelled, the explosions muffled, muted. But there it was. Slowly, as Edan waited for an answer, he felt another energy building. It was the energy from earlier, when this world was created. The energy was filled with a care, a tenderness that was different from the power that was creating the shield. This was what Cygirians were best at. This was what they were intended to do. This was their calling, their usefulness to the universe. This was what they were meant to do.

While overhead, the Neballats tried to hurt them, tried to fight back against whatever they imagined was happening, Edan saw the world begin, just as this one had. In the middle of darkest space, first the eddy, then the swirl, then the form emerging from nothing, a whirl of colors.

This is for you, he thought to the Neballats. He imagined their angry, invisible bodies, their attempts at staying alive, keeping themselves going in order to find a place, a home, a way to be. They had become rodents of the universe, scurrying to what they imagined would save them, not thinking about anything but the most basic survival. *This world is for you.*

No, thought Ava. *This is for us. Our gift to them is for us.*

Yes, Edan thought, amazed at how she understood him, how she'd been with him from about the first second of his idea. She was his double, his twin, his partner, his love. She was truly the woman he was supposed to be with forever, even if forever was over in an instant.

The shield of energy stayed in place, but the world grew, revolved around its sun, sprang to life, the place breathable, livable, full and lush and perfect. Another world in another galaxy, a place just like this world but far enough away that Earth, Upsilia, New Cygiria, and the Neballat world might never have to come in contact again. But now they would know what they brought to each other, what was owed, what was repaid. Earth could spin blindly alone until it caught up somehow, some way, but the most important fact was that Cygiria could reestablish itself, return to the way it might have been.

We will learn from the past, Ava thought. *We will know better.*

I will learn from you, Edan thought, knowing that without Ava, he would know nothing, be nothing, have nothing. All the clichés were true. But he didn't have to think about it. He was here with her now, fighting back and giving at the same time. Changing the course of their lives and all Cygirians'. Moving toward what only had to be better. Was already better.

His heart told him what to say, his mind handing her his thought softly.

I love you.

There was a pause, her hand holding his tight, her pulse against his skin.

I love you, too.

The sky—full of ships—beat metal into the day, and the Cygirians thought on, creating their future.

And the new world spun into full being.

Everything was still. The sky, emptied of ships, was full now of clouds, sun breaking through, casting a golden glow on the Cygirians who stood together, looking upward.

Together, they sent a message, Edan feeling the thoughts coursing through him like blood.

We will negotiate, they thought together, pressing the idea into the sky, into the thinnest of the atmosphere, into space.

We will give you something that you want, they thought even harder, trying to send the truth of their idea with the thoughts. *This is not a trick. This is not about revenge. This is what we can give you.*

Letting go slightly of the communication, Edan opened his eyes, looking out at all of them working so hard to change the animosity of hundreds of years, maybe even of millennia. Next to him, Ava stood still, her face full of concentration, effort, hope.

He wanted to take her in his arms, letting go now of this, all of it. The Neballats could either come to them or not. They could take Cygiria up on its offer or slowly die, planetless, formless, their bodies slipping into the ether, unhinged from body, blood, bone. Unprotected, bitter, the Neballats could sail the emptiness of space until the very last one of them died out, a spindly, desiccated remnant of self.

Edan didn't want that, but it was their choice. Not his. And Edan wanted to choose life. He wanted to choose Ava.

Just as he was about to touch her, pull her close, let the thought vanish from his mind altogether, he heard it, as they all did.

How can we trust you?

The group galvanized, focused, slight anger simmering in the response. *This is not the question* you *should ask. That question belongs to us. But still, we say that we will negotiate. This is not a ruse, a joke, a trap.*

Electrified, alert, Cygiria waited, Edan feeling their need to know what would happen inside him, as if there was nothing else but the question. No heartbeat. No pulse. Just the question.

Send the two to our ship.

There was a pause. *The two?*

The two who are life.

As if his eyes were not open, as if he could see all his people stopping, turning slowly, facing him, Edan knew that the Neballats meant him and Ava. The two who are life. The back and forward of life. While it was true that anyone could do anything with intent, this was what came naturally to them both.

Opening his eyes and taking Ava in his arms, he looked at her carefully, slowly, taking in her beauty as if he'd just seen her for the first time. What happened next could change everything.

What do you want to do? he thought, knowing already what she would say.

Her dark eyes on his, she nodded, slightly smiling, her lips rose, her teeth white, everything about her begging him to force her to stay here. Always a sacrifice, and to sacrifice being close to her? To give up her beauty? To give up her touch, her embrace? To give up what they would have together on this plain of existence? Love. Family. Wholeness?

Ava smiled at him, brought her hand up to his cheek, stroking him softly. Edan felt his mind relax, his breath a slow, strong whoosh from his chest.

Of course she knew what they would agree to.

What we have to do, she thought. *What we will do. We need to. We really have no choice.*

Of course.

Looking at Jai, Mila, Claire, Porter, Garrick, Darl, Risa, Michael, Kate, Odhran, Elizabeth, Mark, Diane, Carl, and all of them, all his people, Edan nodded.

We will go.

Are you certain? Jai thought. *We do not have to negotiate anything with them. We can end this now, if we choose. This is ours to decide. We are in control now. Finally. Always.*

Jai paused, looking at Risa and then back at Edan. *I cannot make this decision for you. No one can. This is yours and Ava's to decide.*

Before Edan could think a word, Ava spoke, her voice light but strong and clear. "We will go to the Neballats," she said. "We will go now."

As she spoke, Edan closed his eyes, feeling for the Neballats' communication, their words, their ideas. Finding them beating like a weak heart in space, he held Ava's hand tight and together, they conjured the power that all Cygirians owned and disappeared, moving through space and time, moving through darkness, moving toward what would finish it all.

* * *

Blinking into the light, Edan at first could only feel Ava's hand in his. The bright light was painful, almost silver, almost slashing into his eyes. But then it slowly dimmed, and he blinked again, his eyes adjusting.

As they had traveled, he'd imagined that the Neballats would produce one of their fancy shows. He'd heard from both Mila and Garrick how theatrical the Neballats were with their displays, at different points giving both of them a dramatic show of the past. He'd known firsthand their abilities with a Simulator, that creative way of controlling minds. But now? What was he seeing? Where were they?

"You are in our prime craft," a Neballat said, his figure clear against the bright light. And he was clear: transparent arms, neck, and face, his blood pumping in pulsing movements under his skin. Edan wondered what the man would look like if his skin had any amount of color, any amount of tint. Or his eyes. He knew from looking at Ava that the color of her eyes meant an emotion to him, simmering, thoughtful, deep, and lovely. The Neballats had nothing but a blue that was white, shocking, targetlike eyes that seemed to depict some other, desperate blankness inside them.

"You found us easily." The Neballat's voice was slow, clear, and accepting.

"There is so much we can do easily now," Edan said, knowing that after saying those words a few times, he would believe them. All this power was right at their fingertips. No, not fingertips. Mind. Anything they wanted was right there.

"Such power could be dangerous to have," the man said. "What you want now is not what you might want later."

"Do you feel that way?" Ava asked. "Do you have something that you fought for and don't want now?"

If the man had had visible eyebrows, Edan knew they would be raised at Ava's question.

"I have the burden passed down from the generation before me," he said. "I have a war I cannot win but must continue. I have a mission that was given to me by my elders that I must finish."

"Even if it means your death?" Edan asked. "Even if that burden, that heavy bundle contains your own end?"

The man shrugged, laughed a thin, hard laugh. "Perhaps. And I see that the end of which you speak is here already. The end is marked by you two coming to our ship. So the question that you ask me is likely moot."

"We are not your end but your beginning," Edan said.

The man cocked his head, watched Edan for a moment, turning to look quickly to his left.

Edan looked around, realizing for the first time that other Neballats stood around the perimeter of the room, almost invisible, the controls and walls visible through their bodies. He turned his attention back to the man, breathing in as he did.

"Do you know Luoc?" Edan asked.

"Oh, we know of Luoc and others like him. Crusaders. Prophets. Criminals. Those who foretold of a new way, a new world. Those who talked of peace when there was no peace. No rest for our kind. Those who broke our laws by contacting and helping you."

Staring at the man, his strange translucent face now somehow bearable to watch, Edan wondered about belief and how it could be so strong that not even imminent destruction could change it. This man hated Cygiria because his parents had, because his grandparents had. As body type and eye color were based down genetically, so was this hate. There was no reason for that hate now, but he clung to it as if he were dangling from a rope.

"Luoc taught me some things," Edan said. "He showed me the way."

The man laughed again, this time anger a ripple in the sound. "So fortunate for us that he did. He must have prophesized our destruction. How wonderful to be right just before death."

"There doesn't have to be death," Ava said.

"Easy for you two to say. You who control it."

"No," Ava said. "We can give you what you need. And then . . ."

Edan finished her sentence. "And then you can leave us alone. Leave us to our lives. And we will leave you to yours. Both our peoples will have exactly what we need to survive."

Slight, sad laughter ringed the room. Edan felt their failure, breathed it in as if it were an odor.

"You would give us this tremendous gift and then just let us be?" the man said. "Like that?"

His arm tight around Ava, Edan looked at the other Neballats in the room and then moved his gaze back to stare at the man. He wanted to tell him that he did not harbor hate. Because of the way the Neballats had chased him and his people to small hidden patches of the universe, he'd learned that there was nothing to fear. During his life of struggle, he learned how connected everything was. Edan and Ava and all Cygiria were connected to the Neballats, and their survival was important. Necessary. Needed.

"Yes, we would." Edan nodded. "Yes."

"You people seem to think that the universe will take care of you."

"But it does!" Ava said. "The universe does take care of us. All of us. You just have to believe in it."

Again, there was laughter, but not quite as much this

time. They knew what Cygirians could do, how they could harness power, so maybe these words were not sounding as strange as they would have just days before. And the Neballats were tired of fighting, tired of war. Like anyone, all they wanted was a home.

"A world," Edan said. "We can give you a world. Very like the one you had us make before."

And in a show that rivaled any that the Neballats had unveiled to a kidnapped Cygirian, Edan presented the world that they would make for the Neballats. The room darkened, space opened its womb to push forth the spinning orb. The planet grew light with colors, light with life. The atmosphere opened up white and blue. A sun shone, the continents below full of only possibility. There in the middle of the room, the world spun in its glistening orbit.

"This," Edan said. "This is what we offer you."

Now there was no laughter. Now there was no sound at all. And even though he could not see their faces in the darkness, he knew they were watching and listening. He knew that they were finally paying attention. For once, they did not want to kidnap, take over, or destroy anything. They'd asked him to make a world once already, and this time they would be able to have it.

"Why?" the man asked. "Why would you do this for us? Whatever could make you want to give this to us?"

Turning to Ava, Edan looked at his love. There she was, next to him, holding his hand, her body warm and lovely, her whole affect calm, even in the midst of their enemies. She was a quiet, constant presence, a *beat-beat* of *yes* and *you* and *us* and *we* and *always*.

Why? the Neballat asked. Why indeed. Such a good question. And the only answer was Ava. Ava was the answer to the question of why Edan would do anything now.

He wanted to live his life with her. He wanted to feel gravity pulling at him; he wanted to feel the sun warming his skin; he wanted to go to bed each night and turn to this woman, turn to Ava, and hold her. He wanted children to pass down what he could learn about his people. He wanted as many years as this life would offer, and in order to wrest those years from this ongoing battle, he had to give to the Neballats. He had to give them back their lives.

So Edan just stood in front of them, glowing, knowing that the answer to their questions was right before them. They were the "life" couple, but they were really just Edan and Ava, twins, doubles, people who wanted to take as much as they could before heading back to the place they all came from, before heading back to the Source.

The man blinked, his eyelids moving over clear eyes, nodding. "All right."

"You must not do anything to harm us," Edan said.

"All right," the man said again. "Agreed."

"And you must let go those of us you are holding captive." Edan wasn't sure about this fact, but the man paused, seemed to communicate with the others around him. "We want them with us now."

After a moment, the man nodded. "Agreed," he said again.

"There's more," Edan said, knowing that the Neballats wouldn't even believe the second part of this gift.

"Yes?" the man asked, his face moving in surprise, invisible skin pulling up transparent features.

"Yes," Edan said, closing his eyes, pulling Ava close, and winging them both back to their people. "There is more. So much more."

Chapter Eleven

"How will we do it?" Ava had her arms around Edan, both of them breathing into the moment of appearing on the new world, the one that would be theirs. That was theirs. The New Cygiria.

How will we do it? Ava looked around as the single thought came from all those about her.

Edan held her tightly, and then moved to face the crowd. As they had traveled back, they'd sent forth the message, the news of the negotiation. Ava had felt the *I don't believe its*, but those thoughts were outweighed by the *Peace at last* thoughts.

"We have this power within us," Edan began.

"To create flesh?" Porter asked. "If that were the case, I know a few people who might want to do a little work on themselves. Or maybe it's the other power they'd need—the old removal of flesh trick. Necks. Get rid of that wattle! Arms. That dangling stomach. That protuberant ass."

"You are the ass," Kate whispered, her thought louder than her words. *Shut the hell up.*

Ava would have smiled, added a thought, but this was not the time, and Porter seemed to realize it, hear Kate's words, and was quiet.

"To create flesh," Edan went on. "To give them back their bodies. To give them the bodies they need to live on the world we will make for them."

There was a rumble, an earthquake of thought as Edan spoke. While Ava and he and many others were for this plan, this peace settlement, she could feel the unease moving through the crowd.

"We would use the same energies we used while creating the world. The intent to heal them would be in our minds, though."

Why should we heal them? came the thought, loud and hard and not without merit. *We are already giving them a world. They didn't think so generously when they slaughtered our parents and grandparents. They didn't think twice about destroying our planet. They didn't care how we were left to figure out our lives on our own. So why? Explain this to us one more time, Edan. Why?*

Inside Ava burned the light that Edan had given her, gifted to her the first time she set eyes on him. The light was an amazing feeling of love, of kindness, of hope that spilled out from his body to her, to the people around them, to the universe. Even to the Neballats. While she knew he didn't have access to this light all the time—things kept him in the shade where most people lived—it burned deep and hard and fast inside him, available to him when he needed it, like right now. And now it was in her, too. She wanted to forgive everyone. She wanted to forgive and live and go on. She wanted everyone to have what she had. This light. This love. This happiness.

So rather than let Edan answer the question, Ava closed her eyes and focused on the light inside her. She knew she wasn't strong enough to share it with everyone, but she could show them. She could lift the curtain and let them peek at it, for just a moment, enough to maybe convince them that Edan was right.

Here, she thought. *Look. Feel.*

The light burned yellow, orange, red, leaping up and out of her heart, into her mind, out of her body, and into the thoughts of everyone around her. It was a light that carried the feelings that could make a world, that could bring people together in love. It was the love of children and family and home. It was the love of the appreciation of the moment, of the instant, of the wonder it was to simply be alive. It was the love of community and people and place. It was the love that created sky and star and earth and water. It was the light and love that created flesh.

The wave of light flowed from her, a flume of heat and power and love. As it filled her, as it flowed out of her, she knew that there really was nothing that could stand in its way. It was stronger than fear, anger, resentment, or jealousy. This light, this love, was the strongest thing of all.

And then she heard it, heard the acknowledgment of it, the acceptance, the understanding.

Yes, some thought.

All right, others thought.

Love, others thought, their collective mind the colors of the Source, the oranges and reds so powerful, so beautiful, so lovely. For a second, Ava imagined them all as they would be in the Source, a bright, unified stream of energy and power.

You, thought Edan. *The colors are you.*

Me? she thought.

You are this feeling in me, Edan thought. *You are my heat, my power, my love. You are my red flame.*

And using that red flame, that beating heart of power, Ava, and Edan, and the rest of Cygiria let the love turn into action. Like before, they created, found the deep, dead spot in space, a place of no life where life could begin. The dead spot began to swirl, to emerge into shape, to slowly spin. And then life started as atmosphere and cloud and sky. Continents formed, seas circulated, spun, moved to the rhythms of a moon now beating its white pulse against the face of the planet, the sun giving it the eerie glow.

Ava couldn't believe how well they all moved together, their thoughts a river contained but driven by nature.

We are almost there, Edan thought.

The world spun blue and green and white, a wonder of elements and chemicals.

We are there, Ava thought, and she felt it as all their minds rested, relaxed. They were still connected, but the power softly hummed instead of burned with strength. She watched the world in her mind, knew that it was as perfect a gift as they could give the Neballats, their enemies.

Former enemies, Edan thought, reaching for Ava's hand.

Former enemies, Ava thought. Everything was former. The old life. The old way of being. Of being so alone, being afraid, her only comfort a place she could not really live in. How long had she wished to simply be in the Source? Was that living? Was that a way to feel about this one life in this body on this plane? Now her entire life was different, changed, new. She wanted to live in her body, in this flesh, on this very ground. She desired it so much it almost frightened her. But she wanted to go on, go forth, try it, live it, love it.

Please don't drop the ball. Now what? Porter's thought popped into the lull. *Pray tell how we start this muscular adventure. I've quite forgotten the entire musculoskeletal system of a human. How am I supposed to build a Neballat? I have quite lost my manual.*

They aren't so much different from us, Edan thought.

*And, Porter, we aren't humans, you know. We weren't born
on Earth, or did you forget?*

Ava could feel Porter's blush from a distance.

Porter can be a little slow, Garrick thought, his words
filled with laughter. *But it is a good question.*

Garrick's idea was mirrored in the minds of all around
them. He went on. *It isn't exactly something we've been
doing for a long time.*

It's all the same, Edan thought. *Everything is all the same.*

Frightfully easy to say, Porter thought, but then he stopped
thinking, caught up in the wide, white swath of feeling and
thought that Edan was casting out.

See, Edan thought, the thin, stick figure of a Neballat in
his mind.

Ava saw the Neballat, too, the figure like the man's in the
ship, the figure like Luoc, the one who had taught them
what they could do, what they should do. There in front of
her was the almost invisible shell of flesh—the skin translucent, exposing organs and veins and bone. There was the
face, the eyes gleaming from the eggshell skull. There were
the hands, reaching out like ghost claws, grabbing, needing,
wanting. A very few of the women carried babies, tiny fe-
tuses that grew thin and colorless in see-through wombs,
sucking on diaphanous thumbs. There was nothing alive or
healthy about any part of any Neballat body.

Give, thought Edan.

And despite their agreement to do so, Ava could feel the
resistance, the tentative nature of the desire to provide such
bounty. Ringing like light bells on the outside of this powerful thought was the anger, the hurt, the fury, the sadness
caused by the Neballats.

Would it ever go away? Ava wondered. Would they as a
group truly ever be able to forgive this group of people?

Give, thought Edan again, and slowly, the tympani of slight thought died away, and in its place was the rich flow that could create worlds. Together, as with the world, their thoughts converged to this task, one task that was split into millions of pieces, energy that flowed out to all the Neballats, everywhere, no matter where they were located.

Ava could see their wraithlike bodies growing from within, cells building, blood and bone and skin growing, filling out, folding over, making whole. Blinking against the vision, this almost horrorlike growth, Ava wanted to cry out. It must be so painful, she realized. It couldn't be easy to take on substance. It couldn't be easy to grow that quickly, that fast.

But she knew it was possible to grow that quickly and survive. Look how she had been able to grow enough to accept Edan. Look how she'd shifted from fear to love. It was possible, and it did hurt. But it was worth it. More than worth it.

Give, thought Edan, wanting them to finish this task, finish it all so that the universe of this ugly relationship could shift. From hate to love. From fear to love. From homelessness to home.

Give, Edan thought, and Ava dropped all of her other thoughts. She stopped seeing what was happening, stopped feeling the power within her. She pressed out and at the Neballats wanting this chapter to close itself, fold in, and become a blank white page.

Maybe it was minutes, maybe hours. Maybe even days. Ava wasn't sure. She wasn't even sure she could open her eyes. Or maybe her eyes were open and all she was seeing was white, a crisp, even dazzle of new sunlight.

"Love," she heard, the voice a kiss in her ear. "Love, wake up."

Trying to turn toward his voice, Ava reached out a hand, feeling Edan's arm, feeling his shoulder, his cheek.

"I'm too tired," she said. "I can't . . ."

She couldn't say anything else, her tongue heavy, her jaw a weight she could not manage.

"Just rest, then," Edan said, and she felt him pick her up, his strong arms around her shoulders, under her knees. Ava relaxed into him, his strength seeming to flow into her, little wicks of healing heat and power. Slowly, her breathing grew deeper, her body stronger, and she opened her eyes.

"Did we do it? Did we finish the work?"

Edan nodded, his arms tightening around her. "We did. I think it took a great deal from us all."

Ava looked up and out for a moment, watching her other people stand, slightly wobbly, leaning against each other, taking in strength from those who had reserves.

"I guess no one knew how hard it was to build a world and a million bodies in one hour."

"We did it faster than that old Earth legend people keep trying to tell me about," Edan said. "I think they should write a story about us. Who needs six days!"

"Do you think the Neballats will be happy?" Ava asked. "Do you think they will leave us alone now?"

She felt his shrug against her body. "I don't know if we really want them to leave us alone. Now that we've formed an understanding, a bond, we can be of use to each other. Upsilia, Cygiria, and the Neballat world together. Maybe someday when Earth comes to, we can include them. There is strength in numbers. There is so much that we could teach one another."

Ava thought about what Edan was saying. In her mind, she saw the four worlds together, all in concert. Suddenly, space seemed almost familiar, the wide vastness of it all a known thing, sort of like home.

He stopped talking, walking away from the crowd, Ava feeling light and happy in his arms.

"Where are you taking me?" she asked. "There's not too much here yet."

Edan laughed, the sound a rumble in his chest. "Are you sure about that?"

"We just made it," she said, letting her head rest against his shoulder. "It's not like we've had time to build a hotel, much less a house. Or even a tent. Look how long it took us to get Talalo up and running, if that."

"A tent?"

"I have very fond memories of a tent," Ava said. "In fact, I want to live in a tent for the rest of my life."

"I have a feeling that a tent can be arranged."

"Are you sure? Making a tent isn't like making a world, mind you. There's a little more to it. I think it's a very delicate operation. It has to be the right tent, with the right feel, with the right—"

"Person," Edan said. "Man, actually. That I can provide at minimal energy expenditure."

Smiling against his shoulder, Ava almost wanted to laugh out loud or cry. So much happiness seemed to be uncalled for, unexpected, rare. But she had it, inside her, around her. This happiness was something she could hang on to, feel in her hands as she pulled forward into life.

"Well, then," she said after finding her voice. "I think it's time we went camping. Take me to your tent, sir."

"My pleasure," Edan said, and Ava closed her eyes again, leaning into him, feeling his strides as he moved into the unknown land of this new Cygiria. At the back of her mind, she heard the thoughts of the others, wondering where

Edan was, calling out for him, but neither he nor she paid attention. There would be time enough to be with the others, figure out their lives here. What they both needed was each other, the skin and touch and feel and scent of each other pressed close.

Edan paused, his mind a whir of memory and imagination. She could see the flickering images of his tent in Talalo, the slight coolness of the inside, the yellow desert light as it shone through the fabric. There was the cot, there was the flap, a slight breeze pushing it open and shut, open and shut. There was the tang of salt and sand, the wood plank floor underneath. And there, in the middle of the image, was Ava. Edan and Ava, together.

Opening her eyes, Ava looked up from her secure perch in Edan's arms, and there was a tent—no, *the* tent.

"Our home away from home," Edan said, carrying her these final few feet. "And I've heard about this custom on Earth."

"What custom is that?" she asked as he stopped right at the tent door flaps.

"Carrying the bride over the threshold," he said.

"Whoa," she said, looking at him, smiling. "I think you've put the cart before the horse, or the bride before the wedding. I don't know what Earth brides are all about, but I'd at least like to have a ceremony. A party. That's the least that we Upsilian girls were raised to expect. So for now, I just want you to walk through, that's all. That's more than enough."

Smiling, Edan did as she asked, both of them in the tent, breathing in the cool soft air. She breathed him in, too, his smooth skin, the tang of salt and sun. She wanted to put her face next to his neck, kiss under his ear, let her lips run down the arc of his neck.

Please. Do something, he thought, his words a smile.

Ava lifted her face to Edan's, and he bent slightly, kissing her, his lips firm and smooth, and clear. He wanted her, just as she wanted him.

Matched, he thought. *We are perfectly matched.*

She let herself fall slowly toward him, each inch, each millimeter that she moved closer like a caress, like a promise. Even the anticipation of him felt good.

And then he was holding her, his arms moving gently over her shoulders, her back, his fingers running gently along her spine. The soft subtle touch made her body tingle, letting her feel parts of her she didn't know could be excited.

I want to excite all of you. Every single part.

"Elbow," she sighed. "Just now. Kneecaps earlier. Then shin."

"I'll keep working at it," Edan said, and he moved his lips from her mouth, down her chin, under her neck, the movement soft and firm and warm. Ava closed her eyes, let herself relax, feeling her nerves become an instrument of desire, each and every ending a chord he was playing. Head, neck, torso, legs, feet. All of her thrummed, and her core throbbed, her nipples almost hurting.

How she knew this language of love, Ava wasn't sure. She'd never let herself learn anything, holding back from everyone, not just men. She'd received so little affection as a child, she was amazed she wasn't damaged, one of those people who ran away from feeling because it is unknown, frightening, unclear.

But this? She wanted Edan, and she wanted him to feel the same way she did. Moving back toward him, her arms now tight around him, she pressed her body close, let her arms follow the strong shape of his muscles, his bones, his flesh, feeling his breath shudder and waver, sharp inhales when she let her hands fall to the arc of his perfect ass.

You know what to do to me, he thought. *Everything you do is perfect.*

What do I do to you? she thought, knowing exactly what she was doing to him, the length of him hard against her belly. She never thought she would enjoy this kind of power, that kind of skill, that kind of ability. Of all the things she'd been able to do—move her whole body, cell by cell, to another chronological age, travel through space, create worlds, add flesh to beings—nothing compared to the reaction in this man standing next to her, his desire made real by his erection. She did that, and that was the most amazing miracle of all.

No, he thought, *you are my miracle. You are the most amazing thing of all.*

And with that thought, he began to slowly take off her shirt, his hands skimming the skin of her ribs as he pushed the fabric up and over her head. At his touch, her nerves flared again, all parts of her reaction to his touch, to the air softly caressing her skin.

More, she thought. *More.*

"Close your eyes," he said as he lifted the shirt off.

And then he didn't say anything, the pause full and deep. Ava opened her eyes, and saw him looking at her, his eyes wide and glistening.

"You are amazing. You see how you are a miracle?" he said, leaning down to kiss her chest, his hands coming up to cup her breasts, his fingers gentle, firm, insistent on her nipples. "There's nothing in any universe like you. Nothing that I've seen or done or felt or known comes even close to this. There is nothing as stupendous as you. Nothing as lovely. Nothing I want to look at more."

Ava wanted to say so much, words with feelings and thoughts she'd wanted to say her entire life. Oh, how she agreed with him, but about him, not her. But all she could do was slip silly and soft into his touch, let the sensations in her body ripple out. He was the thrown stone and she the pond, rings and rings of feeling going on and on, just fading away before yet another stone rippled through her.

Edan let his hands now trace her rib cage, her waist, her hips, her thighs, slowly pushing away her pants, and Ava wasn't sure that she could remain standing this time.

Let's not stand, he thought, pushing away her pants and moving back so that she could step out of them. *There happens to be this handy cot here for some reason.*

Her heart beat so loud there was nothing but her pulse in her ears, everything inside her now a roaring ocean of desires. No ripples now but waves crashing in her. She breathed into his touch on her body, the slightly scratchy cloth under her as she lay down, looking up at his face. He smiled at her, his teeth brilliant white against the yellow-tinged light of the tent, his skin dusky, warm, welcoming.

How lucky she was. There he was, above her, taking off his shirt, taking off his pants, and she lifted her hands to feel him, loving the way he felt under her touch, noticing how he took in breath as she felt the ripped muscles of his stomach. She let her hand slide down, touching him, his heat, his softness, his hardness, moving her hand up and down his length and then only wanting him in her.

His smile gone, his face full of want, Edan lay down on top of her, moving her legs apart with his weight, slipping in between them and then pushing closer to her, all of him so warm. Ava felt how wet she was, how ready for him. She had never been afraid of this with Edan, but now she wanted it. Needed him next to her, in her.

And then he was against her, and then he was in her, filling her with all the feeling her body had been craving.

"You've saved the best for last," she whispered as she held him against her.

"I've saved the best for you," he said, his voice low, soft, hungry.

He slowly moved into her, pressing, letting up, pressing, pushing, letting her ride him, letting his body slide slickly inside her. She held on to him, her lips at his neck, their minds as connected as their bodies.

This, she thought. *Only this.*

Only this, Edan agreed. *Always.*

And together, moving and breathing and feeling each other, they made love on the cot Edan had conjured, in this new world, their new world, Ava knowing that no matter what else might happen to her, she'd had this. Joy. True joy. Had it now. Had Edan, her true love.

Ava let her hand run across Edan's chest, enjoying the feeling of his soft hair under her fingertips. They'd made love twice, and now the bright gold light they'd started off in was a dull umber, the night folding across the sky.

One of his arms was under her neck, wrapped around her shoulder. The other was moving slowly up and down her right thigh, his touch warm and pleasant. She knew that within minutes, they could go from this position to more lovemaking, as they had been all afternoon.

"I don't know about that," Edan said. "I would have to use some of my powers to do that. Four lovemaking sessions in one day might prove to be my undoing."

"We can't have that," she said, kissing his chest. "Even a superman needs a break."

He laughed, the sound filling the tent. Both of them relaxed onto the one pillow, Ava letting her mind move over the events of the day.

"How can we trust them, even now?" she asked. "Does a gift change a whole group? Just like that?"

Edan breathed in, his hand still moving on her. "I don't know if we can ever trust them. Maybe there will be a time when we regret what we gave them. But I don't think they will ever do to us what they did to our parents and grand-parents. How could they? We won't let them. We've changed from the people who allowed such a destruction to occur. We've grown. We've come into our powers. We know who we are and what we are made of. It doesn't really matter if they've changed or not."

Ava took in his words, realizing that it wasn't just she alone who'd had to change. She'd accepted love and her role as a Cygirian. And everyone else had as well. Together, they were more than they'd ever been. Now their lives were what they made of them, how they all decided to use the abilities they'd discovered.

She shook her head, something dark flickering across her mind, a smudgy handprint of thought. "But what about us?"

"You and me?" Edan asked. "There isn't too much question there, if you ask me. We belong to each other."

She smiled, rolling onto her side, breathing in his sun and sand smells. "Not *us* us," she said, her voice muffled. "I mean us, we, Cygirians. We have all this power. We could end up doing things wrong, becoming like the Neballats."

For a moment, Edan was silent, and in his silence, she felt the connection of energy between them. When they first met, she'd felt the connection immediately, but at that time, it was like a river with bridges she had to cross in order to get to him, to it. Now the current was in both of them, moving constantly, both of them flowing together, in synch, in tune, in rhythm.

Edan exhaled. "Power corrupts. I've read through the history of Cygiria when we were at the safe house. I've lived in Upsilia, an almost totalitarian state. I've met people from Earth who have stories of countries and groups invading and sucking up land and resources from those who are too weak to fight back. This is the nature of civilization. I don't know if we are strong enough, evolved enough, to resist the pull."

She pushed herself up, looking down at Edan's face, unconsciously letting her fingers trace his jaw even as his words stung her. "You think we could be as ruthless, as uncaring? Do you think we could destroy an entire planet?"

"Mila, Claire, and I almost did," Edan said. "If it hadn't been for you, we would have cracked open all that we cared about."

"But no one was on it! You weren't trying to destroy. You were trying to stop this fight. This battle."

Edan pulled her back down to him, holding her against his chest, his hand stroking her back. "But we are going to take something away. We were going to break something up. That's the worry. Whatever can build can tear down, too."

The truth of his words flowed through Ava with the current of their connected power. To build. To destroy. The same power.

Turning slightly on her back, she blinked up into the dim light. Who would have given Cygirians such power? What wacky power would have given this ability to anyone? It was too much responsibility. Too much work.

She sighed. "Edan?"

"Hmm?" he said, his voice so warm and sleepy, she almost wanted to stop talking. Who cared about all these questions? She could just go about her life now, knowing enough. But here—in this tent with Edan, where it was safe and warm—she wanted to know. She wanted to figure something out, something that would make all that followed make sense.

"Edan? Are you listening? Are you still with me?"

"I'm still here, as least as far as I can tell."

"I need to know what you think."

He turned a little, looking at her, his eyes shining. "Yes, my love."

"So, if we can do what we did. You know, create worlds. Who—how—how did we get here? Who made us?"

Edan laughed, pulling her closer. "Isn't that the question every sentient being in the universe has been asking forever?"

"Well," she said, pulling up on her elbow, slightly irritated at his laughter. "Isn't it a damn good question, then? Lots of precedent."

"Of course it is," he said, stroking her arm. "But no one has ever had the answer. Even in the Source I never came across the all-knowing, all-encompassing person, power, force that created all this. No spirit, no energy ever led me toward something that was the center."

Ava nodded, but there actually had been something in the Source, sort of a pull toward the middle of it all, a heat, a light, a power. But she'd been too busy being lost, trying to forget her life on Upsilia to search any further for the bright heart of things. That node, that core, though, made her feel that somewhere, someplace, there was the beginning, and the beginning was still there, sending out all the life that any of them had ever known.

"But there has to be some beginning to, well, beginning," Ava said. "All the stories on Upsilia were about the Creator.

On Earth, too, from what I gleaned from the people I met. Usually in the beginning, there is nothing. A sound, a thought, a word. Darkness and then light. But then the story stops dead. No one can figure out how to jump from nothing to the beginning. The tellers didn't seem to have an answer, and then they threw in a creator or a god or a power. And it, he, she couldn't do much more than what we've been doing."

Edan pulled her down to his chest, pulled her tight. "Somewhere outside all this stuff—these planets and black holes and constellations and galaxies and universes—is something else. Something more. I don't think it's a someone. Not a person. Not a being. In a way, I see whatever started life as a pulse, a waterfall, a swirl of molten earth. Who knows? No one knows what it is."

"Are we ever going to find out?" Ava asked, realizing even as she asked the question, she didn't know if she wanted the answer. Living—living well—seemed to be the answer to so many of the questions she'd had. And now that there was the possibility of living well, happily even, she wasn't sure the answer to it all was necessary.

Edan seemed to agree. "Ava, does it really matter? We know what we need to know. And we can keep learning. I don't think we need to have the answers to keep living. To enjoy life. To love. To have this."

He leaned down, stroking her face, kissing her lips softly once, twice, his smile against hers.

"This is pretty good," she said. "But I think there is more. I mean, I have this vague recollection of a something you and I can do together that sort of eclipses all the creation stories I've ever read."

"We do it together very well," he said, kissing her next joke away, something she wanted to tell him about how they created worlds together, knowing as she did that this was the act that always started everything.

It will keep everything going, too, he thought, moving on top of her.

Forever and ever, she thought, opening herself to him, leaning her head back, sighing. *Forever.*

Chapter Twelve

As he had been with his power before he met Ava, Edan felt he had to be careful with his feelings for Ava. He didn't want to relax or focus, knowing that either position could be dangerous. He felt he was holding a fragile dish, something made of the lightest, most beautiful glass, thin as air. But how could he do either? On the one hand, he wanted to either stay in the tent with Ava for the rest of his days, staring at her, touching her, feeling her. Or he wanted to pull her tight and sleep away the time, warm in the tent cocoon he had made. Maybe they could wake up every six or seven hours and make love again. Eat a little. Bathe. And then sleep again, their bodies twinned, their breathing soft and slow and united.

She was so warm, so soft. Edan felt he could disappear in her arms, become the energy outside that he was inside, an orange flame, kindled heat.

But life was calling. Their new life. And they had to go live it.

"Love," he whispered in her ear.

Ava breathed in a little more deeply, moving her head, wrapping her arms around him tight, her arms strong.

"Love, we have to get up. We have to go."

"Hmmmm," she mumbled, slowly pulling her head up, her eyes full of love. "Why?"

"I can hear what's happening. Things are starting. Our life here is ready to begin. They are organizing things. We have visitors. There's Upsilia and Earth to deal with, too."

Ava smiled, the expression fluid and graceful and true. "I think life has already started and, as they say, it started with a bang!"

Edan laughed, leaned forward, kissing her. "You could say that. In fact, maybe Porter would say something just like that. Try not to let him be a guiding influence in your life, if you can."

"He's a bad influence," Ava said. She stroked his arm and then pushed herself up. "But often right. And often very funny."

He watched Ava's sweet back as she reached down to pick up her shirt, her muscles tightening under the skin, the curve of silhouette from her breast. He could feel the weight of her in his hands right now, the soft skin, the full flesh. In his mind, his hands ran along her body, her pulse a rhythm he wanted to follow. Edan closed his eyes, and he was sure he could hear her moan slightly against his ear.

Stop it, she warned. *Didn't you just tell me life had to start?*

She turned to him, pulling up her pants slowly, smiling. *Didn't you just inform me that we had to go?*

"I was lying," he said. "I exaggerate. I am full of nothing but hyperbole. You can't believe a word I say."

"That's reassuring to hear from the leader of our new world," she said, but she stopped her buttoning, and Edan could feel her heat from where he lay.

"What are you lying about now?" she asked, her hands falling to her sides.

Pushing out thoughts of her, Edan smiled. Ava under him, Ava on top of him. Ava's skin, Ava's voice, Ava's feel. And he let her see how he loved all of it, her, them together, the way each of them made the other feel.

"That's it?" she said, taking off her shirt. "That's all you have?"

He pulled her back on the cot. "No. Trust me. There's more. There is so much more."

The tent was gone, evaporated into the particles of energy that were its very origin. With a joined thought, both of them left the impromptu campsite and appeared at the edge of a group of Cygirians, all of whom sat in a newly created meeting area.

Before going to the group, Edan looked around, holding Ava next to him. The new world didn't seem like a new world at all. Everything about it was living, moving, growing, functioning. It didn't seem new, but it was, a miracle of newness. The sun shone high in the sky, the wind carried the scent of flowers and sea. In the trees, fat red breasted birds sang in rain-wet trees. Underground, creatures dug through soil, tunneling for food and shelter. Farther down, the core of the planet roiled with heat and molten earth. What he and Ava did, were doing—what all the Cygirians were doing—was just a natural function of this planet, their planet. And Edan smiled, breathing in, moving toward his people, who were sitting out listening to speakers.

And though Edan carried the warmth of Ava inside him, he stepped into the crowd of Cygirians with some tentativeness, knowing that to them, all of this was new, too. Knowing that he had to be the leader that he was called to be. Knowing that despite the jokes he made with Ava in the tent, he couldn't be anything but one hundred percent true.

Together, he and Ava walked, hearing the sounds of thoughts and voices as they walked toward the front. Somewhere in the crowd, Edan heard a snide *It's about time,* and he knew that Porter was there.

He wanted to reply, but then he realized that Ava had stopped moving.

"What?" he asked. *What?*

You go, she thought. *You go to the front.*

Come with me. You're part of me. You are me, he thought, wanting the feel of her next to him always.

Some things, she thought, *we can't do together. This part of your life—this leadership—is yours.*

But I need you, he thought.

Not for everything. But even if I'm not up there with you, she thought, *I'm here.*

She reached up and touched his temple and then his heart. *Just in case.*

You are always the case, he thought, leaning over and kissing her on the cheek. *Always.*

Edan turned and walked forward, feeling Ava on his lips, in his mind, in his chest. She was warm in him, like the molten center of the planet. With her burning inside him, he could do anything.

As he made his way to the front of the crowd, Jai and Risa turned to him, smiling.

"Here we are," Jai said.

"Yes," Edan said, putting his hand on Jai's shoulder. "Finally."

As he began to walk past Jai, he saw his sisters. For a second, he felt blinded by their light, blinking against something that was inside them, their own molten heat and strength. Mila was holding Dasha in her arms, and Claire stood next to them, her eyes burning dark. Behind them both, Garrick and Darl stood, the other halves to his sisters, the other part that had been missing, needed, wanted, found.

And for a quick second, Edan was back in the ship all those years ago, heading first toward Earth where he would lose them both, and then to Upsilia where he would try to live his life. There with the other children, he'd founder, struggle, fail. Try and fail, until he met Ava.

Yet in this second, he was sitting next to his sisters, their little girl bodies huddled close, the swirl of fear and anxiety all around them. It was dark in the ship, but Edan could hear the sounds of the other children around them—and he knew that somewhere Ava was shivering in fear, alone, upset, so many years away from now. But they all felt the same loss. Voices emerged from the darkness and then disappeared. Fear closed in upon them, the threat of the red, dark, hurtful thing everywhere.

Claire was playing with her animal, and Mila's head was on his shoulder, her thin arms around him. Inside his little boy body, he was shaking, missing those safe, strong people who had put him in the ship, whispering quick thoughts to reassure him.

"It will be all right. We will always be with you," they said, but then they weren't. Then they were nothing but gone.

But he had to be strong. That's what he'd been told to do. So he was. Turning to his little sisters, he told them things would be all right, even though he didn't believe it, even though he knew more than they what they were going to lose.

We've found it again, Mila thought now. *We've found all we lost before. And now it's ours to lose.*

Close call that way! Claire thought, smiling. *Thank God we didn't blow this place up. This would be the happily ever after we've been waiting for all this time.*

They shared a thought of them all in a ring, holding hands, wishing for the world to explode. But it wasn't the world they'd wanted gone but the past that seemed impossible to fix. Without Ava, they'd have done it, and this moment right now would never have happened.

Go, Edan, thought Mila. *Let's do this life now. It's time. It's time to live.*

Claire nodded, and so did Garrick and Darl. Looking a bit away from them, Edan saw Porter and Stephanie and Michael and Kate. In such a short time, they had brought him into the fold of Cygirian life, shown him what it was to be part of a group. A little farther back, he saw Whitney and Kenneth, Odhran and Elizabeth, people who had helped him and his sisters, people who wanted this same life.

And without meaning to, he thought of Luoc, the Neballat who had taught him so much, shown him how power could create, how power could harm, how power could be just like this, about life.

Thank you, Edan thought out to the skies, to space, to the newly made planet, where he hoped Luoc lived now. He hoped that the Neballat was living his life in his new body, unpunished for the help he gave Edan. And without Luoc, none of the Neballats would have the life in front of them. Edan could only hope they could see things that way.

Taking in a deep breath, Edan nodded, and he walked to the front, held up his arms, feeling the new sun on his skin, feeling his sisters' fire, Ava's heat inside him.

"People," he said.

My people.

The thought shocked him as it always did, hard this time. And there they were. There, right in front of him, were his sisters, their families, his love, Ava. There were the friends he'd made, the people who would be with him while he was on this plain.

"Let us make this world a world that lasts," he said, throwing out images of how this new, safe, protected Cygiria could work. He conjured towns and cities and countries and continents. They wouldn't need too much space at first, but there would be more of them. In some millennia, this world would teem with Cygirian life, people, culture. He pictured that time, a future unmolested from the outside world, safe in its fluid, solid governance. It could happen. It must.

Looking closer, he saw the families, the groups, the clusters of organization, education, commerce, government, a way of living that was fluid and easy and natural. He saw that in this time, people would not necessarily need a twin, a double because all powers were possible. There would be no need for the polar opposite power as all the powers were merged, were one. Of course, there would be that need for connection and feeling, but the need wouldn't be as desperate. The time before would not be as lonely, bereft. With training and time, all of them would be able to harness their energy and do what was necessary to live. All of them would be able to love.

Still there would be that feeling. That intense, lovely feeling.

Still there would be Ava. Ava feeling. Ava everywhere.

Of course, the group thought. *Yes.*

Edan loved the word *Yes*, remembering how Ava had said it, thought it. It was a word of promise and hope and growth. It was a word that built and did not tear down. It was the word they needed to go forward and change their lives.

Together, all the Cygirians who had survived the journey from Cygiria and the Neballat attacks and abductions and use, all the Cygirians who had fought and then banded together to create—all of them thought one word, one sound ringing in all their heads.

Turning to look at Ava, Edan smiled, the *Yes* in his head, the *Yes* in his heart, *Yes* all the way to the end of everything and beyond.

It was late at night, the only activity Edan could really feel or hear was the beating of his own heart. Ava was asleep against his shoulder, still and smooth and silent.

At first, he'd thought he'd been unable to sleep because of the excitement of the day, the heady rush of adrenaline of the Cygirian success, the whirlwind of structure building at the end of the day. The toasts and joy and connection he'd felt all the way up until he and Ava had walked into this room to sleep.

But that wasn't it, and after he and Ava had made love, he'd found himself staring up at the ceiling. Maybe it was this constant, passionate connection with Ava keeping his heart banging against his ribs, his mind racing, his skin prickling with nerves. After having missed it, her, this, his whole life, he barely wanted to sleep, unable to pass up moments of her mind, skin, being to unconsciousness. He didn't want to waste one moment.

But that wasn't what was keeping him up. He knew that now. She was here, by his side, in sleep or in wakefulness. He didn't have to worry about missing her when she was here. That's when he realized what he had to do.

He had to go. He had to go back to the Source, at least one more time. Now.

No one had talked about the Source during this day. Those who had been there—who had been forced there by the Upsilian government—seemed to prefer to focus on the here and now, this alive life, this temporal, corporeal reality. Edan understood that desire completely. So much of what had happened to them on Upsilia had been like a punishment, a curse, and he could see why those who had endured it would want to be here and only here.

But there was something calling to him like a night bird, something keeping him from sleep. Slowly, trying to move without waking Ava, Edan slipped out from next to her, moving out of her sweet arms and then off the bed. In the darkness, he walked to the door, grabbing his clothes as he did, finding pants, shirt, jacket, shoes, dressing as he went along.

At the door, he turned, his eyes adjusted to the dark, and he could see Ava, the gold glint of her hair, her smooth curves under the blanket. It hurt to leave her side; he could almost feel the place on his side where she'd lain nestled. If he woke her, she would come with him, too, but he knew this was a journey he had to take by himself.

Quietly, he opened the door, moving out into the hallway, and then closed it behind him. He would be back before she stirred, he promised. She wouldn't even know he'd left.

Outside, the night was crisp, mostly clear, only a thin line of clouds a faraway landscape in the moonlit sky. Bats looped through the air, the hum of insects and night creatures a tiny tympani. The grass underneath his feet was wet, the earth a damp, musty loam. In the nearby bushes, animals scampered away from his steps, their eyes luminous lights in the darkness.

Edan walked toward a tall tree, something huge, a pine, a sequoia, a redwood, a tree he couldn't name yet because of night and newness. A group of Cygirians would have to define the names of things, giving a title to plants that could clearly exist without any names at all. Like everything, however, a name defined made clear what was obvious but unknown. Now, though, Edan knew that the tree was there, that its bark was smooth, and he leaned against it, closing his eyes.

The Source. The place from which they all came. Edan focused on the feel of the wide expanse of everything that was the Source, the steady, strong current of energy, the oranges and reds flowing around him. As he focused, he felt himself leave his body, move from imagination to reality, the reds and oranges flowing around him and in him, moving against the current of his own energy, his own soul. Opening those soul eyes, he found himself in the Source, the place he'd escaped to, loved being in. The place that had made the most sense until he'd found Ava.

This time, he wasn't going to be content to float, to meet up with whatever energy that came his way. He wasn't hiding or being punished or being put away from the daily life of a "normal" society. No, he was looking for something very specific, needing to complete a circle he had not begun but that he could finish.

Yet this place was so compelling. For moments, Edan would forget his purpose, the reason for leaving Ava's arms to walk outside and fling himself in here. This silky, smooth ride through energy was like warm water, like soft air, like being satisfied after a good meal, like lying in Ava's arms. Safe. Comforting. Happy. Joy.

This place was the reward for everything, and yet . . . and yet it wasn't life. It wasn't where he was now.

He took hold of himself, pressed forward through the streams, ignoring all the other compelling energies around him. In the eddies of energy he saw his sisters' energies, his friends'. In a distant patch of blue, he was sure he saw Luoc, and he was compelled for a moment to stop and talk with the man, to thank him.

But he didn't have time to spare. Edan called out, called them forth, needing finally to be able to see them, to tell them what had happened, to ask them if it was the right thing, the thing that was supposed to happen.

You were supposed to happen, came the answer.

Stopping, slowing the movement, the reds and oranges circling around him, Edan looked over to his left, and then his right. There were two solid forms, light purples, dark reds, heavy with thought and memory and feeling, energies that were all here, in the Source.

Mata? he thought, using the old term, the one he knew from his dream, from memory, the word in his heart.

Pata?

Yes, they both thought, their forms coming closer, their energy thick with gold flecks. *It's us, Edan.*

All the questions he'd wanted to ask evaporated, and he felt tears everywhere. This life of his—the life he had now with Ava and his sisters and his people—was because of his parents, because of the Cygirians who gave up their lives for their children. And they'd lost what he had, the time in the body, the time of watching their children grow up and live.

Everything has worked out exactly as it should have, Edan. There isn't anything that we would undo. Even if we could, his mother thought. And with her thought came the memory of lilies, lavender, vanilla, smells on her skin, smells from her kitchen. He could see his hand reach up for something sweet that was on a counter. He could taste it even now, the sweet crunch of her baking.

But you had to let us go. You had to—had to die.

Nothing ever dies, thought his father. *Here we are.*

I know you are here, Edan thought. *But what I mean is you can't be with us. With Mila, Claire—Sophia—and me.*

We are with you. Always. And we will come back. That's just the nature of things, his mother thought, her energy moving closer to him, the tendrils of her moving around him purple and gold and red. *That's what you have to remember. Remember that we are here, and don't be sad. Don't worry because really, always, everything is as it should be.*

Edan knew that what she was thinking was true, but nothing seemed as real as gravity, as the body, as the new world that they had created. He wanted his life to be complete, wanted his parents, everyone's parents and grandparents, to be there to complete the circle.

The circle is complete, his father thought. *You completed it today. And then another circle will begin. The cycle is unending. So stay with Ava. Live your life, Edan. Let us go because we are here. We love you and your sisters, and do not regret anything. This is the answer we hoped for when we put you on that ship.*

His father moved closer, his energy aqua, maroon, bronze. *Take what you have and appreciate it. And know there is more and more and more. It's not the same each time, but it never ends.*

For a second, both his parents moved even closer, and Edan could barely keep his eyes open, the light so dazzling, so pure. In the embrace of their light, he felt the love he'd known all those years ago, back in the time before the spaceship. He'd felt nothing like it until the moment Ava opened her arms and pulled him close. But this amazing light embrace was an older love, a love that he knew had to recede.

Go back, Edan, his mother thought, her light slowly fading. *Go back and live. This is a fine and lovely place, but it's not the place for you now. Know that it's all right. Everything, no matter how grim, is all right.*

Love, his father thought. *Love well.*

And with that last thought, his parents' light merged into the stream and flow of the Source. Edan watched until he saw the last flicker of gold.

He wanted to pull them back, to call them for more conversation, for more answers, but he simply watched until there was nothing but the fabric of energy all around him, a swatch of red and orange.

It was time. Edan closed his eyes, let the Source fade into itself, let his essence return to his body.

Slowly, slowly, he found himself back on the planet, his spine hard against the tree, his face wet with tears.

Blinking into the night, Edan breathed in, feeling as though he'd been underwater. The night was slowly fading into gray, the mountains around him dark figures slumbering on the horizon. Soon it would be morning, and the new day would bring the rest of his life with it. The new day would turn into more days, then weeks, and then years, generations of life stretching out connected and whole. This night, this visit with his parents, would have to be tucked away so that life could go on.

He pushed back away from the tree and walked back to the building, carrying a little light in his heart, the knowledge that his parents were there, with him, with his sisters still. One day, he would tell them both about this, but now he wanted only one thing, one person.

Walking into the building and then down the hallway,

Edan put his hand on the door of the room where his love, his true love slept. She was light. She was love, the love that his father talked about. He would love her well. He would live here on this planet truly and well and he would love Ava with everything he had.

Turning the doorknob, Edan smiled, his whole body filled with the same feeling he'd had in the Source. Ava was his warm water, his soft air. And Edan opened the door, smiling to himself, and closed it behind him, knowing that nothing would ever be as wonderful as this.

If you liked this Jessica Inclán book,
you've got to try her other titles,
available from Zebra. . . .

BEING WITH HIM

They are here among us . . .

Far from home, gifted with special abilities, hunted for their powers. And they are desperate to find their other, the one who completes them . . . before it's too late. . . .

Sometimes, time really does stand still. . . .

Mila Adams has always known she was different. For as long as she can remember, she has had the ability to shift time, and who would believe that? Certainly not the obnoxious blind dates her mother keeps foisting off on her. But Mila can't help feeling there's someone out there for her, a soul mate who might understand her unique ability. And when she looks into the dark eyes of financial whiz Garrick McClellan, she can't help but feel that her time has finally come.

Any man would lust after a beauty like Mila, but the moment Garrick touches her—feels her shifting time just as he can—he recognizes her as his partner in power. Their connection is immediate, passionate, raw, and beyond anything either has ever experienced. But who are they? What is this gift that joins them so intensely? Are there others like them? And why do they feel that time is running out?

"Your painting," he asked, his words coming from him slow, as if he had to pull each word out of his mouth by a string, "the one with the purple swirl?"

"*The Ride*," she said, changing her gaze, moving it from his hands to his face. She was startled by his pointed expression. "What about it?"

"What does it mean?" he asked. And when Mila looked at him, she could see such an intense curiosity burning from behind his indifference, she wished she could open the car door and fling herself out. No one had ever looked at her like that before, not her parents, not a lover. No one ever paid that much attention to her, all at once. "What is it saying? Where does it come from?"

"It's just something from my imagination. Something I think about. All the time."

"Why? Why do you think about that shape? That color? What do you think?" He was leaning forward now, his face alight, his eyes filled with something like heat. "It's like there's movement there. Like the shape is going some place. Like it's carrying people, important people."

Mila blinked, startled. She'd only ever talked about *The Ride* with her art instructors, the museum gallery director, her classmates. "I don't know why you care. You certainly didn't show any interest earlier."

"I—I . . ." Garrick stopped talking, shaking his head. He jerked his head up and noticed where the car was. "Never mind. I shouldn't have done this. I never should have come, Linda or not. Driver."

"His name is Mr. Henry."

Garrick leaned forward. "Mr. Henry, you can let me out here."

Mr. Henry didn't turn but said, "It's a mile yet."

"That's fine. Right here. Let me out here." And when Mr. Henry didn't seem to slow down, Garrick almost yelled, "Stop."

Mila sat flat against her seat watching this beautiful angry man do everything in his power to get away from her. If it wasn't so upsetting, she thought, she'd be able to craft some kind of story about it to tell her friends at the beginning of open studio, recounting the evening with verve and style, a jaunty yarn about the blind date from hell. The man who endured asphalt raspberry burns rather than ride a final mile in a one-hundred-thousand-dollar limo with her.

"Here we go, sir," Mr. Henry said, and Garrick opened the door, and he started to push through to the outside. He stopped for a second, and she could see him take in a big breath.

"Look," he said, turning back to her, one foot already out on the pavement. "It's not about . . ."

It's not you, it's me. Yadda, yadda, yadda, Mila thought. *Get out of the car, jerk.*

Garrick stopped talking, and she thought she heard him laugh. But his eyes weren't happy.

"Good luck with your painting," he said, leaving for real this time, the door closing heavy and hard.

As the car pulled away, Mila watched him as long as she could, until Mr. Henry turned left down the hill, heading toward the Mission District.

"Well," Mila said finally as they sailed through traffic. "That was so much fun, I hope I can do it again next Saturday!"

"He seemed a little strained," Mr. Henry said. "A little tense."

"He needed—well, he didn't need me, that's all I know."

Mila sat back, letting the ride home take her over. If she wasn't laughing, she would cry. And vice versa. It was too ironic. Here was a man who if he hadn't acted like such an ass, she actually would have loved to see again. And for no good reason, except for a strange feeling she'd had ever since he walked into her parents' living room. Some kind of zing, a flurry of energy in her body.

But his good looks and some kind of chemistry weren't enough to overcome his clear lack of manners or caring. So now it was over. She'd survived the dinner, her mother would likely not try a setup for months, and Mila could scratch another San Francisco bachelor off the long list her mother seemed to keep on file. Maybe now after this debacle, Mila thought, it was a good time to kiss that list good-bye.

She didn't even have a chance to look at the clock before picking up her cell phone, fumbling in the dark bedroom to find the button to answer it.

"What?" she asked, blinking into the early morning light, her blankets piled around her.

"I have to see you," he said.

Mila forced herself into total consciousness, taking in small breaths, keeping her eyes open. What day was it? Or what night? Was it the weekend? "Who is this?"

"It's Garrick. Garrick McClellan."

Mila rolled onto her back. "You have to see me? Didn't—didn't you just jump out of a car to get away from me?"

There was a pause, and Mila wondered if she'd fallen back to sleep, but then he said, "I'm—I'm sorry. I want to explain. And I want to ask you something about . . ."

"What? About what?" Mila asked.

"Us," Garrick said. "Us."

Sitting up, Mila leaned against her pillow, her mouth open slightly. *Us?* What was he doing calling her like this after a night like that? After he almost made himself roadkill rather than sit next to her? She wanted to laugh at him. To tell him to take a hike. But then, through the phone, she felt so much that she wanted to lie down flat on the bed and weep. Images were coming to her, feelings, thoughts. Garrick's. So much hurt and loss and pain. He had been so alone. So afraid.

"Oh," she said, trying to find words. "Oh."

"Can we meet?" he asked, unaware of what she was pulling in from his mind.

"Yes. Yes," she said. "We can meet."

"When?" he asked.

What time was there? she wondered. What time was there but this moment? She knew from wasting time how valuable it was.

"Now," she said. "Come over now."

INTIMATE BEINGS

When you least expect it, love finds you. . . .

Lately, Claire Edwards feels like she's floundering. A ho-hum teaching job, a string of terrible dates, nights spent with only Netflix, and bizarre dreams of spaceships for company. . . . Life isn't working out the way she hoped. But Claire has an extraordinary secret ability—she can go any-where at all, just by wishing it. And if the intensely attrac-tive man who suddenly materializes in her car one day is any indication, Claire's not the only one. . . .

Ever since Darl James learned of his true origins, he has been searching for his partner and life mate, the one whose gift will complement and complete his own. Now that he's found Claire, he vows to never lose her again, or their soul-searing, sensual connection. But keeping her safe won't be easy when they've been marked for destruction by an evil, power-hungry race. A fierce battle is brewing, one that will test Claire and Darl's new bond to the limit, and decide the future of all their kind. . . .

*O*kay, she thought. *Okay. Just a few more miles and all this will disappear.*

As she rounded the park, heading toward Stanyan, she wished for the nth time that her mother were alive. Like so many things, she wouldn't be able to tell her mother about the voice, but she could at least sit by her and maybe watch a TV show. Or work out in the garden, digging up weeds or planting the latest in heirloom vegetables. Anything to take her mind away from the craziness.

But, of course, her mother wasn't here anymore, and there wasn't a person she could confide in. Claire was pretty sure that Yvonne would listen politely and then call 911. Ruth would likely do the same. Maybe it was time to go to a therapist and just spill it all and wait to see what a trained professional would suggest. Maybe she would do it. Maybe she would just finally take care of this problem.

"You don't have a problem, you nut," the voice said.

"Stop it!" Claire shrieked, braking hard at the corner of Stanyan and Hayes, a Muni bus squealing to avoid hitting her.

"Shit, shit, shit," she said, turning right onto Hayes and stalling right behind a FedEx van.

"You need to stop this car right now," the voice said.

Breathing in small, shallow breaths, Claire pulled over, parking in a rare open spot, ignoring the stares from passersby and the FedEx driver. The voice might be a product of her own imagination, but it was right. She was a danger to herself and others.

"Who are you?" she whispered, convinced now that she was talking to nothing but her own sad thoughts. "Where are you?"

"Due to the powers of others, I have managed to render myself invisible this once," the voice said. "But I don't hear that well."

"Who are you?" she asked again, her voice louder, clearer, even though she felt her heart pounding in her throat.

She looked down at her hands in her lap, shaking her head, almost wanting to laugh out loud. Was she this lonely and sad that she was conjuring up a voice? A male voice. A man. A man who was focused on her. She had finally cracked. All these years she really had been crazy. Those times she thought she'd gone to another country or town or place had been psychotic breaks. A psychotic break. She had been delusional, was so right now. When she thought she could hear other people's thoughts, she was merely deep in some horrid fantasy of her own creation.

She was paranoid, schizophrenic, maybe bipolar with an affective disorder. Top it off with panic and anxiety, and she was a psychiatrist's dream. A master's thesis. A doctoral dissertation.

So it was clear. She had no choice. No more debate here. Nothing else to argue about. Claire knew she needed to drive herself right now to Langley Porter Psychiatric Institute at UCSF and check in. Forever. Get some kind of commitment. What did they call that? A 5150. At least she'd never have to deal with Annie and Sam again.

"Oh, what a drama queen!" the voice said, and as she heard the words, a body began to take shape and form in a waver of pixilated air.

"You are a jerk," faded from her tongue, and she blinked, tried to focus on what she could hardly believe was happening next to her in the passenger's seat.

For the moments it took for him to appear, Claire knew that even though she had felt odd her entire life—even though she'd made herself appear with a *poof!* all over the place—she'd never really believed that magic existed. She never really thought about the concept of super powers or abilities. Everything truly odd was contained in her and her alone—she was the holder of the world's weirdness. Actually, she thought she was some kind of genetic anomaly, a creation of some weird fluke in a DNA strand. No one else was like her. No one on the planet.

"I would have to say that no one is like you. But you aren't alone in this power business," said the man now sitting next to her. "Believe it or not, soon you are not going to be all alone anymore, ever again."

Claire couldn't focus on what he was saying. Instead, she slowly moved her gaze from his thigh (a very nice thigh in what seemed to be cotton pants) to his body (strong), shoulders (stronger), neck, and then face. His face. Claire wanted to stop breathing because if she did, she would die, and she wouldn't have to sit there completely embarrassed, her body roiling in heat, her mind just about everywhere.

"You are just some kind of delusion," she said, relieved in a strange way that at least she knew what she was dealing with. "Some kind of sad last gasp of hope in me."

"Really?" the man said. "Strange how I feel so *here*. You know, like in my body."

"Sorry. You're not," Claire said. "It's all about me. Finally, the cliché comes true. Hold on to your hat. We're going to Langley Porter. It's close by, so that's good. Put on your seat belt."

"I don't think that's where I want to go. From the sound of it, there are madwomen screaming in the attic there," he said, and for a brief second, she allowed herself to look at him. He was so—so perfect. His eyes were dark, looking at her with an intense humor. Like he liked her and wanted to laugh not at but with her. His dark brown hair hung in soft curls to his shoulders, gleaming in the sunlight coming through the car window. He smiled, his teeth white, his lips full. As if hearing her, he licked his lips, his eyes sparkling, his hand almost reaching out to touch her.

"Whoa, buddy." Claire started giggling, laughing, resting her forehead on the steering wheel and then sitting up and looking back at him. "Keep your fake hands to yourself. If I'm going to be crazy, I'm not going to add to it by letting the figment of my imagination touch me. Haven't you ever seen that movie *Fight Club*?"

When the man didn't answer, she answered for him. "Of course you did, because I did and you're me, so you did. I've split my psyche. If there were a movie of this car scene, I'd be talking to air. It's Brad Pitt and Ed Norton all over again. The next thing you know, I'll be hitting myself thinking I'm beating you up."

"This is not going the way I wanted it to," he said slowly. "It would be easier if you would just be quiet for a minute."

"So you have practice in this?" Claire wondered how many other unfortunate women were out there, all certain a handsome man had just appeared one day, especially for them.

The man sighed, shook his head, and put his hands on his knees. Turning to face the street, he sighed.

"Look, I know this is weird. And I tend to be a pain in the ass. So can we start over here?"

Claire stared at him, breathing in quick breaths, nervous and scared and amazed. And then she smelled it. Him. He smelled like soap and something citrus, the tang of whatever he used to shave filling the car.

Do hallucinations have smells? she thought. *Is this a multisensory projection of all my sorrows? Can I hear, smell, see him? God knows if I could taste him, and I didn't let him touch me. But smell?*

"You know," he said slowly, "I haven't had much practice with this. You are the first person I've rescued. And, of course, I have a vested interest. But I really would like to start over. If I get out of the car, would you promise not to drive away?"

As he spoke, the man seemed to become more real. His movements had weight. He filled the car space with what Claire could only call maleness: smells, words, muscles actually rippling under his clothes. Rippling. She'd thought it was only a cliché, the men she'd dated skinny or maybe filling out their Dockers a little too fully around the middle, their expensive leather belts pulled tight.

He smiled again, his eyes so bright, dark but seeming to be full of pinpoints of light. "Do you promise?"

Claire nodded, took her hands away from the wheel and folded them in her lap. What would it hurt to listen to him? Maybe once he left the car, he would simply disappear. Hallucination over. A wonderful hallucination all gone.

"I promise," she said.